"Fans of *Where the Crawdads Sing* and *Before We Were Yours* will find much to love in this evocative and thought-provoking debut. Church reaches into a shameful and little-known pocket of the past to give us a heroine who is plucky, tender, and determined to fight for her autonomy and dignity against insurmountable odds. This book will change the way you feel about the simple question of 'Where is home?'"

—Kim Wright, author of *Last Ride to Graceland*

"In this piercing novel, Meagan Church depicts one of the most disgraceful episodes in American medical history: forced sterilization. As a physician, I am deeply ashamed of the real-life actions of the medical community fictionalized so eloquently in this book, but as an author and a reader, I'm grateful for the opportunity to envision it. *The Last Carolina Girl* is a powerful and thought-provoking story."

—Kimmery Martin, author of *Doctors and Friends*

PRAISE FOR
THE LAST CAROLINA GIRL

"*The Last Carolina Girl* is a heart-wrenching and authentically rendered glimpse into the portal of a state's secret dark culture, family ties, and the fierce strength of a young girl's grit and resilience. Church is electric in her delivery of loss, longing, and place. Unforgettable—this a powerful debut to savor."

—Kim Michele Richardson, *New York Times* bestselling author of *The Book Woman of Troublesome Creek*

"Meagan Church has written a compelling and aching debut. *The Last Carolina Girl* is both a story of love and a tale of abuse set in the shadow of the Depression. There, a girl's blind obedience to her circumstances—a kind girl uprooted by her tender daddy's death—comes with a devastating price. Leah's life as an orphan takes her far from the comfort of sand and sea, yet she is armed with tenuous hope and a plan. Gradually, she puts together the puzzle pieces of her fractured life and uncovers truths: family can deceive and betray, but love offers salvation."

—Leah Weiss, bestselling author of *If the Creek Don't Rise* and *All the Little Hopes*

"Leah's story is both humbling and inspiring. Church's ode to the natural world, to the often elusive feeling of home, and to the friends who become family provokes profound reflection. A dark spot in history warps Leah's path, but her resilient and unassailable character prevails. *The Last Carolina Girl* is a breathtaking read, and Leah Payne an unforgettable character."

—Lo Patrick, author of *The Floating Girls*

"*The Last Carolina Girl* is lyrical and atmospheric, a true masterpiece of Southern fiction that will earn its long-standing place among greats on our bookshelves both for its exploration of a horrific piece of history often overlooked and for its insistence on hope. Church's debut is a must-read."

—Joy Callaway, international bestselling author of *The Grand Design*

"While readers will surely find all of the characters in Meagan Church's debut compelling, the true beating heart of *The Last Carolina Girl* is its fourteen-year-old protagonist: a girl tied deeply to her natural landscape whose abrupt uprooting after the death of her beloved father comes with devastating consequences. Leah Payne and her indefatigable spirit will break your heart and put it back together again. I tore through this haunting and emotional story."

—Erika Montgomery, author of *A Summer to Remember*

"This spirited, coming-of-age debut whisked me straight to the heart of the Carolinas in the 1930s. I couldn't tear myself away from Leah's journey, from the piney, isolated woods of her childhood to an often bewildering life in the foreign world of the suburbs where appearances are everything. Church so beautifully interweaves the connections between Leah's deeply sunk roots in the rural South with her search for belonging and her bravery in the face of unspeakable loss. This is a story that will stay with me; I knew little about the eugenics programs that had taken hold in American culture in that time period, and Church's tale left me wanting to research and understand more of this broken, devastating piece of America's history."

—Lisa DeSelm, author of *The Puppetmaster's Apprentice*

THE
LAST
CAROLINA
GIRL

THE
LAST
CAROLINA
GIRL

A Novel

MEAGAN CHURCH

Published by Sourcebooks Landmark, an imprint of Sourcebooks
P.O. Box 4410, Naperville, Illinois 60567-4410
(630) 961-3900
sourcebooks.com

Library of Congress Cataloging-in-Publication Data

Names: Church, Meagan, author.
Title: The last Carolina girl : a novel / Meagan Church.
Description: Naperville, Illinois : Sourcebooks Landmark, [2023]
Identifiers: LCCN 2022028710 (print) | LCCN 2022028711
(ebook) | (hardcover) | (trade paperback) | (epub)
Subjects: LCGFT: Novels.
Classification: LCC PS3603.H8835 L37 2023 (print) | LCC PS3603.H8835
   (ebook) | DDC 813/.6--dc23/eng/20220702
LC record available at https://lccn.loc.gov/2022028710
LC ebook record available at https://lccn.loc.gov/2022028711

Printed and bound in the United States of America.
LSC 10 9 8 7 6 5 4 3 2 1

To Matt, who will always be my home.

"We are all strangers in a strange land, longing for home, but not quite knowing what or where home is."

—Madeleine L'Engle from
The Rock That Is Higher

Prologue

HOLDEN BEACH, NC
1935

The last time Daddy and I stood at the ocean's edge together, there had been a storm most of the day. Even so, Daddy insisted on making it to the shore of Holden Beach before the sun retired for the night. We always went when he was missing Mama.

I can't say I ever minded the pilgrimage. Living a few miles from the ferry, it didn't take much time to get to shore, but time was what we had—even though we didn't have much else.

The ocean breeze, blowing strong and cool that night, didn't seem to bother Daddy much, though it rattled my bones and set my hair to dancing. As I looked to the sand and squished my toes into its millions of granules, Daddy called my attention to above the rolling Atlantic waters.

"Wait for it, Leah," he said with his eyes to the cloud-heavy horizon. "There's more coming."

And he was right. Perhaps because he'd always lived close to nature, Harley Payne had a way of knowing these things. Along a sky that had moments ago been monotone, a complete double rainbow bent from the coast and into the ocean. It stretched high and plunged into the water. I wondered if the fish below could see all the colors.

It was a sight the likes that happens once, maybe twice, in a lifetime, each of the seven colors—the start, the finish, and all in between—lighting up on full display. As the rainbow faded, the setting sun lit the remnant clouds with brilliance. Oranges and yellows over the coastline mixed with blues and purples that hung suspended above the ocean. The few fishermen on the shore that night looked more to the heavens than they did to their poles.

Daddy never let me swim at dusk, nor near where the fishermen cast their lines, but I couldn't help but dip my toes in the cool water, causing my arms and legs to turn to gooseflesh. I liked to stand in one spot, let the water wash up to my ankles and then rush back to sea. I'd see how long I could stay in that one place before sinking too low as the sand washed away with the waves.

During one of the washings away, I felt something under my foot. I screamed and jumped out of my sinking hole, and, when I looked down, I saw what Daddy called sand fleas. They looked like sea bugs to me, about the size of the cicadas that buzzed in the trees outside our windows. Their gray bodies matched the sand. With each wave that rushed back to the ocean, they would bury themselves only to have the next crashing surf expose them again. The water tossed and turned them, dragging them farther than they wanted to go. They scurried to latch onto the earth, to cling to it and find safety within it. But those relentless waves kept coming, kept pulling them from their homes.

As the water washed out to sea, I couldn't help but wonder if the surfacing fleas could find their friends. With each motion of natural forces, did they know where their mama was? Could they find their daddy? Or maybe the constant beating of the tides left them all too scattered to notice, too alone to have family or friends, even when they were surrounded by each other.

As I was busy wondering, I missed the final colors of the sunset. In mere moments, the oranges and purples faded, and a blanket of deep blue settled overhead. Maybe I should've been disappointed to have missed the last moments of majestic lights, but how was I to know I should've lingered in that moment with Daddy? How could I predict the oncoming waves and all their ripples?

When I recall that night, my memory fades with the setting of the sun. I don't recall the ride home, and I know it's not because of one of my flashes—those wrinkles of moments I couldn't control or explain, when my body froze and held me captive, still in the world but temporarily absent.

What I do remember of that night was later on at our home, the little overseer's house on the mainland where Daddy and I lived. The one with only one room, one table for two, one bed shared between us. I recall Daddy's prickly whiskers pressing into my forehead as he whispered, "Good night, Mouse," before he turned over in the bed, tumbling just outside my reach as if the wave of sleep pulled him from me.

That was the first night after a long Carolina summer that we needed Mama's quilt. The beach breeze had been stiff. The storm could've explained the drop in temperature, but the impending change of season, the start of a new school year, the sun that began to set earlier in the evening, even a thirteen-year-old knew what it all meant. Change was coming, a new season entering whether or not we were ready.

But I longed for more than the quilt to wrap around me and offer me assurances I didn't even know I needed. I rolled closer to Daddy, crawling into his warmth, basking in his closeness, searching in him for the only home I had ever known.

Part One

BRUNSWICK COUNTY, NC
1935

CHAPTER ONE

Most mornings, Daddy was already gone by the time sleep released me. But when I heard the rain pinging the rusted metal roof a few weeks after we saw that double rainbow, I knew before my eyes even opened all the way that Daddy would still be sitting at the kitchen table. Soggy mornings meant his lunch pail went unpacked and each sip of coffee was slowly savored. Being a lumberjack depended on the weather. Neither the Carolina summer heat and humidity nor the winter cold snaps affected his schedule. The clearing to develop Brunswick County and the barrier islands kept moving forward through those conditions. But the rain did make work difficult, and I could count on it to give me a few more minutes with Daddy. The horses struggled in mud-soaked woods, their hooves sinking, their legs straining to pull the timber from the forest floor and into the clearing.

'Course Mr. Barna could always find odds and ends for Daddy to help with on those rainy days. As his employee, and with the housing arrangement Mr. Barna had given my folks in that time before I was born, Daddy obliged his requests and reassignments, pitching in at the farm, sawmill, or country store when he couldn't be working in the woods. Daddy said Mama used to help around the Barna's house, even stitched a quilt and needlepointed Mrs. Barna's good handkerchiefs. I wished I had my mama's skills to make something ordinary into something beautiful. Daddy said I may not have picked up stitching like she did, but I got her spiritedness.

That rainy morning, the steam still curled off the grits when I sat down to the breakfast table. Typically, Daddy left the remainder of breakfast in the pan on the stove for me to dish out before I left for school. The steam twisted toward the ceiling as I sat down to my bowl of warm cereal.

"Mornin', Mouse," Daddy said as he kissed the top of my head, smushing my curls, wild from sleep. He placed his finger atop the biggest freckle on my nose and paused for a moment before giving it a little wiggle.

The bowl held more than grits that morning. As I stirred my spoon, I unearthed a few buried, salmon-pink additions.

"Is that shrimp?"

Daddy nodded, a slow smile creeping across his sunburned lips, revealing the gap in his front teeth.

"Did you catch them?" I asked, but Daddy shook his head no. "Bought them? That wasn't in the budget."

"Mr. Barna had a job down at the shore yesterday. He brought a few extras for us."

"Where's your shrimp?" I looked at Daddy's bowl. He always used the one with a chip. He kept his eyes on his bowl, his spoon in a constant motion from grits to mouth and back again. He didn't even pause when he said, "Already ate it."

"You did?"

Daddy nodded, his head bobbing the affirmative. His hair did not move at all. A layer of oil kept it firmly in place. He raised his dark-brown eyes to meet mine.

"You always tell me not to lie," I said.

"Do I now?"

"Yes. And I think—"

And then I must've paused. Daddy always said I'd become like a statue, pausing all motion, my mouth slightly open in an O, my green eyes staring blankly, yet focused, in the distance somewhere. If I had been aware, maybe I would've seen his smile fade, fall from his face like a glass slipping from wet hands and shattering on the floor beneath. I may have been in the room, but I was as distant as a sandbar on the other side of the riptide of parting waves.

And as the moment released me, I gasped for breath, shook my head, and recognized the blip of my reality only when I saw Daddy's expression.

"Mouse? You back?"

I shook my head again, my curls bouncing against my shoulders. I always shivered after coming to.

"Yeah."

"You good?"

"Mm-hmm." I looked down at my bowl and circled my spoon in search of another shrimp. I wanted to gobble them all up immediately, but I also wanted to savor them, save them for the final bites, fool myself into believing that every bite I had taken had been filled with the delicious morsel.

"Was it a long one?" I asked.

When he didn't answer, I knew. But what did the length or even the frequency of such episodes even matter? We didn't know a proper name for them, so we called them flashes. They acted as pauses in time, but they didn't hurt. Being a child who not many gave attention to, my flashes often went unnoticed, a benefit I didn't much mind.

"Now go on and finish up your breakfast." Daddy always moved on from my flashes quickly, not wanting to give them the satisfaction of attention. "Don't want to be late for school."

My head dropped, my shoulders slumped, and my tired body longed to be under the quilt again.

"Maybe I need more rest." I knew better than to directly ask Daddy to stay home. But from his raised eyebrows, I knew he was onto me right away.

"What else you gonna do on a day like today? Woods are too wet for exploring. Sand's more like mud after all that rain. Besides, you still got learning to do. What's it I tell yuh?"

Together we said the words he'd been speaking to me since he walked me to school my first day. "Let 'em teach me what they can, but don't go forgetting who I am."

Daddy put his finger on top of my big freckle and gave it another wiggle. "You're a smart girl, Leah, but you gotta know more than the trees and the tides to survive."

Jesse dawdled on the porch that morning, trying to stay out of the rain as long as possible. His mother insisted we walk the mile or so to school together, and being a good Southern boy, he obliged her, even if together meant him marching a few paces ahead once the schoolhouse came into view while I trailed behind. No use in letting everyone think we were friends. That was reserved for when it was just the two of us running through the woods or chasing after the chickens on the Barna's farm.

As I emerged from our overseer's house that sat in the shadow of Jesse's family's two-story home with tall pillars and a wrap-around front porch, he began to walk down the road. He nodded a hello in my direction, our typical morning communication. Just like in the afternoons, some mornings we'd be full of words and others we'd be fine in each other's presence without feeling the need to speak. Growing up beside one another since babies, we'd gotten used to each other, knowing how to act when it was only the two of us and realizing our different roles with others around. That's why most mornings I would let him go on ahead before the others saw us.

But this morning, I wanted to warm the chill that kept trying to get to my bones while seeking a few moments of freedom and movement before having to sit at a desk for more hours than I wished to count. So I began to run, feeling the wind whip across my cheeks as my heart pounded and my lungs begged for air.

Soon Jesse started running too. Beside each other, we raced toward the schoolhouse, aiming for the shortest distance to our goal, stomping through the puddles that had been forming all night. His stride was longer, but mine was quicker.

"Don't let a girl beat you, Jesse!" a chorus of boys called as the trees broke away and revealed the schoolyard.

The girls—of an age when they had put away such foolish notions as foot races—offered no encouragement. Instead their focus was on the puddles before them, carefully stepping to avoid splashing and spraying their stockings.

With the school building in sight, Jesse began to slow. I kept my pace, catching him at the flagpole and lunging ahead of him as we crossed onto the school lawn.

I raised my arms in accomplishment. Daddy always said it wasn't kind to gloat, but it wasn't often that I had opportunity to, so I figured just this once would be okay.

"I wasn't racing," my opponent said, as he sucked in air and tried to slow his breathing. Even with the cool in the wind, he'd worked up a sweat that dampened locks of his brown hair and stuck them to the sides of his forehead.

"I was," I called back. We'd had enough races through the Barna's acreage of yard and forest for me to know that he could've taken me. He won most times, especially since he'd gotten so much taller than me, but he didn't that morning, and I wasn't going to let whatever reason it was stop me from enjoying the moment.

But that feeling of victory soon faded. Miss Heniford didn't like it when I came to school sweaty. She said girls should glisten, not sweat. I thought the rain would hide it that morning, but judging from her pursed lips and furrowed brow, she could still tell the salty perspiration from the precipitation. As she passed out the themes we had written the week before, she smiled and applauded Jesse for so eloquently explaining why he wanted to own the country store, a farm, and a sawmill, just like his daddy. She even told Jean-Louise that being a mother was the blessing of all blessings. I couldn't help but roll my eyes.

Most of the girls in the class chose to write about motherhood. Each talked about how many babies they wanted and what their names would be. Some even wrote about who their husbands would be and what they would do. But Daddy always said, "The only thing that stays the same is change," so I figured how could I know what I'd be in five, ten, or twenty years? There was only one thing I knew I wanted and so I wrote about it. I even illustrated it, the nubby pencil shading and shadowing all I ever hoped for.

"Remember, students," she said as she approached my desk. "You were graded not just on your grammar, but on the feasibility of what you want to be when you grow up. Who can tell me what 'feasibility' means?"

That Jean-Louise's hand reached to the ceiling, as if her fingertips could scratch the tiles overhead. Leave it to Jean-Louise to be the first with something to say. She and I never had been what you'd call friends, especially after she asked me what kind of a name Leah was. It wasn't so much that she asked, but the way she said it, her hands on her hips, her jaw sticking out, her lips pursed together and eyebrows high. I thought about telling her it was the name my mama whispered as she hemorrhaged on the birthing bed, and I cried with uncertainty. At least that's how Tulla tells the story. She was the only one in the room with Mama after I was born. Mrs. Barna had already run out of the house, calling for help. But I knew better than to tell my business to Jean-Louise, so when she asked about my name, I told her it was the kind that was strong, not a mouthful of nonsense like hers was.

"I recall, Miss Heniford," Jean-Louise said, her arm still stretched high. "It means what could really happen. What's possible."

"Thank you, Jean-Louise."

Miss Heniford dropped my essay on my desk. She tapped her finger on the red letter at the top. "Feasibility, Leah. Feasibility."

Above my title, "When I Grow Up I Will Live on the Beach" was a letter C with a note below: "A bit unrealistic. Remember your capitalization. Your spelling still needs work."

Leave it to Miss Heniford to think my notions weren't feasible, but in my defense, the assignment had been to write about what we wanted. And that's what I did. Just because she saw a house built upon the sand as impractical, especially for a girl like me who lived in a house her father didn't have the means to own, didn't mean it wasn't what I wanted.

Jesse had liked my idea just fine. He wished he'd thought of it for himself. 'Course, we knew enough to know that parts of our futures held certain predeterminations, Jesse's more so than my own, especially when his family's name was painted on a few buildings around town. When I told him what I wrote about, he asked if we could still be neighbors. I said that'd be hard when he'd be taking over for his daddy and I'd be in a cottage where the ocean met the sound. But, I informed him with a smirk that it'd be okay if he visited sometimes.

I drew the landscape I envisioned, wanting to show Miss Heniford how much consideration I'd given the assignment. But the illustrated waves below the essay had smudged and smeared, smoothing out the lines and blurring the image into a gray mass. Below it, the red note continued, "This isn't art class."

Daddy didn't know about that essay. He didn't need to. He knew about enough. Miss Heniford sent home notes all the time, even though he never responded, said we didn't need to concern ourselves with her tendency to nitpick. As long as I kept learning, he was satisfied.

The sun began to peek through and shoot sunbeams onto my desk. That was the way of Carolina weather; the blue skies never stayed absent for long. With the passing clouds, Daddy would be headed to the woods. It would still be wet, his boots caked with mud when he would get home, but there were more trees to cut, more land to clear.

I watched the clouds as they rolled away, the charcoal fading with puffs of white moving in and dotting the blue sky, thinking about how Daddy said the clearing would bring more people, more visitors, more homes to our small town of Supply and the surrounding Brunswick County. Of course "town" was a loose term. We existed more as a collection of homes within a few miles of one another, a handful of businesses to meet the needs of our community, and only a couple of stop signs along our few miles of roads. Farm animals far outnumbered the population of people, and trees surrounded us except in the places on the edges of town that had been cleared for tobacco fields.

Daddy said someday we'd have to share the sand dunes that had so far been our private Sunday resting places. But of course they weren't ours. They never belonged to us at all, just like the woods behind our house and even the house itself. The property all had Mr. Barna's name attached, but how could a man ever really stake a claim to something that existed before him and would continue on long afterward?

CHAPTER TWO

To this day I can't say why I did it. Motivation and inspiration are fickle matters, I suppose. I didn't wake up thinking I'd start some trouble, and even as I was doing it, I wouldn't have said I was doing anything wrong or in need of correction. Like the orange and yellow leaves dropping from branches only to get caught up in a breeze, I suppose I got carried away, swept up in the moment.

Daddy worked late that evening. As I walked onto the back porch after school, Maeve met me there, meowing and purring. Daddy always said you can't choose an animal; they choose you. Maeve chose me alright. Even though she loved Daddy, we all knew she belonged to me. She'd sit on our porch and meow good-bye and hello to me each school day, begging me to let her nug—that's what I called it when she rubbed her cheek into me as if hugging without her arms.

I don't recall when she first started hanging around our place. So many cats that would wander up to our house lasted merely a season or less. Not Maeve. Sometimes Daddy would bring home a kitten he found lost in the woods, but if the kitten didn't know enough to find his own food, he wouldn't survive long because, truth be told, there were few scraps for us to share.

Maeve's continued presence was a curiosity since she came to us with a bum paw that never quite bent as it should. It hung sorta limp and, though she could walk on it, it pushed her saunter to one side, making her sway from shoulders to tail with each step. But it never stopped her from hunting a mouse or taking a bird clean out of the air. Good thing, since her survival depended solely on herself. Though, sometimes, instead of eating what she caught, she'd leave it on our back porch beside Daddy's work boots. When he'd go out in the morning to put them on, she'd walk figure eights between his legs. She'd stretch her head in the direction of his hand, waiting for a pat of approval. With it, she'd purr even louder.

That afternoon, I couldn't open my hand quickly enough. I'd tucked away a bit of the fish Daddy had caught and fried up for dinner last night. Her tiny triangle nose picked up the scent, and she persistently meowed to let me know.

"Got something for you," I told her as I unfolded my hand. Maeve didn't hesitate. She climbed onto my lap and began licking at my palm, her sandpaper tongue tickling, so I couldn't help but giggle.

"Miss Leah, what are yuh feeding that cat?" I knew the voice well, plus Tulla was the only one who called me that. "Miss Leah," she'd say, "you know Mista Jesse don't have to be friends with no girl" or "Miss Leah, you can't give a cat a child's name." I didn't understand why not. I thought it was an honor to name something after someone. After all, Maeve was the friend I had at school before her daddy decided there were better jobs in the mountains and moved the family west. But Tulla preferred Tiger, an obvious name given the cat's orange and white stripes.

I looked across to the Barnas' backyard. Tulla was standing at the clothesline where a few of Jesse's pants danced in the breeze. She dropped a shirt into the laundry basket on the ground,

tucked the clothespins in her apron pocket, and walked through
the line of azalea bushes into our yard. Well, it would have been
a yard had it any grass. Compared to the lawn on the other side
of the azaleas, our side of the bushes was mainly sandy forest floor
with lumps of roots twisting and turning along the ground, some
grasslike weeds, and a bit of ivy.

I answered her question as she walked toward me. "Just a taste
of fish."

"Fish?!" She put her hands on her hips, tilted her head to the
side, and raised her voice in disbelief. Her accent always seemed
thicker when she questioned the things I did. "Why yuh givin' a
cat any bit of fish?" Daddy felt the same way as Tulla. Treats like
that should be reserved for people, not animals. But hearing Maeve
purr as she licked my hand clean, I didn't regret sharing with her.

"You keep feedin' that cat, she's not gonna know how to
survive on her own. Plus, you're the one who needs meat on
her bones," she said, her shawl slipping from her shoulders. She
gathered the ends of it and hugged it around herself.

Of course Tulla was right, but it was a small piece. Satisfied
that she had licked every last bit of fish from my palm, Maeve
plopped herself down. She never was one for taking up a lap, but
she would rest beside me. Her purr began to fade as she busied
herself with her own washing, starting with her paws before rubbing them over her ears.

Tulla decided to take a seat for a few minutes before she had
to get the rest of the laundry from the line and dinner finished.

"The air's a-changin'," she said with her chin pointed to the
sky and her eyes closed.

I looked ahead of us to the row of live oaks that lined the path deep into the woods. Had they been a different variety of oak, their leaves would have turned colors by now and started dropping to the ground. But their name came from the fact that their leaves clung to their branches until the spring, always looking alive, regardless of the season. They didn't drop off and leave the trees barren. They stayed green and swayed in the breeze until the new growth budded each spring.

The three of us sat on the porch as the breeze rustled the oak leaves. The tall pines swayed back and forth, their fronds of needles reaching into the blue sky. They didn't offer the same shade as the oaks, at least not individually, but together their quantity darkened the forest floor.

"Do you ever dream of being someplace else?" I asked.

Tulla took a moment before responding. "Can't say I dream about much anymore."

"But if you did, where would that be?"

Tulla closed her eyes for a minute. She inhaled, her chest puffing up and holding in the air before she smiled and said, "Sitting in the porch swing with my mama."

That last word made my stomach drop. 'Course I'd want to be anywhere my mama was, if that was ever possible.

Wanting to stop thinking about her just then, I asked, "Know where I'd be?" I didn't wait for her to answer. "On the beach."

Tulla let out a little snicker. "I'll never understand your fascination being in a place with all that sand. Look around here. There's enough sand as is. I'm always shaking it out of Mista Jesse's socks and pants. Imagine it blowing inside all the time. Couldn't have the windows open. And then the salt water. It's pretty to visit, but it ain't for living."

I had heard her deliver this speech before, but it didn't matter how many granules of sand I had to sweep up. I longed to be in the place where I could hear the water sing to me with every crash of a wave, look out for miles with nothing in sight but a cresting dorsal fin or two, stand beside Daddy as he fished and smiled and seemed the most content out of anywhere.

But I didn't say any of that to her, not on that day. Home looked different to each of us, but at that moment, neither one of us imagined what Miss Heniford would call "feasible."

After a few moments, Tulla said, "I nearly forgot. Got somethin' for yuh." She moved aside the fringes of the shawl so she could reach into her apron pocket. She held her hand in a fist in front of me, slowly opening one finger at a time as the gift was revealed.

"Where'd you get those?"

"You know Mista Jesse. Has more than he needs. Doesn't use 'em anyways. Thought you could."

I thanked her as she dropped the crayons into my hand, giving me as much of a gift as she ever could. Her fingers brushed my palm, sending a chill through me like cold ocean spray on a winter day.

"Sounds like yuh daddy'll be home late tonight."

"Yep."

"Get the fire goin'," she said as she pulled the yarn shawl higher on her shoulders and wrapped it tightly around her body. "Gonna be a cold one tonight."

She stood from the porch, placed her hands upon her hips, and curved her stomach outward. She groaned and swayed for a minute before wiping the dust from the backside of her dress. I always wondered how old she was. I tried asking her once, but she told me that was nobody's business but her mama's.

"Be over a bit later with some drippin's from tonight's chicken," Tulla said as she walked away, staggering at first as she took a few steps. She always said she had to warm up those hips before they were alright.

"Thought you said if we feed Maeve, she's not gonna know how to survive," I called to her as she walked toward the row of azaleas. It would be months before they'd be full of blooms so heavy their branches would sag toward the ground. Each year I'd pluck a few to bring them into the house and put them in a glass of water. Their pink the only other color within our four walls besides Mama's quilt. But they never lasted long, maybe a day, before wilting and withering.

Tulla waved her hand in the air, keeping her back to me as she walked. "You're right," she hollered above the rustling of the oak leaves, "but sometimes yuh gotta love even when it don't make sense."

The fire started easily, much to Maeve's delight. I'd invited the cat inside for what I'd said would be a few minutes, but of course we both knew better. She stretched out on the hearth, rolling from back to stomach every few minutes as if trying to warm all sides of herself equally.

The wood stove sat in the corner of the living room, which was also the bedroom and part of the kitchen too. That's the way houses like that worked. They offered protection from the elements, not rooms and compartments all for different things.

A gust whistled through the walls, and I suddenly got to thinking of a different storm. A while back, the wind and the rain blew in from the coast, and the water dripped through our roof. Daddy struggled to light the fire, the sparks not wanting to catch on the damp firewood. He said something that I could barely hear over the pings of the drops falling into the buckets and bowls we had scattered about the house.

"How's that?" I asked.

He raised his voice above the din and said, "I'm sorry!" I didn't know what he was apologizing for. Before I could ask, he interrupted. "We wanted—" he paused for a few beats, the only sounds filling the house were the mismatched pings of the rain, a discordant harmony. Then he finished his apology, "—more."

We wanted more.

That's what he was sorry about? Wanting more? Back then I couldn't for the life of me figure out what more we needed than what we already had. My face never was good at hiding what I was thinking before I was even saying it. Daddy looked at me and knew I had questions to ask, but before I could, he said, "We were young. We thought we knew things."

That's when the wind blew open the front door. The latch never fastened all the way. As I helped Daddy move our dresser in front of it, I looked at the picture on top, the photograph of Daddy and Mama. So young. So happy. Daddy didn't have the creases beside his eyes yet. He didn't have the silver threaded through his hair. He smiled big. He looked like a man—and still kind of a boy—who thought there would be more.

The night of that big storm, I hadn't understood what Daddy had meant, but now, while I waited for him to come home and as the glow of the fire reflected on the floor, radiating an orange shimmer about it, I looked at the crayons and wondered. The firelight brightened their colors, made them flicker as the flames grew and shifted and danced inside the stove.

Maeve reached a paw toward them, bumping one so it rolled away from her. Her tail twitched like, maybe, she'd pounce. Maybe she'd get up and go after it like she would a mouse or a squirrel or a bird in the bush. But instead, she stretched, arching her back, rolling so her belly would face the fire as it took its turn at getting warm.

She pushed the crayon toward me, encouraging me, maybe? I had some time before I needed to start dinner, had plenty of time before Daddy got home, had only a little bit of time before the sun fully set and the light stopped coming through the windows.

I didn't have a pattern in mind when I started, but I had a vision to work from. I thought of the rug in the Barna's front hall, the colors and patterns, the movement of lines and shapes that repeated and rotated, none of them intersecting with one another but working alongside the other shapes to create a pattern of color and design. I started drawing, using each of the colors, making lines and shapes, extending the creation from the hearth and into the living room, making a rectangle of color in an otherwise wood-toned living space.

I looked to Mama's quilt on the bed for some inspiration and direction, but just as each quilt maker chooses her own style, I did the same. I thought of what I'd want in my own beach cabin one day, thought about sweeping sand off it in the doorway like Tulla said, and drew in some blue waves and designs. This rug wasn't going to be warm and soft and purposeful like the one in the Barna's entryway, but it would be colorful. I suppose that was the purpose it would serve; it would bring color and life to our home.

I finished well before Daddy got in. I let Maeve out the front door as he came in the back, the latch still not tight enough to keep out hurricane winds. Maeve growled at me for moving her out of her warmth. She flopped in my hands like a fish hooked and pulled out of its safe waters. I didn't have time to comfort her or ease her transition to the outdoors. I barely had the front door closed again before Daddy walked in.

"Hi, Mouse," he said as he stepped out of his boots and hung his coat and hat on the pegs beside the door. Sawdust sprinkled down like snow, dusting the floor around his feet. On warm days he'd shake out before coming in, but on this cold night, he came inside first, figuring he'd sweep up the mess later.

"Hi, Daddy!" I didn't run to him yet to give him a hug. I knew to give him time, let him get settled, put on a clean shirt first. After years of it being the two of us, we had gotten to know each other's rhythms. "Soup's ready when you are."

I don't know how I'd forgotten what I'd done or maybe I just thought it wasn't going to be a big deal, but my back was to Daddy when he saw the fruits of my creativity on the floor beneath his feet. I'd ladled one bowl of soup and was preparing for the second one when I heard him.

"What's this?"

Now that phrase can be said in many ways, good and bad, soft and loud, curious and furious. Just as I knew Daddy's rhythms, I also knew his tones, and his voice had more ferocity in it than it did curiosity.

With a ladle full of steaming cabbage soup, I stopped, trying to figure out what to say and what I'd done.

"Leah. Explain yourself."

He turned to look at me, waiting for me to respond, the flames of the stove behind him casting a shadow over most of the hand-drawn rug I'd spent my afternoon creating.

"I...I...I wanted to make something colorful."

"On the floor?"

"I don't know." My eyes began to sting as the words came out of my mouth. Truth was, I hadn't questioned the creative urge, but as Daddy demanded I explain myself, my mind made sense of what my heart had kept hidden. In that moment, I began to understand what he meant that night we battled the hurricane winds. Until then, I'd been fine with what we had, but while coloring a rug onto our floor, I realized that I'd entertained thoughts of wanting more too. "It's just," and then I started hiccuping, "so dark"—hiccup—"and brown"—hiccup. "Tulla gave me the crayons and—"

"No, now don't you go blaming Tulla for nothing. You did this. You admit to it and don't you go blaming nobody else."

I wasn't crying because I was afraid of getting a licking. That's not what my daddy would do, but sometimes I wonder if that would've been better. I certainly tested boundaries of permission, not intending to do what he'd call "unacceptable," but there were times he'd set me straight. The tears escaped as I felt a hole inside myself that had once seemed fully satisfied. And I cried because I didn't want Daddy to know that perhaps somewhere deep inside, I thought he wasn't enough.

"You know this isn't our home." He walked toward me and

looked me in the eyes. "This doesn't belong to us. We can't be making it our own like that."

"I just wanted"—what was the word? Ah, yes—"more."

Daddy closed his eyes and took in a breath, his face and shoulders softened and fell. He wrapped his arms around me, the sawdust still clinging to the folds of his shirt. With his chin on top of my head and my face in his chest, he said, "I know. But this place isn't ours." He held me as I hiccuped and then asked me the question he'd been asking me for years. "Where's your home?"

"Right here," I said as I melted into him even more.

"That's right. We're all each other has." His voice caught on the last word as he forced it out over the emotion, as if to remind both of us.

And I hoped that would be the last of it, that those would be the final words about my masterpiece, my homemaking, but I knew better. He gave me a minute to sink into his arms before he said what we both knew was coming, what I wished would've been replaced with a licking and a moving on. "Now you know what you need to do."

Unfortunately I did know, but I didn't want to. Why couldn't this have been left to just the two of us? Why couldn't he let me figure out how to clean it up and wipe it away so no one would ever know what I'd done? Instead, we put on our coats, more sawdust sprinkling out of Daddy's sleeves as his arms went right back inside the coat they'd just left. We walked next door and climbed the front steps onto the porch. He made me knock on the door, but he spoke when Mr. Barna answered.

"Would you mind getting Mrs. Barna? Leah's got something to confess," Daddy said. And as we waited for her to leave the dinner table and come to the door, I looked at that rug in their entryway.

Daddy made me look the Barnas in the eyes when I apologized for marking on their property. As the Barnas thanked my dad, I looked again at the rug that was on the floor in front of the grandfather clock that chimed as we stood there. Down the hall was the kitchen, across the way was the parlor and the dining room. So many walls. So many rooms. So much warmth spilling out of the house that night. I knew Daddy was my home, but sometimes I also wanted a porch and stately pillars, a beachfront view, a bedroom with a door and even a staircase if I was dreaming big. And definitely a mama, even if she looked at me like Mrs. Barna did as I confessed to trying to make myself a home, even if she was disappointed in what I'd done.

When Mrs. Barna thanked me for my honesty and reminded me that I'd be responsible for cleaning up what I'd done, my eyes couldn't hold back the tears. I only let go of a few, but I was embarrassed by even that many. I wanted to control them, suck in those tears like Daddy did the night that storm blew in, be strong even when I ached for something more.

CHAPTER THREE

My birthday was on a Sunday in 1935. I remember because Daddy was home all day. We lingered under Mama's quilt and then over weak cups of coffee. I knew not to rush Daddy on that day. He had both a mourning and a celebration to honor.

As I waited for Daddy to finish his now-cold grits and coffee, I focused on the still-lit flame of the table lantern, willing it to warm me. I cleared our breakfast dishes and dunked them into the basin. The water that I had warmed on the stove that morning was beginning to cool.

"You're a good girl, Mouse," Daddy finally said. He paused for a minute and looked at me, his brown eyes taking in all my features, looking over me like he hadn't been looking at me every day since I was born. I knew to give him time, a minute of silence. Though he wasn't talking out loud, I knew he was thinking, and when he got like that, quiet was what he needed.

"You look more like her every day," he finally said. "Even your freckles are just like hers."

"I've been counting more of them," I told him. And I had. Seemed like every day a new one popped up on my arm, cheek, nose, even my hands, covering my skin like the stars on a clear night. "Tulla says they're touches of an angel."

"Does she now?" That's what Daddy always said about one of Tulla's sayings.

"Says every time an angel touches me, I get a new spot."

"Well, I don't know about no angels, but your mama did pray for your protection every day from when she found out she was pregnant until—" This was one of those silences that wasn't about contemplation or thinking. It was about trying to forget. "Now about your birthday."

Daddy walked to his dresser and pulled open the top drawer. It always stuck when I tried to open it, the left stubbornly holding as the right side glided willingly. Daddy could always open it in one swift motion, whereas it took me a few tries of open-close-jiggle-pull before I could create enough space to place his clean undershirt within the drawer.

I knew what the two newspaper-wrapped gifts were before he even opened the drawer. Every year, without falter, was the same.

"One for the past and one for the future," he said as he placed both before me on the kitchen table.

While the gifts remained the same each year, I varied which I opened first. This year I chose the future. I reached for the flatter of the two, the one shaped like a rectangle, the paper loosely cradling the delicate contents. As I pulled back the newsprint, the deep-green leaves came into view. This year's find was a magnificent one, but not for its size.

"It's so small, but how'd you find one with the acorn still intact?" I pulled the southern live oak sapling from the wrapping, the roots rocking back and forth like the pendulum of the grandfather clock in the Barna's front hall.

For the first time that morning, he smiled. "A lumberjack never tells his secrets."

"How tall do you think she'll grow?" I asked.

"You think that one's a she?"

"Of course. Look how beautiful she is."

"I'd say probably taller than Three, but not as tall as Five."

The forest of our creation started at Mama's grave site, the one marked with the wooden cross and surrounded in the ever-growing pattern of seashells, knobbed whelk shells to be precise. The line of oaks stretched toward our house, each year getting a few feet closer to our back door. Lined in a row, we could identify which birthday each sapling represented. Five was the tallest, surpassing even One a few years into her maturing. She towered over Four even when we planted her, but Four isn't one we talked about anymore. We'd skip that empty spot when counting, silently recalling it but not speaking it aloud. That's the trouble with planting live things to remember the dead; sometimes what you plant doesn't live as long as you'd like either.

I reached for the second gift, and judging from the size of the package, this one was also smaller this year. But it would be hard to beat last year's whelk that was the size of the squirrels Maeve would chase up the trees and sometimes leave on our porch when they couldn't outrun her.

I pulled back the wrapping to uncover the shell. While not impressive in its size—its length barely longer than the palm of my hand—it was perfect in its wholeness. Finding a shell clear of any chips, cracks, or breaks was not easy. But finding one with the perfect coloring was even more rare.

The shell morphed from cream to clay-orange, creating a

symmetrical pattern around each turn and swirl. I ran my fingers across the lines of orange, tracing the polished smoothness.

"It's not the biggest," Daddy said, "But the color—" He didn't finish his sentence. Instead he reached across the table, his chapped hands pulling one of my ginger curls out straight and placing it alongside one of the orange lines of the shell. The colors matched perfectly.

As he released my curl, it bounced back into place, hanging beneath my shoulder. And as he sat back into his chair, he said what he said every birthday, "I couldn't give you the beach, but for now, you at least have part of it."

And I did what I did every year. I smiled and nodded. He knew we weren't the Barnas, nor the Holdens. Lumberjacks didn't own shops and islands and legacies. But that year I said something I hadn't before.

"It's okay. I'll see to it for myself one of these days."

Daddy's eyes squinted, the lines beside them scrunching together, as he smiled before saying, "I don't have any doubt that you will."

"We'll have a place on the eastern tip where the sun rises each morning while we eat shrimp and grits and drink our coffee. Nothing but you and me and Maeve and the wide-open sea."

Sitting at the kitchen table the morning of my birthday, I couldn't imagine dreaming of anything more.

We made room for Fourteen, her roots, acorn, and all. She was by far the smallest Daddy had ever given me. In the earliest years, Daddy had dug up adolescent trees, transplanting them and coaxing them to take root, but as the years went on, he found smaller saplings, telling me that we needed patience over time. Our forest couldn't be accomplished in only a few years. It would take decades or longer for them to grow tall and reach wide, providing shade and shelter. They'd go on growing long after we stopped walking the path, belonging to generations who would live well beyond us.

Sand clinging to my hands, I clapped them together before wiping the remainder of the dust onto my dress. In one hand I held the shell. In the other was Daddy's hand. We walked along the path, both of us silently counting the oaks. The farther we walked, the farther their branches curved and reached, making space for themselves in a wood otherwise full of spindly ever-greens that stood tall and narrow with the only signs of green at the top where they brushed against the blue sky.

The mound of shells lay just a few steps from One. Daddy walked up, leaned over the spiral of shells, and straightened the wooden cross. There was no name, nor date. The ones who wanted to know where Emma Payne was laid to rest knew where she was.

I walked around the mound until I found the spot for my shell. I smoothed out the sandy soil and wiggled it into place, making sure it had a solid positioning. And then it was time for the third gift. Daddy would tell me a story about Mama. Of course there were some stories he wasn't ready to tell me, some questions he had yet to answer. "When you're as old as your mother was when we got married," he'd say, meaning when I turned seventeen, he'd tell me all I asked. So for now, I wanted the story that led to their elopement.

"Tell me 'bout when you first met Mama," I said.

"Didn't I tell you that one last year?"

He had. But I wanted to hear it again. I wanted to hear about how the War had ended and the entire city of Raleigh flooded the streets. How men and women hugged people they didn't even know. How mothers cried and hoped their sons were about to come home. I wanted to hear about how Daddy saw Mama's red curls through the crowd. How he walked up to her, grabbed her hand, pulled her close, and kissed her before saying a word. And how she said, "Now that's a proper introduction," before she told him her name. I wanted to hear about how he took her hand, pulled her away from the crowd and her family. How they found a park bench under an oak tree and talked until sunset. How the girl raised in proper high society kissed Daddy's cheek before she went home. Daddy trailed behind at a distance so she couldn't see him, making sure she got back safely, not knowing until later how her parents scolded her for worrying them sick.

Daddy sat outside Mama's family's two-story home. He saw her father leave for work the next day in his suit and overcoat, his gold watch chain hanging from his vest pocket. When Mama left for school, Daddy stepped out from underneath a tree, and they spent the rest of the day under that same oak.

Maybe I wanted to hear that story more and more because I was only a few years away from being their age. Or maybe because it was a beginning that defeated the odds and expectations—a penniless son of a sharecropper and a debutante with a full dance card.

But if I'd have known that was my last birthday with Daddy, I might've asked more. I might've pushed for more stories, more memories to remind me of who Mama was and who I might become. Instead, I simply held his hand as we walked back to the house, progressing from One to where we had placed Fourteen. There was still more room to go, more space for future saplings.

As Daddy washed up our supper dishes that night, I went looking for Maeve. When I couldn't find her in her usual spots, I decided to lie down in the grass in the only place where the trees separated enough to see the night sky. I looked up at the sparkling lights, breathing in the crisp air as I counted as many of the stars as I could see. I wasn't done counting when I felt Maeve brush up against me and rub her fur along my arms before nugging her cheek against mine. Her motor started, her purr coming loud and happy. She nugged and rubbed until she curled up beside me.

She paused her purr when she heard Jesse say, "What're you doing out here?"

I kept on staring upward while answering, "Looking for Maeve."

"Looks like you found her."

As he sat down beside us, Maeve settled back into a nap, her purr starting up again, but this time with a little less motor.

"Isn't it kind of cold to be looking at the stars?"

I shrugged and asked, "What're you doing out here?"

"Taking scraps to the chickens."

We sat in silence for a bit. We usually didn't have problems being quiet around each other, but I felt like saying something, so I told him, "Today's my birthday."

"Really?"

"Yeah."

"I didn't know."

"I know."

"I'll be right back," he said. I thought that was an interesting way to wish someone a happy birthday.

Once again in silence, I heard the rumble starting off in the distance followed by a whistle. Of course we heard passing trains multiple times a day, but the silence of that night conjured a memory I didn't think much of anymore, the day Jesse and I never talked about. Even though we didn't share words about it, there's no denying that was the day things changed. He changed.

Living next door to one another and attending school together, we had certainly known each other before that day. Perhaps you could say we had played together some, but never on purpose or in a planned way. Back then, our differences felt too sizable, perhaps. We'd play sometimes when he'd catch me following him, hiding along the bushes or behind fat trees, keeping an eye on him—the quiet neighbor boy who always did his chores before adventuring off. Most days he'd not noticed me, or maybe ignored is a better word. On rare occasions, he'd call me out and maybe we'd strike up a game of hide-and-seek. Of course I'd usually win, having spent more time peeking from behind hidden places.

One of his favorite places to go was the railroad tracks back behind his daddy's property. His mama didn't like him going back there, said it was too dangerous and he was to stay within the property's boundaries. But that didn't stop him from sneaking away from the house, past the barns, deep into the forest, and out the back side to where the tracks cut along the edge of what they owned.

I really don't think he knew I tagged along with him that day, following from a distance so he couldn't hear my feet rustling the fallen leaves, or if he did, he'd blamed a squirrel. When he got to the tracks, he stepped atop, putting one foot in front of the other and balancing along the rail. He walked this way and that, back and forth, arms held out as he wobbled a bit from side to side. His feet slipped a few times, but he kept standing back up and balancing again.

Now I don't know why, but for as smart as that boy was, he couldn't seem to get a handle on fastening his shoes. Mrs. Barna and Tulla were always reminding him to tie them up right. Apparently he ran out the back door without them seeing him, without them warning him to tie those laces good and proper, because when he slipped that last time, he didn't rise back up and start his balancing again like he had before. Keeping my distance, I couldn't see at first what he grappled with on the ground, but I could make out his pulling and tugging. And that's about the time I heard the rumble starting up in the distance.

"Jesse!" I yelled, giving away my hiding place as I began running through the leaves. When he heard his name, Jesse looked in my direction and when he quieted himself to hear me, that's when he also heard the rumble for himself, probably felt the tracks start shaking.

"Train!"

He looked from me to the path of the oncoming train before trying to tug himself loose again. By the time I reached him, the laces held so tight that he couldn't pull out his foot. He used all the strength his eight-year-old body could give him, but it only bound him more tightly to the tracks.

"Stop pulling!" I told him. I reached for his laces, trying to loosen their grip on him, but he kept pulling on the one free length of lace. "Stop!" I said again. "Stop pulling!"

I don't know if he finally decided to listen to me, or if it was the sight of the train rounding the corner and coming toward him that made him finally freeze, but he stopped pulling long enough for me to get my fingers under the Xs of his laces to loosen it enough to pull his foot free of the shoe.

The train blew its whistle, startling the birds out of the trees and Jesse off the tracks. Together we tumbled backward before standing to our feet and running for the cover of the forest as the train rolled fast and loud over his shoe that was still bound to the railway.

After the engine and all its freight cars passed, we walked up to the tracks to find what remained. Neither of us said anything. The metal wheels of the train had broken the lace, so the flattened, torn, and barely recognizable shoe—or what was left of it—was free.

Jesse took it in his hand, slowly examining all sides and pieces of it. He did his best to put it over his foot, hoping he could cobble it together so maybe his mama wouldn't notice.

I don't know if she ever did notice. I don't know how he went about explaining only having one shoe to wear, but I suppose he had others to choose from to get him by. But I do know that it was after that day that I started to get to know the boy I had lived beside my entire life. Sure, we may have been more barnyard than schoolyard friends, but I never was one to mind keeping a secret. Certain parts of ourselves didn't always need to be known by all.

The train had passed before Jesse returned to me in the yard, this time saying, "Happy birthday," as he reached toward me with something in his hand. "Mama and Tulla said to tell you happy birthday too."

Still caught in that memory of a few years ago, I hesitated.

"Did you have one of your spells?" he asked.

That was Jesse's word for my flashes. As much time as we spent together, there was no hiding them from him and while they bothered him the first few times, he had grown accustomed to them, having patience until I returned and not calling me strange for leaving in the first place.

"Not this time," I said before looking at his extended hand and asking, "What's this?"

"A biscuit. It's not cake, but it was all Tulla had."

I sat up and took the biscuit from his hand. The scent thick with baked buttery goodness floated upward and into me, making me inhale slowly and completely, my eyes closing and a smile coming across my face. Maeve didn't appreciate the smell or the disruption of my movement, so she headed off toward the barn.

I took a bite before finding my manners. "Thank you," I said with my mouth full, a few crumbs spilling out as I spoke.

"You're welcome," Jesse said. He lay down, his arms crossed behind his head, looking upward while I finished the treat. "Don't you wish we could see the stars any time of day?"

Of course I did, but I felt I needed to set Jesse straight. "That's not how they work," I told him, as I wiped the final crumbs from the sides of my mouth and licked my fingers clean.

"What's that supposed to mean?"

"The brightness of the sun outshines them in the day. We can only see the stars in the dark."

I expected Jesse to say a "yeah, but." But he didn't. Maybe he was thinking about what I said. Or maybe he was giving me a small birthday present by not picking a fight just then. Quiet and cold surrounded us for a few minutes before he spoke again.

"Look at that one there," he pointed. Just over the tops of a silhouetted tree, a star shined orange. "It's the same color as your hair." He was right. And then he continued, "That's your birthday present. I give you that star."

"I'll take it," I said. "Daddy says the stars stay still. We may move, but they always remain. Sometimes we can't see them the first time we look, but they are there, just as steady as always."

We lay beside each other in the grass, pointing at stars, making lines and designs, and imagining different shapes until Tulla called for Jesse from his back porch. The coolness started to rattle me, the chill getting stronger when he walked away, so I decided to go inside. I could look at stars another night, find that orange one Jesse had given me, but right then I needed to warm up, to crawl under my quilt as I thought about the day, the gifts, and the planting, imagining how tall Fourteen would grow. I drifted off to sleep with thoughts of growth and maturity, of reaching limbs and green canopy. But how was I to know that would be the last sapling we'd plant along that path?

CHAPTER FOUR

A few weeks later, on a morning when I needed him, Daddy left before I woke. He didn't hear me cry out from a nightmare. I bolted awake, sitting upright in bed so quickly my head spun and my body rocked as dizziness swooped and swirled. Sweat dripped from my forehead despite it being so cold that I could see the puffs of my breath in the air like shadows floating through the darkness. I pushed back the quilt and touched my toes to the dusty floor beneath.

I shivered as I walked to the pitcher Daddy had left on the kitchen table. I took a drink, hoping for refreshment, but the chill of the water dripped down into my body filling my insides with an icy dread. I called out for Daddy, but then I remembered he had gone to the woods. Mr. Barna wanted him out early, wanted him to beat the storm that was sure to come. Daddy was probably hitching up the horses next door, getting them ready for a day's work. I should've gone to see him that morning, to hug him and inhale his scent. But I knew Daddy didn't like to be interrupted at work. It wasn't safe work, he always told me. The sharp edges of the axes, the horses, though tame, still strong beasts meant for work and not play. Besides I needed to get to school.

The grits were cold on the stove. Of all mornings, I needed

something to warm my bones. As I scooped my breakfast into a bowl, I saw Maeve sitting in the kitchen window. Her meow came through the thin pane. Daddy wasn't there, so what was the harm? As I walked to the front door, she jumped from her perch and met me there. I picked her up, put her on the bed, and crawled underneath the quilt. She leaned into me, purring, both of us seeking warmth in one another as I ate my breakfast. When I was done, I placed the bowl in front of her nose. She sniffed and then licked it clean.

"Don't tell Daddy," I said.

I remember walking to school like normal with Jesse that morning. The cold didn't seem to bother him much, but he had a coat with sleeves that went all the way to his hands. Plus, he had mittens. And a hat. I tried to pull my sleeves over my hands, or at least to my wrists, but there was no budging them any farther. A few months ago, Tulla had let out the shoulder hem as much as she could. "This'll do yuh," she said as I tried it on, but we both knew it wouldn't.

Truth be told, I remember most things about that day, as typical as it was until it wasn't anymore. The moments play with a clarity like none other, even as simple and typical as they were, as if I was storing up what happy looked like. After all it's not until something worse comes along that we can look back and realize we had something good all along. If only we hadn't been so foolish as to miss it at the time.

Miss Heniford surprised us with a math quiz that morning.

"What?" Tom protested. He was the boy who liked to call me

orphan. I'd always remind him that I still had a daddy, but he'd say that didn't matter. "You didn't tell us about no test."

"Any, Tom," Miss Heniford said. She held the stack of papers in her hand and licked her finger before taking one from the pile and placing it on each wooden desk. "'You didn't tell us about *any* test.' Class, you will have thirty minutes to complete this. That's plenty of time. Don't rush. Take your time and turn it in when you're done."

A math test. I was afraid it was going to be another one of those grammar quizzes. Or maybe a theme we had to write right then. Miss Heniford and I didn't see eye to eye on imagination stuff. But when it came to right and wrong answers, I stood a better chance.

Jean-Louise was the first one done. She stood up, straightened her dress, and walked with her shoulders back toward Miss Heniford's desk.

"Thank you, Jean-Louise," Miss Heniford whispered.

"You're welcome, Miss Heniford," Jean-Louise responded at full volume before turning on her heels so quickly that her dress twirled outward and her blond curls whipped around. She strutted back to her desk and took her seat, carefully smoothing her dress underneath her bottom as she sat. She stretched the top of her skirt, so it made a perfect half circle over her legs. She brushed the curls from her shoulders before looking at me and smiling. I rolled my eyes at her.

"Leah!" Miss Heniford didn't whisper my name. "Eyes on your own paper."

I could feel my cheeks burning as I looked back at my test.

It wasn't that I wasn't good at math or that I didn't know the answers, I just needed more time than most of the others. Miss

Heniford should've known that by then, but her five-minute warning always seemed to imply, "Hurry up, Leah. Everyone else is already done." But she said we had thirty minutes, and I was going to use as much of that time as I needed.

I finished with a whole minute left to go. When I stood to turn it in, Tom said, "'Bout time."

Miss Heniford didn't hear him, but I know she could've. I was closer to him than she was, but he didn't say it in any sort of a quiet voice. He looked away from me as I walked closer to his desk. Some of the others were still snickering. Miss Heniford kept on grading everyone else's papers. At least until she heard me fall.

Trying to avoid looking at anyone else, I held my paper up. I couldn't see anything in front of me, but there was nothing in the aisle to see. Even still, my foot got tangled as I passed Tom's desk. As I took a step, my foot caught on something. I put my hands down to brace myself as I fell to the floor, my left knee hitting before anything else.

"Leah! For heaven's sake!" my teacher called.

I rolled from my stomach to my back and rubbed my knee. *Don't cry. Don't let him see you cry*, I kept telling myself.

"You've got to watch your step," Miss Heniford said. The room had gone from snickering to silence to full-out laughter in that one minute I still had left to be taking my test.

"Yeah." Tom leaned down so only I could hear him. "Watch your step. These desks are known to jump out atcha."

I grabbed my paper from the floor. The fall had wrinkled it. I smoothed it out as I limped to turn it in.

On the way back to my desk, I chose another route and took my seat. Thankfully it was reading time, so I sat my book upright on my desk and leaned down so no one could see the tears that refused to stay in my eyes.

It had been spitting rain most of the morning, but as I kept behind my book, the rain started making a little tinkling sound when it hit the window. Tiny water crystals sparkled across the glass and reflected back the classroom lights.

I was lost in a trance of my own making, thinking about Daddy and me running away to that beach, leaving Tom and Mrs. Heniford and Jean-Louise behind, when the crack erupted. It was a boom that started in the sky and rumbled until it felt as though it was all around us, above us, below us, beside us. It rumbled and it echoed. It crashed to an end. A few of the girls in the classroom screamed. And then it was over as if nothing had happened, nothing had changed, and life was just as it should be.

Jesse and I kept to the ditch alongside the road on the way home, the road itself being too slick with ice. The grass and weeds within the ditch gave us a bit of traction so our feet didn't slip quite so much. Jesse stumbled and fell a few times, grabbing on to me as he went down, nearly pulling me with him when he'd try to stand. His wobbling about made him look like Maeve's litter of kittens one year, before they grew big enough that their legs stopped wobbling and heads stopped bobbing when they took a step.

"How can you stand on this stuff?" he asked.

"Slide. Don't walk," I said. I showed him how to scoot his feet along, adapt to it instead of fight against it. But he kept trying to push through with strength and speed, though neither got him far before he ended up on his rear end again.

As we neared his house, I didn't hear Mrs. Barna calling for me at first. When I finally did hear her voice over the tinkling of the falling ice, it sounded different.

"Leah!" she called, waving her arm and motioning me toward the house. I kept waiting to hear her say more. Her voice was quieter than usual, her eyes glassy, I assumed from the cool air. "Careful on the steps," she said as we walked to the porch. I paused for a minute wondering what she needed. "Hurry up, child, before we all catch the death of—"

That was all she said. No more words came out, but a small hiccup escaped. She clutched a handkerchief to her lips and extended her other hand to me. She pulled me up the steps, walked me to the front door and opened it, waiting for me to move forward.

"Inside?"

She dropped the handkerchief from her mouth and said, "Of course."

As I crossed the threshold, I stopped, afraid to step off the rug and drip water onto the hardwood floors. I never got tired of looking around that house. The staircase climbed to the second story, the wooden banister shining even in the dim light of the overcast day. I looked to the lighting fixture above us that must've glowed brighter than all of our lanterns combined. Standing in the foyer, I was blocking the others from entering.

"All the way in, child."

I moved so we could all stand in the front hallway. Mrs. Barna started pulling on my coat sleeves, trying to remove my soaked outer layer as I looked to my left and right. On one side was a dining room with a table that wouldn't even fit in our house.

More chairs lined its sides than people Daddy and I knew, or at least knew well enough to have over for dinner if we had any food to share. To the other side was a room with davenports, chairs, and tables with lace doilies and knickknacks on top of them.

Mrs. Barna continued to tug on my sleeves, trying to release me from my overcoat, but it wasn't until I stopped looking around and started helping her that we finally got the coat to budge. She hung it upon a hook by the door before telling Jesse to go run along upstairs. She ushered me to the kitchen table, where Tulla sat with an expression a lot like Mrs. Barna's. Except her eyes held a few more tears. Mrs. Barna placed her hand atop Tulla's and gave it a little squeeze before asking Tulla to bring me some hot tea.

Tulla sat a delicate cup in front of me, one with no chips, no partial handle. It was complete, whole, and painted with pink flowers that reminded me of Mrs. Barna's prized azaleas. Steam curled toward the light over the kitchen table as Tulla poured tea into the cup. Still chilled from the ice, I didn't wait for it to cool before I took a sip. I was about to take another when Mrs. Barna reached out and laid her hand atop my own. I sat perfectly still, but my hand began to shake a bit, nervous as to why she'd called me to have tea, wondering what she had to say. The more I focused on hers, the more my hand trembled.

"There's no easy way to say this, Leah," she began. Tulla no longer sat at the table with us. She busied herself at the sink, turning the faucet off and on as she washed up the dishes. She didn't have to heat water on the stove first. She just had to turn a handle. I had asked Daddy why we didn't have a sink like that. He shook his head and said, "be thankful for what you do have."

"Leah, you know what your daddy does?" she asked. I nodded my head before remembering my manners. Speaking to someone like Mrs. Barna, Daddy always said I needed to use words, but before I could say, "yes, ma'am," she continued. "You know it's dangerous work?"

This time I was able to unstick the words. "Yes, ma'am."

"Well, today there was an accident," she said.

Over the years, I've pieced together the details of the day from conversations, retellings, and questions I asked, creating a picture show in my mind, a playback of the events. There was the woods and a team of horses. And there was Daddy beside them. A layer of ice covered the ground around him so slick the crew fought to stand. Daddy had the trailer hitched up to the team, logs piled high. They had gotten a lot of work done that day before the storm started, but the fierce weather blew in hard and fast before they could get the load out of the woods and back to the mill. Daddy's hands were red from cold, but he still pulled and tugged on the rope, trying to secure it in place. He bent down low near the front of the trailer. Something was caught. Something wasn't working right. If he couldn't tighten the load, the logs on top would shift once they started moving the horses and they needed to move them quickly before the ice made the journey impossible. He leaned down to look closer. And that's when the thunder clapped.

Winter thunder doesn't happen often, but just like that double rainbow at the beach that one evening, the weather can surprise us.

Chestnut reacted first. I'd named him because of his coloring. He always was the most beautiful of the Barnas' horses but the most fickle as well. He never did like loud noises. That clap, the boom, was what shook the classroom that afternoon. The foretelling of what was to come. Well, it spooked Chestnut. He reared onto his hind legs, which only made the others follow suit. The horses' movements shifted the wagon. Daddy called whoa. I know he did. I know he tried. But the pelting of the ice, the neighing of the horses drowned him out. He tried to stand up, but he hadn't tightened the load. One horse's rear led to another and each of them shifted the load of hard work they had stacked that day.

Daddy tried to step out. His feet slipped like Jesse's on the way home—no small, short slides, but unbalanced efforts that only left him even more off-balance. Until he fell.

If the load had been secured, he would've been fine. He would've stood up, grabbed the reins, gotten the horses under control. But it wasn't secure. The timber shifted. The tall pines he felled hours earlier moved and rolled and dropped from the top of the wagon onto the ground below. Onto the man slipping and sliding and angling for his footing. Until he was still.

Mrs. Barna finished delivering her short version of the story. She didn't tell me all the details then. She did the best she could to tell me what I needed to know at that moment. She did it through hiccups, apologies, and her own grief. Her tears rolled steady like the ice outside the window.

"You'll stay here for now," she said. "You'll use the extra room upstairs next to Jesse's until we sort things out. This'll be your place until we find another."

And that was when I finally spoke. "With all due respect, Mrs. Barna, my place is next door."

Tulla and Mrs. Barna turned their attention to one another, mouths hanging open before Tulla said, "Now, Miss Leah, how's about we go on and get you settled?"

She wiped her hands on the tea towel that hung from her waist apron, as she walked toward me. She pulled out my chair and took my elbow to help me stand. I wondered how Tulla did it, each day, waking in her little bedroom, making a bed that didn't belong to her, cooking meals with food that wasn't hers with pots and pans and spoons owned by someone else. She knew what it was to exist in someone else's place, to live within a house without ever really having a home.

As I let Tulla walk me out of the kitchen, I caught sight out the window. The ice continued to fall, but through the distorted window panes, I could see Maeve. She sat on the porch, looking in, not perched in the window like she did over at our place. Mrs. Barna didn't see her or she would've chased her off. At least on a normal day she would've. Maeve didn't meow. She sat with her tail curled around her, her fur matted to her body, wet from the weather.

I wanted to break free of Tulla, to run to Maeve and tell her to get in out of the cold. I knew I shouldn't worry about her because, just like Daddy always said when I'd sneak her a treat, "She knows how to survive." But part of her surviving was finding family. She had chosen me, but right then I had nothing for her. And in that regard, the two of us became kindred spirits, two strays without a place to call home.

CHAPTER FIVE

That night, I lay alone in the Barna's upstairs bed, waiting for sleep to take away the hurt. But sleep slipped from me like the minnows my hands never could quite capture. I heard every tinkle of the last falling ice pellets, each creak of the house, every snore of Mr. Barna, the random ramblings of Jesse in his sleep. As the clouds finally began to move away and the moonlight dripped through that upstairs window, I wrapped a blanket around me like a cape and tiptoed out of bed, down the stairs, and out the back door. I'd only taken a few steps off the back porch when Maeve darted between my feet.

The moon lit a path, guiding me to the place I wanted to be, and Maeve came along for the adventure. I stepped over limbs the ice had pulled down, hearing the crack of a falling tree too weighted to stand any longer. I knew the threats of an ice storm, how it turned the protective tree canopy into a danger. I sought my shelter, hurrying through the back door of our house, the cold not much different inside than it had been outside.

One of Daddy's flannel shirts hung beside the door. I dropped my blanket cape and reached for it, pulling it to my nose. I inhaled the combination of sawdust and musk, and that was when the tears flowed out of me with hiccups that turned to heaves. I melted to the floor and cried into Daddy's shirt. I cried so loudly I was certain the startled owls outside flew deeper and farther into the woods. As I curled on the floor and let the grief wash over me, Maeve began to circle, rubbing on what skin of mine she could find. Her sandpaper tongue slowed my tears as she licked clean the bridge of my nose right where Daddy would push against my freckle.

Maeve walked to the bed and I followed. She waited for me to pull back the covers and climb in before she jumped up. She walked in circles beside me, positioning herself just so before plopping down, her body pressing into mine. I fell asleep to the sound of her steady purr and escaped into a world free of feeling.

I remained so lost in sleep that I didn't hear their distant calls the next morning. I didn't know of their panic until Tulla shook me awake, repeating my name until I answered. Once I told her I was quite alright, she ran to the back door and shouted.

"Miss Leah's here!"

She came back inside, pulling the shawl around her shoulders.

"Why'd you give us such a fright?"

I rubbed my eyes free of sleep. "Didn't know I had."

"What'd you expect when we found an empty bed and no sign of yuh?" Honestly, I hadn't thought of them looking for me. She clasped her hands together and blew into them. "You slept here all night? You lookin' to catch a cold?"

"I had Maeve with me."

"And that's another thing. You think the missus wants to see you sleeping with a cat? You know how she feels about animals and their place being the barnyard." She reached for the blankets, but I grabbed at Mama's quilt and hung on. Her voice gentled at the gesture. "Come on now," she said. "It's time to be getting on to school."

I could hear Mrs. Barna's voice through the windows. I shook my head. "Let me be." Tulla again tried to pull the blankets back to coax me out of bed, but I held on tighter.

"Now, Miss Leah, it's time you get up and get on with your day."

My fist tightened around the quilt. The only energy I had was for staying put where I was. I couldn't even think of sitting at my desk, swinging my legs like any other day as Miss Heniford explained the difference between a pronoun and an adjective. Then I thought of Tom, and I knew that if he called me an orphan again, I'd have no defense.

Mrs. Barna's voices grew louder. Any second she'd walk in. I released the quilt and put my hand on Tulla's. "Please, Tulla," the tears pooled heavy in my eyes, "don't make me go."

The door creaked open and sunlight began to pour in. The weather had changed and birds sung their songs as if yesterday's storm had never happened.

"Leah! There you are!" Mrs. Barna came rushing to the bedside. "What on earth were you thinking?"

I grabbed the quilt and dabbed away the wet tears that had fallen down my cheek. "I'm sorry," I said. "I couldn't sleep."

Mrs. Barna shivered, "But it's so cold in here." She looked around the room, her eyes moving quickly until she saw my artwork on the floor. She kept on looking at the crayon work I hadn't yet washed away. "Well, let's get back inside now. Some breakfast'll help warm you up."

"Missus," Tulla began to speak, "Leah's saying she's not feeling up to school today."

"Oh, yes, well, I suppose I can understand that, but how about we don't decide anything until she gets some breakfast in her?"

"I'd rather stay here," I said. "We still have some grits I can cook up."

"No, now, Tulla's already put together your breakfast. Come on with yourself and let's go where it's warm."

Mrs. Barna walked out the door, expecting Tulla and me to follow along behind her. I had every intention to hesitate, but Tulla took my hand, pulled me upright, and wrapped the quilt around my shoulders. Before she could lead me out the door, I walked to the dresser and grabbed the photo on top, hugging the rigid frame to my body, the corners pressing into my chest.

As we walked outside, the sun hit my eyes and warmed my cheeks. The trees shined brighter that morning, the last bits of ice still glistening on the branches as the melt dripped to the ground beneath. Fallen branches lay broken across the landscape of the yard. Soon there'd be no more of yesterday's ice, only remnants of the destruction it had caused.

Tulla and I trailed along behind Mrs. Barna. "I forgot the Barnas' blanket," I said.

"You can go back for it after breakfast."

She barely finished her sentence before we heard a crack echo through the yard. A flock of birds flew into the air and cawed as the sounds of the breaking tree rumbled through the air and caused Maeve to dart ahead of us and scurry under the Barnas' back porch.

Tulla and I both cowered to the ground, looking behind us to see what the noise was all about. We looked back to see the fronds of the falling evergreen slide through the air before the tree bounced to a rest on the house where, moments ago, I had been tucked away in bed. A whoosh of air sprayed melting ice and pine scent in our direction, the force so strong it blew my hair away from my face. As the mist quickly dissipated, we caught sight of what was left. The house remained standing, but the tree cut through the front edges of the roof, blocking the front door while tearing planks off the wall.

"Good gracious!" Mrs. Barna called as Mr. Barna came running toward the three of us, asking if we were all okay.

Tulla tried to hold on to me, but I broke loose from her, running back in the direction of my home.

"No!" Tulla and the Barnas called, but none of them could catch me, except for the one who took me in nearly every foot race we had. I felt Jesse's hand on my shoulder before I even knew he was in the yard that morning.

"Leah! It's not safe!" he told me, as he slowed my momentum.

"But—" I tried for words, but nothing came.

"It's not safe. You don't know how many other trees might be coming down along with it."

He was right. These trees lived in a community, roots intertwined beneath the soil's surface, strengthening one another. When one fell, it was possible another would follow.

All I had left in all the world was my quilt and the picture I'd taken from the dresser before we'd walked out the door that morning. I held both against me as I fell to my knees, a sobbing heap of nothingness. The ice had taken both my daddy and my home. There, in the wet sandy soil, Jesse knelt beside me. He wrapped his arm around me and let me cry, recognizing who I now was: motherless, fatherless, homeless.

———————

A few days later, we laid Daddy to rest right alongside Mama. The ceremony was a simple and quiet affair. The five of us stood around the sandy mound, bowing our heads. No preacher read any scripture. Mr. Barna held his hat over his heart as he said what a hard worker Harley Payne was—the best he'd ever had. Mrs. Barna said my daddy was a good man. She could see it in him from the time he and Mama showed up at their door, asking if they knew of a place to stay or a job that needed to be done. Tulla said he was kind, just like his wife. Jesse didn't need to say any words; he just stood by me, shoulder to shoulder. Sometimes the strength you need comes in silence.

When Mr. Barna put his hat back on, everyone else seemed to know the ceremony was over. They all headed back to the house, but I remained, moving the shells back into place after they'd been moved to make room for Daddy. And I'd return to that work over the next few weeks at the Barna's whenever I began missing Daddy so much that I didn't know if my lungs could breathe.

After a bit of time, Mrs. Barna decided that I didn't need to go to school anymore, at least not until "things" got settled. In the weeks I stayed with them, she spent a lot of time figuring out my situation. I explained to her that all I wanted was to stay in my house, but the tree lying on the front of it made her side much easier to argue. Plus she said the state had a say in things, and we needed to do as they said. I soon learned to stop listening when I figured out my voice didn't matter.

Tulla tried her best to distract me, said idle hands were the devil's playground, so she asked me to help with some chores. I peeled a few potatoes and tossed scraps to the chickens. The last day she asked me to help her, she'd handed me a dusting cloth and told me to go dust Jesse's room. She walked in a few minutes later to see me holding a whelk shell I'd found on Jesse's dresser. I had picked it up and wiped the dust from the top of it, but I couldn't put it back down. It looked exactly like the last one Daddy had given me, but much larger, larger than my hand. I held it to my ear. The sound of waves closed my eyes and swept me away from the Barnas' house. I stood at the shore, feeling the warm sun that we hadn't seen much of in the time since the ice storm. I felt the spray of the ocean water rolling down my cheeks, the memories and the longings making my nose drip.

Tulla's voice pulled me from the shell's hold on me. She told me to put the shell down, to run along outside and she'd call me for lunch. I didn't want to go outside. I wanted to stand at the water's edge. I wanted to feel the smooth hardness of the shell, rub it against my cheek, feel the coolness of it. But I did what Tulla told me to and I headed to the only place that did feel like home.

Every time I walked out the back door, Maeve sat perched on the porch, her tail wrapped around her body, waiting for me. We spent our days back at the grave site, rearranging the seashells to cover both mounds of dirt. After Jesse would leave for school, I'd go out there and work on the design, changing it only to go back the next day and start all over again. But with every new design, I left that one whelk with the orange, spiraling lines on Mama's grave.

But there was something I wanted for Daddy's grave.

I tried to stay away from his room. Even still, the ocean pulled me in, whispering its song in my ear, calling me to come find it, take it, and give it to Daddy as the only homage to our past I could ever give him.

Though time meant little to me, there were rhythms to the day that I came to recognize while I was there. They mostly had to do with when meals were served. I suppose I should've known when Jesse was about to come home, about to walk through the front door and call for his mama. Maybe I was figuring that call would be the alarm to warn me. But I didn't hear it. I didn't hear him come in the house, nor climb the steps, nor walk to the threshold of his bedroom. The first thing I heard was him saying, "Leah?"

The second thing I heard was the shell smashing onto the floor and shattering into shards. We both stood motionless in the room, staring at the broken pieces on the floor until Mrs. Barna ran breathless into his room.

I waited for the punishment, for the tone, the look, the yell, any sort of reaction to the thing I'd just done. Nothing came. Instead Mrs. Barna turned to Jesse and said, "I'll have Tulla clean it up."

I walked across the hall and into my room, closing the door behind me, sliding down the door and onto the floor, my head resting in my hands.

I didn't come out of my room until Tulla called for dinner. When I did, I walked past the dining room, careful to not look at the Barnas sitting around the table. That night, I sat with Tulla, and we ate in silence. As soon as I was done eating, I walked out the back door, through the yard and azalea bushes, and into the tree-lined path, but someone had beaten me to it. Standing at the grave site was Jesse. He must've left through the front door before I had finished eating.

"Is this where you go all day?" he asked.

I shrugged my shoulders and we stood shoulder to shoulder, staring ahead at the mounds before us, the shells spiraling atop them.

"You don't talk much anymore," he said. I shrugged again, so he tried something different. "Miss Heniford yelled at Jean-Louise today."

I sucked in my breath. "No, she didn't."

"Did so. She caught Jean-Louise sassing at Tom."

"Well, I'm sure he deserved it." Not that I typically sided with Jean-Louise, but in this case, I could understand why she'd done it. Jesse knelt to the ground. "I've missed you."

"I've been right here."

He began smoothing out the dirt, picking up my pattern where I'd left off. "It hasn't felt that way." Then he started talking about the day, what happened at school, who got in trouble, and what Miss Heniford had been trying to teach them. We worked shoulder to shoulder, our knees darkened from the sandy soil by the time we finally headed back to the house. Winter sunsets happen early, and the darkness had come when we weren't looking. I had to lead the way down the oak path, warning Jesse of any roots he needed to avoid.

"I didn't even know these oaks existed until we came out here for your daddy."

That was all he said about the path, and at that moment, I didn't give him any explanation as to where they'd come from. I wasn't ready to give away certain parts of me just yet.

After that day, Jesse'd come home from school and find me in the woods. He'd tell me about the day's happenings as we'd work together, passing shells to one another, smoothing out the dirt with our hands, creating new patterns before heading back to the house for dinner. At least that's how it was until Mrs. Barna "sorted things out."

CHAPTER SIX

I heard talk of my situation one afternoon when, instead of taking the typical path, I moseyed through the woods on my way to visit the chickens. The Barnas stood outside the barn, talking to one another, not noticing me peeking from behind a tree. I hadn't been able to walk into the barn since before the ice storm. I couldn't bring myself to see those horses.

"She says they have room for her," Mrs. Barna said. At first I thought they meant the horse Mr. Barna wanted to get rid of. I had wanted him to release Chestnut, but he was too much of a worker horse for Mr. Barna to want to lose him. Instead he hoped to find a place for the weakest one, the one that cost more in feed than she contributed to the logging.

Mr. Barna lifted his hat and scratched his head before saying, "Well, I guess that's what we've got to do, then. Did you tell Leah?"

I paused when I heard my name. They hadn't been talking about the horse at all. I crouched down behind a bush a bit closer to the barn, hoping I could hear better. I looked through the leaves, watching the Barnas, stretching to make out their conversation.

"Not yet. Girl's been through a lot. Didn't want to say too much before they found a place for her." I knelt down lower and got as quiet as I could though my heart pounded loud in my ears. "Wish she'd be closer, for Jesse, but guess she's got to go where there's space." Mrs. Barna turned into the wind so that the strands of hair that had come loose from her bun flew free of her face.

"Distance'll do her good," Mr. Barna said. "She doesn't need to be reminded of this place."

Mrs. Barna nodded her head. They both stood silent as I tried to understand it all. Mrs. Barna had explained finding a foster family. 'Course I couldn't help but think of the little girl in town—I think Carrie was her name—the only survivor of her family's house fire a few years prior. When I'd asked Daddy who would care for her, he said she'd be sent away to a foster family— strangers who agreed to take her in. At the time, I wondered what that would be like to leave all you'd known to move in with someone else and get on like you were a family, but really, you'd be strangers. I hadn't spent too much time thinking about it, though. I hadn't needed to then.

"Sounds like they have three kids, a girl close to Leah's age," Mrs. Barna said.

"That'll be good for her."

"I hope so." Mrs. Barna paused again. She lowered her voice so I could barely make out the next part. "I just hope it works out. Especially with those spells of hers. What happens if it doesn't?"

Mr. Barna put his arm around his wife. "It will."

Mrs. Barna's words came out muffled, but I could still hear the question. "And if it doesn't, would they send her to a children's home?" The last words sent shivers down my spine.

"I know you promised Emma you'd make sure she was taken care of." My mama's name caught my breath. I leaned in, causing the bush to shake, but the Barnas didn't seem to notice, too focused on each other to know how close I was. "That's what we're doing. It's what we have to do."

Mrs. Barna turned into the wind again. "We can't keep her," she said as she looked into the woods, right over the top of where I hunched to listen. I gathered all the strength I had to keep from shouting out and asking why not. "I can't even look her in the eyes. I keep thinking of that day. How long she labored. If I'd called the doctor sooner—" She began to shake as her voice caught. "Or Harley. If he hadn't gone to the woods that day—"

"You can't go on thinking like that," Mr. Barna warned his wife. She nodded like she understood, but she put her hand to her mouth, as if trying to hold in the emotions that wanted to burst out. He put his arm around his wife again, and together they turned to walk into the barn.

Once they were out of sight and I could get my legs to work, I left my hiding spot and headed deep into the woods. Running helped my body let go of the shock, my heart pumping hard and fast, my lungs aching for air, trying to cleanse myself of the dread I felt. But no matter how fast or far I ran, my mind didn't stop playing that conversation over and over, trying to figure out how to protect myself.

Out of breath, I finally sat down on a fallen tree. Two squirrels darted through the dried leaves, chasing one another up and around trees, jumping from one branch to another before running down a tree trunk and around another. Those two squirrels seemed as content as ever to chase each other. They didn't have anyone telling them where they needed to be or where they had to go or where their home could and couldn't be. They ran free and wild. I watched them as I thought about what I'd heard, as I tried to prepare myself for what I'd be asked to do next: leave the only place I'd ever known.

In that moment I wanted to run farther. I wanted to head to the tracks and try to hitch a ride on the next freight train to go rumbling by, ride it until I felt like leaping off and starting new. But of course I couldn't. Trains never slowed enough for me to jump on. Besides, what would I do once I got someplace different? I had no money. No skills for a job. No way of making a place for myself. Plus, what would happen when I got found out? Would the foster family that was willing to take a girl with spells be as willing to take a runaway?

I knew I had no options. Those squirrels could do as they pleased without the threat of being snatched up and thrown into an orphanage. It may've been called a home, but I knew enough to know it was no place for a life.

Before I could think too much about it, I heard Mrs. Barna calling for me. I wanted to stay put, to ignore her and keep my distance. But as her voice grew louder, I figured being more agreeable would better serve my situation.

"Come help me with the azaleas," she said as I walked out of the woods. She carried a pail of coffee grounds and egg shells, a spade resting on top.

When we reached the line of bushes that separated our homes, Mrs. Barna got on her hands and knees and told me to do the same. She moved the soil at the base of the bush with her shovel before scooping up some of the coffee and egg shells. She worked at mixing the scraps into the dirt, patting it down once it pleased her.

"You know who taught me how to do this?" she asked, a bit

out of breath from the gardening work. I shook my head no. "Your mother." I stopped staring at the ground and looked at Mrs. Barna. Her eyes had lines beside them like Daddy had, but you could see hers even when she wasn't smiling. She sat back on her heels for a minute and wiped stray hairs away with the backs of her wrists. "You should've seen these plants before your mother moved in. They were nothing to write home about. One day I found her out here, working coffee grounds and broken shells into the soil, and wouldn't you know, next spring these bushes had the most blooms I'd ever seen."

She stood up and moved to the next bush. She didn't tell me I had to, but I followed her, and when she handed me the shovel, I copied her movements.

"Your mother was a kind, wise woman." She let me feed the roots, not saying anything else until I had finished. "I think you've got her touch with nature. Now it's time to move on to the next."

I worked the soil a bit before I asked, "Did you know Mama well?"

"I knew her a bit. Not sure I'd say well. We'd talk some when she was helping around the house, but your folks were both quiet. Guess you could say that made 'em good neighbors." A chuckle escaped her, and when her smile faded, she continued, "From the moment I met them I could tell they were kind, just a bit down on their luck."

I mixed the shells and grounds into the dirt and patted it down, and together we moved to the next bush before Mrs. Barna said, "I know you've been a bit unsettled since the incident, but it sounds like soon your new place'll be ready."

I kept working the dirt. "I'm quite alright here," I said.

"I know, but that's not how things are working out."

I crawled to the next bush, digging deeper, harder, and faster, bumping into roots and nearly cutting through some of the smaller ones with the shovel. "I've been thinking," I began, "What you said about quiet neighbors, well, I believe it's time I move back to my home."

"Leah, you know that ole place isn't safe." Mrs. Barna said.

I paused my digging and looked at her. "That ole place's all I got."

"There's a way of doing things," Mrs. Barna started saying as my cheeks heated up. "You're still a child."

"I've been cooking and cleaning and tending that house since before Jesse could even tie his own shoes."

Mrs. Barna's eyes grew wide. "You're right." She reached for the shovel in my hand before continuing, "But there's a family waiting for you."

"What good's a family to me if it ain't even my own?"

I didn't give her time to respond before I stood up and took off running. I headed back for the woods, not wanting her to see where I was going. I heard her call, but she didn't chase after me. I ran to the back of the property and then walked the boundary that brought me to the back of the overseer's house.

Until that moment, I had listened and obeyed. I had stayed away from the house, knowing it wasn't stable, but it was the only refuge I had at that moment. I peeked around a tree to make sure no one saw me. No one was looking, so I stepped out of the woods, onto the back porch, and through the back door. Light poured in through the ceiling and the front of the house where the tree had wrecked it. Branches and drying fronds hung like chandeliers in the living room. I took a moment to look around, realizing that, other than the tree, the only difference since the morning I'd last been inside was that the Barnas' blanket was no longer there.

Maeve eventually found me, walking through an opening near the front door. She nugged me to say hello before chasing after specks of dust that the afternoon sun illuminated as it shined through the window. We stayed in the company of only one another until someone knocked on the door a while later.

I didn't answer until I heard Jesse's voice.

"How'd you find me?" I asked as he walked inside.

"When you weren't with the shells or back by the railroad tracks, I figured this was the only other place you'd be."

He looked around the house. At first I thought he was examining the tree damage, but he moved his eyes around every part, pausing longest on my hand-drawn rug. That's when I realized in all the time we'd been beside each other, he'd never actually been inside our home.

"I think I'm leaving soon." The words flew out of me like the gush of wind the falling tree had caused.

Jesse walked farther into the house, moving to the edges of my artwork. He knelt down and ran his fingers over the lines. "You did this?"

"Yeah."

Jesse stood up, stepped back, and took a long look before he laughed and said, "I bet your daddy wasn't happy about that."

I laughed and shook my head. Jesse turned away from the rug and walked past me to the back door.

"Where are you going?" My voice climbed higher than I meant it to. "Did you hear me? They're sending me away!"

Jesse opened the door, stepped out, and then right back in, holding something behind his back.

"Whatcha got?" I asked.

Jesse's lips turned up into a smile as he brought his arm around the front of his body. There, balancing on his hand was the shell. The pieces it had broken into were put back together like a puzzle with glue, still sticky, holding it all together.

I reached for the shell, but left it in Jesse's hands. I feared how fragile it was, and I didn't want to damage what he had put back together. I touched my fingers to it, feeling the broken smoothness as gently as I could. When I looked him in the eyes, he smiled and said, "Let's go finish arranging things."

We worked side by side, Jesse telling me once again about school lessons, brown nosing, and schoolyard scuffles. We talked and laughed. We let the sun set and the bats come out for their evening snacking before we gave into Mr. Barna's calls to come in for dinner. Jesse led the way down the oak path, now knowing for himself where the roots lay and waited to trip us up. As we walked into the clearing above our joint yards, the stars met us.

"Mama already told me you're leaving," Jesse began. "She told me about the family. Said they have three kids, a girl close to your age."

"I don't want to go," I said, but Jesse interrupted.

"Listen, we both know you don't have a choice," he grabbed ahold of my hand and turned to stand in front of me, making sure I saw his eyes even in the dim light. "I know you don't want to hear this, but give them a chance." I rolled my eyes and pursed my lips together. "Let them give *you* a chance." I didn't expect those words. "We both know how—free—you can be. Let them see the Leah I know."

He wouldn't let go of my hand until I made the promise. It took me a minute and a few huffy breaths, but I told him I'd try. As we resumed walking, Jesse pointed to the sky. "There's your star." It always looked different than the rest, the one that glowed bright and orange. "You know what I like best about it? It's not like the others."

And then he took off running, calling for me to try to beat him. We raced to the back porch, acting as though this night was no different than that morning racing toward the schoolyard. Other than Jesse's advice, we didn't talk about my leaving. Maybe we should've, but instead we chose to carry on, as if that day was like any that had come before and any that would follow.

The next morning, as Tulla prepared for me a plate of eggs and a thick, warm biscuit smothered in her homemade muscadine jam, the phone rang in the front hall. Mr. Barna spoke in mumbles too quiet to hear. After a couple of minutes, he returned to the table, sat down across from me, and said, "After breakfast, I'm to drive you to your new home."

"What?" I asked as a part of my breakfast fell out of my mouth and onto my plate.

"It's all settled. They're waiting to meet you and asked that I bring you right away."

I looked to Tulla, who paused spreading the jam on her biscuit. A tidal wave of questions hit my mind all at once, but the only one I could get to come out of my mouth was, "Is Tulla coming?"

Mr. Barna took a drink of his coffee and said, "No. Just you and me."

"Jesse?"

He shook his head from side to side. "I'm afraid he's gone to school already."

"Why can't I stay here?" I asked.

Mr. Barna and Tulla looked at one another. "We've got instructions."

"I can live in the overseer's house. Help with the gardening and cooking. Maybe even the dusting."

Tulla placed her plate on the table and put her hand on my shoulder. "Miss Leah"—I could hear the quiver in her voice—"This is the way of things right now. Go on and eat your breakfast, and I'll help you get your things gathered up."

She nodded to Mr. Barna, who took one long sip of coffee before putting on his hat and walking out the back door.

I ate nice and slow that morning, but no matter how slowly I chewed, I couldn't stop what had already been set in motion. After clearing my plate, Tulla took me up the stairs and began packing my things for me. Packing meant putting sleeping clothes and an old school dress into the center of the quilt before folding it up. Of course, I also added the framed photograph.

"I remember when your mama made this," Tulla said, as she gathered the patchwork blanket together. "The way she pieced together the bits of old fabric and made something beautiful." She clucked her tongue and continued, "I always thought it matched her spirit, a bringing together of things."

Tulla turned toward me and uttered, "Be a good girl for your new missus." She grabbed me and hugged me. I melted into her arms. Since Daddy's passing, people only ever touched me on my shoulder. And it was usually quick and fast. A pat, a sigh, and then they'd move on with what they were doing.

With Tulla's arms holding me, I reached around her back and grabbed my wrists, forming a belt at her midsection. She moved to let go once, but then squeezed me again. Feeling her strong, slender arms around me, a flood of tears broke through the dam and poured over my eyelids.

Once I started gasping and hiccuping, Tulla let go. She got right at my eye level, and her big brown eyes as dark as her skin looked straight into mine. She put one hand on each cheek and spoke slowly, "Miss Leah, there's no use cryin' over the past."

Snot dripped from my nose and mixed with the stream of tears that flowed down my cheek. Tulla pulled a handkerchief from her apron pocket and wiped the mess off my face. "You're a good girl, Leah Payne. I see the same light in you like I saw in your Mama and Daddy. Don't yuh ever forget that."

With the mention of my parents, the sobs rolled out of me again, tears flowing round and heavy down my cheeks. Tulla let me hold her a minute longer.

As she turned to leave, the hiccups finally released my voice, so I asked, "But what about Maeve?"

"Why're you worried about a cat?" her voice slow with each word falling into the next, a laugh fighting to come out. As she waited for me to respond, her laugh disappeared, her head tilted to the side, and a deep exhale escaped her. "You don't worry about Tiger. I'll see to it that she's alright."

Tulla left me alone for a minute to get myself together before going downstairs. I didn't want to be left alone. I hated being alone in that room, the mattress cold, the walls and shelves decorated with pictures and keepsakes that meant nothing to me. All that ever felt like home was gone.

I reached for the quilt, bunched it up, and slung it over my shoulder. I could hear Mr. Barna starting up the pickup truck, but I needed to say good-bye first.

I raced down the steps, through the front hall, and out the back screen door.

"Miss Leah!" Tulla gasped before the door flapped shut behind me.

Maeve leaped from the porch railing and caught up with me before I even made it to the azalea bushes. It had rained overnight. The trail beneath the oaks was wet and slippery. I slowed down and walked to the grave site. There in the middle of the newest mound was the shell we'd placed there the night before. I picked it up and held it to my ear. There were no waves, whooshes, or crashes this time, but the ocean of my imagination met me there in the woods. My eyes fell closed, and I could see the surf. I could even smell the salt water. I saw my Daddy standing beside me, looking out at that surf. Mr. Barna's voice broke through the waves and hollered, "Leah! It's time to go!"

But before I could go, I closed my eyes again and brought Daddy back to mind. His hair flapping in the ocean breeze, the gap in his front teeth showing through his smile. "Daddy," I called to him, "They're sending me away. I don't wanna go, but I have to." I swear I smelled the salt water and felt the sand on my toes before Mr. Barna's voice broke through again. Before running to him, I had one more thing to say to Daddy: "I'm gonna try to be a good girl, like you taught me. But I won't go forgetting who I am."

That was the most certain I'd been since the ice had taken Daddy. I said good-bye to all I knew, but I stored it up in my heart. I didn't know what was on the horizon, but if Daddy had taught me anything, it was that home existed not simply in place but in the arms wrapped tightly around you. 'Course I didn't know then the motion of natural forces, the beating of the tides that I'd have to swim against if I'd ever find home again.

Part Two

MATTHEWS, NC
1936

CHAPTER SEVEN

When I asked Mr. Barna how far we'd be going, he'd told me it'd take a couple of hours. He put the truck into gear and headed out the driveway. As we picked up speed, we passed my house, still blocked by the collapsed tree. I turned to watch it out the back window as long as I could until the trees and the distance took it from me. I wished with all my might that I'd have taken more from the house, even one of Daddy's flannels to keep me warm despite Tulla saying it wasn't right to wear the clothes of the dead.

We bumped along in Mr. Barna's truck for a few hours. I'd never been that far away from home before. The beach was the farthest I'd traveled, and that was only a few minutes' drive. But where we were going that day was the opposite direction of the beach. Instead of the evergreens giving way to sand and shore, the trees grew denser and the roads longer. We began to dip and climb, and in the distance, we could see different hues of leaf-barren trees rising and falling along hills that stood out against the bright blue Carolina sky. I asked if those were mountains, but Mr. Barna said that we were still a few hours away from the Appalachians.

Sometime after I ate the sandwich Tulla had packed for me, I rested my head against the truck window and closed my eyes. I wondered about this family I was about to meet. How old were

they? What was their house like? Did they eat the same food as
me, or did they have things like liver and onions that set my
stomach to rolling? I dreamed of my room, wondering if I'd have
a bed of my own. In my imaginings, I pictured a place more like
the Barnas, a family of means who was kind enough to share
with someone. While that seemed good and a blessing I should
be thankful for, I stopped myself from being too excited with
possibility, because allowing hopes of wealth to woo me seemed
like betraying Daddy.

The thoughts, possibilities, and steady rocking of the truck
lulled me to sleep. By the time I woke, I was uncertain of how
long I'd been asleep, what I had missed along the way, or where
our journey had ended.

As Mr. Barna pulled alongside the curb and placed the truck
into park, my eyes tried to adjust to the new surroundings, taking
in the straight, paved street outside my window, lined with sym-
metry in both natural and man-made structures.

"Where are we?" I asked.

This street looked nothing like the one back home, the tunnel
carved out between tall pines that interconnected, touched, and
fought with one another to reach the sunlight above them. This
street held a single line of leafy trees on either side of the road.
And sidewalks beneath them. Houses lined up beside one another
with thin strips of grass between and in front of them. White
picket fences separated one yard from another but remained low
enough to allow you to see what was going on next door. There
were no wide-open yards with orchards and chickens and space
from the few neighboring houses.

"Matthews," Mr. Barna answered.

"We still in North Carolina?"

He laughed. "Yes. We aren't in Brunswick County anymore, but we're in North Carolina." He put his hand on the door handle and said, "Wait here till I call you."

The hinges squeaked before the door slammed shut and shook the truck. I watched Mr. Barna walk around the front of the truck and to the sidewalk. He hadn't dressed up that day like he did most days when he wasn't working in the woods, at the mill, or checking in at the country store. He had on his work boots, denim overalls, and brimmed field hat. He was taller than Daddy and had lighter hair, though he had a shiny bald spot on the top that he tried to cover with a long patch of hair that had to continually be reminded of where it should be. As he walked toward the front steps, he took off his hat and swooped that long hair up and over the hairless circle, patting it down, though it popped back up the second it could.

The porch spread long and deep, wrapping around the house before disappearing from my view. I think my own house could've fit beneath its overhanging roof. One side of the house rounded out from the rest, almost like a fancy silo with curved windows I'd never seen before. Its roof was a round and pointy hat. The rest of the roof had straighter lines, though it too had some peaks above upstairs windows with shutters that framed them all. For a moment I let myself wonder which of those windows might be mine.

I don't know how long it took for someone to come to the door. I got distracted looking around at the outlines of the house, the bushes, and the winter-barren trees. But when I stopped, I saw who I supposed would be the missus of my foster family. I didn't know what to call her—the Barnas hadn't told me that.

From a distance, she looked typical enough, her hair pulled up, her dress hanging below her knees, her slight heels still making her shorter than Mr. Barna. She stood outside the threshold of the house, facing Mr. Barna, who waved for me.

I took a deep breath and reminded myself of what Jesse had said. *Let them give you a chance.* Then I grabbed the handle of that old pickup truck and lifted it, but couldn't get the door to budge. Daddy had always opened it for me. I lifted the handle again and tried to push. Still nothing. With my left hand holding tightly to my quilt, I lifted the handle a third time and this time put the weight of my shoulder into the side of the door, which flung open with a cry of the hinges. My full weight had shifted into the door, and as it swung open, I fell out and onto the ground beneath.

As I stood up and wiped the dirt from my school dress, I looked at the two adults standing on the porch. They both stared back at me, but neither made an effort to help. Eventually Mr. Barna turned his back to me as he and the woman continued to talk.

A corner of the quilt dragged on the ground beside me as I approached the house. The closer I got, the more I saw that the house's beauty I had first glimpsed from a distance wasn't all there was to see. Upon closer inspection, I saw details I had overlooked on first inspection. The paint was cracked. The hat that topped the silo was missing a few shingles. The shutters above the second window from the right on the second story were crooked. Cobwebs reached from the porch roof to the pillars. And the third step leading up to the porch sank as my slender frame stepped onto it.

"Mrs. Griffin, this is Leah," Mr. Barna said as I ascended the fifth and final step with the quilt still dragging on the ground.

Mrs. Griffin looked me up and down. Her dark hair was pulled into a tight bun atop her head with just a few wisps of bangs hanging along her temple. Her dress cinched at the waist, giving her an hourglass figure. She had been smiling at Mr. Barna, but as I stepped closer, the corners of her mouth fell.

"Hello, Leah," she said, fixing that smile back in place behind closed lips.

"Hello, ma'am," my voice squeaked. I then attempted a curtsy, but my left foot got tangled in the overhanging quilt and my pleasantry ended in more of a stumble than a greeting.

"I'm not sure if they told you," Mr. Barna said in a hushed voice, as he fidgeted with the brim of his hat, "but she's a pretty quiet type."

Mrs. Griffin watched me for a minute before saying to Mr. Barna, "Thank you. And thank you for helping get this matter settled." That was when I got a good glimpse of her smile up close, her pink lips parting to show crooked teeth, whiter than any I'd seen before. "I hope the drive out today didn't trouble you much."

"No trouble at all, ma'am. I was happy to do it. Gives me an opportunity to see about some business out this way."

"I see."

Mr. Barna smoothed his long, flock of hair onto his bald spot before dipping his chin and saying, "But I do wish we'd met under different circumstances."

"As do I," Mrs. Griffin said, with a side glance in my direction. "Does she have more in the truck? Perhaps a suitcase?"

"No, ma'am. They had little, not much of worth. Not even a suitcase to put her things in."

"I see," she said quietly, her eyes getting squinty. I thought it was maybe from the sunlight, but she stood in the shadow of the porch. "Can I offer you some tea and perhaps a biscuit before you leave?"

"That's very kind of you, ma'am, but I'm afraid Mrs. Barna is expecting me home for dinner, so I should be on my way."

My stomach began to rumble with the thought of a warm cup of tea and a light, fluffy biscuit. My eyes started to sting as I began to realize how far away I was from Tulla's cooking, from Maeve, from my home. I took a deep breath, blinked fast and hard, and hugged the quilt to my chest.

"Of course. Again, Mr. Griffin, I thank you for all you've done, for troubling yourself."

"It was no trouble at all," he said. Then he paused, looked at the ground, and said, "Don't hesitate to write if there's anything—"

"I'm sure we'll be fine."

"Of course." But he didn't finish his sentence. As he turned to me, he kept his eyes focused on the floorboards below. "Be well, Leah." With that, he put his hat on his head and walked back to the truck.

Before he could get all the way down the sidewalk, I turned and, with desperation boiling up inside of me, I put all my might into making my voice heard, "Tell Jesse I said bye!" Birds took flight at the sound of my voice echoing down the quiet street.

Mr. Barna paused, turned back, and bowed his head in my direction, but he didn't say anything else.

"Quiet type, huh?" Mrs. Griffin muttered as she gave a final wave to Mr. Barna. Then she instructed me to, "Come along," before she turned to go inside.

The wooden floorboards creaked as I stepped inside the front entryway. It reminded me of the Barnas' house—a climbing wooden staircase, a runner on the floor pointing the way in—but thanks to the shadows of trees that blocked the sunlight and the clutter of stuff placed and piled about, walking inside felt like entering a cave.

I caught a glimpse of the front parlor and the dining room as Mrs. Griffin guided me into the kitchen. Potatoes, carrots, and a cutting board covered the table in the center, with dishes, pots, and pans scattered over the counters.

"Let's get your things settled, and then you can help me get dinner set," Mrs. Griffin said. I turned to leave the kitchen, to walk back in the direction of the front staircase, but the missus kept walking through the kitchen, to the back door. "Where're yuh going?" she asked me.

I turned around to see her holding open the back door. Turns out, my room wasn't behind any of those windows I had seen outside. It was behind a door on the back porch. The door squeaked as Mrs. Griffin opened it. A spiderweb hung diagonal across the top of the doorframe. I was certain Mrs. Griffin's bun would brush through it, but she missed by only a few hairs. I followed her into what looked like a haphazardly constructed closet, an afterthought assembled in the corner of the porch.

Stepping inside, she walked to the center of the dark room and pulled a string. A light bulb turned on. The room was only long enough to fit a bed—smaller than any I had ever seen before—along one wall. Beside the bed stood a makeshift dresser with a small rectangle of a window well above it. Only a few rays of light broke through the window and came into the room. At the tops of every corner was a spiderweb.

I stood in the doorway, clinging tightly to my quilt, wondering about this closet of a room that was supposed to be mine. But this being my first moments with my foster family, I worked to fix my face before the missus turned to look at me.

"This'll do," one of Tulla's phrases escaped as I put on a smile and hoped my eyes didn't show the shudder I felt inside. I stood in the doorway, not ready to cross the threshold quite yet.

"Take a minute to get settled and then meet me in the kitchen." Mrs. Griffin looked at the balled up quilt I still clung to. "I'll start introducing you to your helpmate duties."

I nearly dropped my quilt, picture frame and all, onto the floor. *Helpmate?* I looked at Mrs. Griffin, who was trying to squeeze by me in an effort to leave.

"Helpmate?" I finally said out loud, my voice cracking on each syllable.

"Why, yes." Mrs. Griffin tilted her head to the side. "It's why you're here." Mrs. Griffin straightened her back. "Given your," she searched for the word, "situation, you've come to help with domestic duties."

I stood in the doorway, still blocking the missus from leaving. My mouth hung open. My body frozen. My heart beating so I could hear and feel it. Mrs. Griffin watched me, her eyes growing more worried with every second I remained quiet. When I finally said, "What?" she exhaled and moved to step around me.

"Don't worry about all that just now. Get settled then meet me in the kitchen."

The door squeaked on its hinges as she closed it behind herself and left me alone in the closet—my new room. I grabbed tighter to the blanket I had been holding all morning and hugged it to me.

Helpmate?

Did the Barnas know?

How could they send me to this place to be someone's maid?

Did Jesse know?

I walked to the bed and plopped down, the mattress squeaking beneath me. I sat alone in the darkness, other than the glints of sunlight that filtered through the one window. Turns out when I'd been dreaming of having a room of my own, I hadn't thought to also wish for a family to go along with it.

CHAPTER EIGHT

With my place being outside the house itself, walking inside felt like barging into someone else's space, even more so than my situation already warranted. Before I tapped on the door's window, I took a deep breath. I remembered what Jesse had said and what Tulla had told me that morning; I needed to be a good girl for this new missus. So I got myself right before I knocked.

She didn't come to the door and open it for me. She sat at the kitchen table and waved me in.

"You don't need to knock," she said, keeping her eyes on the carrots she had been peeling.

"Sorry, m——," I didn't know what to call her, and with this being my foster family, I assumed she thought of herself as a mother of sorts to me. I tried to make that word come out, but it stayed low inside me, not wanting to call anyone but my own mama that word.

"Mrs. Griffin," she said for me. "Call me Mrs. Griffin or ma'am."

"Yes, ma'am," I said. I closed the door behind me, and when she didn't give me specific instructions, I took it upon myself to sit down at the table and begin peeling potatoes. I'd done plenty of that with Tulla. I worked hard and fast, wanting above all to make a good impression. And I do think that's what I was doing up until a potato, still wet from being washed, slipped enough so that the blade of the peeler hit my thumb instead of the skin of the spud.

"Ow!" I put my thumb in my mouth, sucking on the blood, trying not to cry in front of the missus, who stood from the table, wet a cloth, and brought it to me.

"Wrap this around the cut and put pressure on it." She handed me the cloth and sat back down across from me. I wrapped my hand around my thumb, squeezing so much I could feel a throbbing. Once the bleeding stopped, I reached for the peeler again, this time not trying so hard to do such quick work.

Mrs. Griffin kept her eyes on her own task when she said, "Fast isn't always good. Slow and steady will sometimes get you further. I'll finish up here. You go on and wash up. Kids'll be home from school soon." She said this as if she'd told me about her kids already. "I'll call you for dinner once it's ready. Tomorrow we'll get you acclimated to the house and show you your duties."

Despite my best efforts to control myself, I know a look of disgust shot across my face before I could right myself again. I could only imagine what duties this woman had planned for me, what tasks she'd expect me to do. While I wanted to be free to run through the woods and sit on the porch with Maeve, I took in a deep breath and reminded myself that at least I wasn't in a children's home.

It took only a minute to wash up and, not knowing what to do with myself, I went out back. I didn't want to sit in the darkness of my room, so I walked into the backyard, stepping out of my shoes so my toes could touch and feel the grass, the crunch of the leaves, the coolness of the soil beneath the dormant blades.

I'd missed the view of the backyard when I'd followed Mrs. Griffin to my quarters, too focused on where she was taking me to see anything else. It was much smaller than the yard I'd always known. Neighboring houses sat close over the fence line. I wondered where kids had space to run and move, especially when accounting for the trees, bushes, and garden plot that took up their own stretches of the place.

I walked to the center of the small plot of yard and lay down. The clouds overhead rolled and twisted fast, looking like a rabbit at one moment before morphing into a jack-in-the-box. I watched cloud after cloud swirl by, colors of white mixing with grays before hints of pinks seeped in. I listened to the birds chattering in the trees, the squirrels scampering over fallen leaves. Though this town held more houses and buildings than back home, the animals still found their way around, making homes among the humans, tucked away and hidden in plain sight, like the squirrel nest tucked into the tip-top branches of the sweet-gum tree. I watched it sway in the breeze, wondering how it felt to have your house rocked with each passing wind.

A while later Mrs. Griffin opened the back door and called me to come for dinner. I walked into the kitchen, blinking as my eyes adjusted to the light. Mrs. Griffin was standing over the stove, dishing boiled potatoes from the pan and into another bowl. When she turned and looked at me, she nearly dropped the bowl. "Do you have some proper clothes for dinner?"

I looked down at my dress. Tulla had scrubbed it as best she could before I came, but there was no getting out all the dirt and stains from running around the land and arranging the seashells. She had patched the few holes I'd gotten, some of them from Maeve's claws getting stuck. But she couldn't get it as clean as she'd wanted to.

"I suppose we'll have to see about getting you something to wear. Thing's too short for yuh anyways." Her words were a blend of the Southern drawl most of the people from Brunswick County spoke and the Northern influence like Miss Heniford spoke, you's and yuh's mixed into the thought without much reason for choosing one over the other. It was as if her words were fighting with one another, all trying to escape to cover up for the other one. "And where're your shoes?"

"I must've left them out back," I said. "Just wanted to feel the grass between my toes."

"Well," Mrs. Griffin began, "we wear shoes in this house, as people do. Run along and get them. Then have a seat at the table."

Before I walked back into the house, I did as I had done before entering the kitchen that afternoon. I took a deep breath, telling myself to be on my best behavior, to show the side of me that made Jesse and Maeve my friends, not the one that Jean-Louise rolled her eyes at.

My body shook a little as I walked into the dining room, assuming everyone'd be waiting to meet me. The man I figured was Mr. Griffin sat at one end, but I couldn't see much more than the top of his head that poked above the newspaper in his hands. From the table setting, it looked like Mrs. Griffin would sit opposite him. A boy who I guessed was older than me sat to the man's left. Opposite the boy was a girl who looked to be my age or a smidge older. Beside the boy was a girl young enough that I guessed she'd still say "and-a-half" at the end of her age.

I took another deep breath and walked into the room. The kids all paused. I willed myself not to trip, not to flash right then, to be as normal as I could be. The older girl swung around to see me, her dark ringlets bouncing just like Jean-Louise's. But when she saw me, she smiled instead of scowling and finally my legs stopped shaking.

"Hello!" the girl with the curls said. "Here! Have a seat right next to me!" I pulled out the chair and sat down, relieved to no longer be standing in front of everyone. "I'm Eva Jane! I'm so happy to meet you!" she leaned over to hug me, pinning my arms to my body.

"We'll do introductions in a minute. Right now it's time for the blessing," Mrs. Griffin said as she took her seat at the head of the table, opposite her husband. "Franklin, I said it's time for the blessing." The man behind the newspaper didn't move at all. "Franklin!" Still nothing. "Franklin!"

"What?" Finally two eyes peered over the top of the paper.

"I said it's time to pray."

"Right." Mr. Griffin folded up the newspaper and placed it next to his plate. He looked older and paler than both Daddy and Mr. Barna, with more gray hair than either and a lot of it piled high on his head, sticking out a bit on the sides. He adjusted his wire-rimmed glasses, pushing them higher up the bridge of his long, narrow nose before folding his hands together and bowing his head.

Everyone around the table folded their hands together and lowered their heads as well, even the littlest one, who sat across from me. But during the prayer, I saw her peeking at me through squinted eyes that she tried to pretend were closed. When I winked at her, she squeezed them shut and smiled.

After the "amen," Mrs. Griffin started the introductions that went something like, "Franklin, Michael Henry, Eva Jane, and Mary Ann, this is Leah, our new helpmate. Now, let's eat."

The family all nodded as if that made perfect sense. Mrs. Griffin plopped a boiled potato onto Mary Ann's plate and her own before handing the bowl to me. After hearing the missus describe me as nothing more than a helpmate, I didn't know that I had much room for dinner, but I also knew it'd be rude to pass. So, I took a small potato before putting the smallest piece of meatloaf I could find on my plate.

"No wonder you're so skinny," Eva Jane said as she put two helpings of meatloaf onto her plate. "Mama wishes I'd eat less. Gotta fit into my dress in a few months, she keeps saying. But Daddy says I'm a growing girl and it's fine. Mama says I'm growing the wrong way. But what does she know?" She let out a breathy laugh as she forked another piece of meatloaf and began moving it toward her plate.

"Eva Jane, that's quite enough," her mother's voice was low, her eyebrows high.

Eva Jane's chin dropped toward her chest as she put the third helping back on the platter and passed it to her father.

Mrs. Griffin went on talking to her husband. When she wasn't looking anymore, Eva Jane turned to me and rolled her eyes. She then giggled, but I saw the pink in her cheeks and the water pooling in her eyes even though she tried to blink it away.

After dinner, we moved into the front parlor. Mrs. Griffin said I could retire with the others for that night; she'd take care of clearing the table this once. She didn't have the energy to show me the way of things just then, so she'd just do it herself, like she had been doing since the last helper had left some weeks ago—some person named Alma.

"Come sit beside me!" Eva Jane said as we walked into the sitting room. She plopped down on the settee in the corner and patted the cushion beside her. "I just love your hair." She reached up and touched my curls. She ran her fingers over them softly. "I wish I had curls. Mama can't stand curls, but then what does she make me do to my hair? Curl it! I have to sleep with my hair tied up in rags. Or try to sleep. Do you know how hard that is? Well, of course not. What am I saying? You don't have to do that. Your hair is already curly, so why would you have to try to force it to be? But Mama insists."

She talked more than Jesse. I struggled to keep up with all she said, and I couldn't help but wonder how she ever caught her breath. But the whole time, she looked at me and smiled. She might not've asked me my thoughts, but she at least acted like she thought I was okay.

"Hey, blabbermouth, how's about letting her talk some?" Michael Henry sat on the footrest near us. His manners put me in the mind of Tom, at least the way he spoke to his sister. But he was different with me. He put his elbows on his knees and leaned toward me, his knees nearly brushing against my own. "Where you from?"

Eva Jane repositioned herself in the settee, angling herself in my direction. She folded her hands in her lap and smiled, waiting for my response.

With their eyes on me, I whispered, "Supply."

"Where's that?" she asked before I'd even finished speaking.

"Brunswick County," I said.

"What do you mean 'where's that?' Don't you know nothing?" Michael Henry said.

"Shut up, Michael Henry! As if you know where it is."

"As a matter of fact, I do. And if you ever got out of Mecklenburg County, maybe you'd know too."

"So where is it?" Eva Jane asked her brother.

"Well, it's, I'll let her tell you," he said, pointing to me.

"On the ocean."

"The ocean?" Eva Jane gushed. "You've seen the ocean? Daddy keeps saying he's gonna take me someday, but he hasn't yet. I can't wait to see the ocean. I bet it's just beautiful!"

"Why would you want to go to the ocean, birdbrain? You know what lives there?"

As Michael Henry began to name all the sea creatures, some real and some made-up, I looked across the parlor. In the corner opposite us, Mr. Griffin sat in a wingback chair, his feet propped on the footrest in front of him. His head lay back against the head rest, his jaw hanging open, and a small, yet audible snore came out in a well-timed manner. Mary Ann sat on his lap, curling her body into his, her head resting against his chest, rising and falling with each breath he took in and let out. A wave of grief threatened to drown me. What I wouldn't have given to have one more moment like that with Daddy.

I looked away and distracted myself by taking in the rest of my surroundings. All the chairs angled toward a fireplace that looked as if it hadn't been used in years, perhaps even before I was born.

On a winter night like that one, Daddy would have to light the stove and we'd huddle around it for whatever warmth we could pull from it. But in this house, though the wind blew outside the window and the fireplace went unlit, the cold—or at least most of it—stayed away.

I looked out the window beside me, watching cars go by as the wind blew the tree branches. I'd never seen such a steady stream of cars before. In just a few minutes' time, more cars passed by than ever would in one day at our little house.

"I'd still like to see the ocean someday," Eva Jane said as their argument wound down.

"My daddy used to take me all the time." The words came out of me before I realized I was speaking. This statement finally made Eva Jane stop talking, looking like she had just seen a ghost. And then I kept saying more. "He and my mama used to go there together a lot, even got married there. I want to live there someday."

"Is it—" Eva Jane started to say but paused, choosing her words carefully for the first time that evening, "Is it okay to talk about them?"

"Eva Jane!" Michael Henry said before I could respond.

"What?" she asked, her cheeks blushing, her shoulders shrugging.

"It's fine," I said.

"Mama said they died," Eva Jane continued. "I didn't know if it might hurt too much to talk about."

I took a deep breath. Truth was, it did hurt, but it hurt whether I spoke of them or not, and having been trained in grief since birth, I knew there was no use in ignoring it. "I'm sad, but,"

I inhaled to slow my heart rate, "grief's the love we carry with us. Ignoring it only makes it hurt more."

The only sounds in the room came from Mr. Griffin's and Mary Ann's deep, harmonious, sleep-heavy breaths, but Eva Jane couldn't let the silence go on for too long.

"How old are you anyways?" she asked.

"Fourteen."

"A year younger than me! Michael Henry's nearly seventeen, and I turn sixteen in a few months. That's about when I get presented. Mama's making such a big deal out of it. I just don't understand the fuss."

"Who are you kidding?" Michael Henry laughed. "You love the fuss. Fuss is your middle name."

"What's your middle name?" Eva Jane asked.

"Emma."

"Leah Emma. There's a lot of uh's in your name." Eva Jane tucked a curl behind her ear and turned in my direction again. "Say, are you smart?"

Michael Henry inhaled, rolled his brown eyes into the back of his head, and said, "What kind of a question is that?"

"I'm just thinking that you may be younger than me, but if you're smart, then maybe you could be in my class at school. Wouldn't that be fun?"

I hadn't been missing Miss Heniford and a good portion of my classmates, but I had been missing the rhythms of my day, the certainties that came with routine, the hope that came with the diploma Daddy never did manage to get for himself. Perhaps my life could go back to something resembling normal.

"I mean, Mama could tell them what class you should be in."

I scooted myself up in the chair and began to smile, but Mrs. Griffin interrupted.

"Go wash up for bed. Tomorrow's school."

"Mama! I had the most wonderful idea!" Eva Jane began to explain her hope—our hope. Like pulling a loose string from a hemline, the plan came out easily. It started with me sharing Eva Jane's room, since she had plenty of space in her bed. Plus since we'd be going to school together, we could wake each other up in the morning. But the proposal didn't fully develop before it began to unravel.

"Oh, Eva Jane," she laughed to herself, "Girls like Leah don't go to school, do yuh?" Mrs. Griffin looked at me like I knew what she meant by it. I admit that at the Barnas, I had no desire for schooling if it meant butting heads with Tom and the others. But here, in this big house with this new family, maybe I'd like it. I'd gotten swept up in Eva Jane's talk and thought that things could be different in Matthews.

Eva Jane went on to argue that I could do my chores in the morning and evening and go to school in between. At least that's what I think she said. I was too busy feeling like I'd been hit in the gut to hear her words for certain. Since I'd overheard the Barnas talking, I'd thought they'd found me a family who wanted me to be a part of it, but as I sat in that parlor and as cars full of people I didn't know drove by outside, I realized I'd come simply to fill a position. To work.

But still I felt a glimmer of hope. Maybe this Eva Jane could change that for me. Maybe all the Griffin kids could help make me a part of the family, help move me out of the room on the porch and into a home. Trouble was, I couldn't figure out for myself if I wanted to be one of them or who I'd always been in the place I'd always known. I needed time to choose for myself and then hope they chose me in return.

When Mrs. Griffin refused to give in, Eva Jane cried, "But Mama—"

"No buts," she said, the quiet lilt of her voice lifting to a tone that woke her husband and youngest child. "You know I need help around here. Now, wash up and go to bed." With those directions, she left the room, walking back toward the kitchen.

All three Griffin children filed out with a murmuring of good night, their heads bowed and their footsteps heavy, leaving me alone in the room with Mr. Griffin. He folded the newspaper in his lap and spoke to me for the first time, "Before you go to bed," he began, "I'm traveling most weekdays. Vivian needs help around here, especially after we had to let the last one go." My palms began to sweat, wondering if the last one had also been an orphan, and if so, where had she gone? Why was she gone? "I'm sure you'll be a good helper."

I didn't like the words he spoke, but the kindness in his eyes, paired with a soft glimmer of curiosity, as if he were trying to figure me out, softened the irritation I felt deep inside. "Yes, sir," I told him.

"Good. Mrs. Griffin'll tell you more tomorrow." He unfolded the newspaper and said, "Better go on now. When Vivian speaks, it's best to listen."

On the way to bed, I stood on the porch, my arms hugging my body as the wind blew cool, chilling my cheeks where the tears streaked down them. The clouds blocked any stargazing that night, leaving the sky empty and muted. I crawled into bed and curled up under my quilt, inhaling the final scents of home. Exhausted from the day's events, I hoped sleep could rescue me from this unwanted reality, suspend me in a place where someone wanted me for more than service.

CHAPTER NINE

Those first few nights especially, I couldn't sleep much in that closet of a room they put me in. The silence was so loud, my mind couldn't rest. Winter was always quieter without the sounds of frogs, crickets, and cicadas, but never had I heard such silence. When I finally would drift off to sleep, my own movement would wake me, the squeaking of the bed springs pulling me from my shallow rest.

In the morning, I'd get tired of being restless in that bouncy bed, so I'd go sit on the back porch, watch the stars fade into the lightening sky, and see the birds come out for their breakfast. I'd try not to think too much while I sat there, other than to enjoy what was in front of me. If my mind started in with the questions—*Why was I here? Who was Alma? Was she an orphan like me? Where was she now?*—my mood would be sour all morning. And Mrs. Griffin always had a way of noticing, even if we still hadn't warmed up to each other enough to be conversational.

On the weekdays, once the light would switch on in the kitchen, I'd head into the house to begin breakfast. But I thought Sunday might be the day I didn't have to go inside too quickly. After all, Sundays with Daddy had always been days of rest. He didn't care to spend the time sitting with a congregation and listening to a preacher, though he did believe in observing the commandments, even the one about taking a Sabbath. Those lazy days were always my favorite. Daddy didn't have to go to the woods and I didn't have any school, so we could dawdle over cups of coffee, the sun already risen before we even woke those mornings. Sometimes we'd drive to the beach or walk down the tree-lined path out back. But mostly, we took those days slow, savoring every minute.

The Griffins felt differently about Sundays. That first one I had with them started with Mrs. Griffin knocking on the kitchen wall, the pounding coming into my room right over my head. I took a minute to shake the sleep from my body before I went inside the house. That morning was the first time I'd noticed the lock on the inside of the bedroom door. I wondered if I should use it the following Sunday morning. Maybe I could say it accidentally slid shut, but I knew that wouldn't stop Mrs. Griffin from banging until I woke.

"Sundays are not for being lazy," the missus informed me as I entered the kitchen. "Get yourself dressed for church."

She pointed to a shapeless, colorless cotton dress that lay draped over a kitchen chair. She'd apparently pulled it from the back of Eva Jane's closet. At least this one had no holes and dirt stains like my everyday dress. I'd seen prettier dresses in that closet, so full the doors barely stayed shut. Eva Jane had taken to having me up to her room in the afternoon when she got home from school. Listening to her talk about her day, nodding along like I was hanging on every word, I passed the time observing her belongings, including the dresses. There was a blue one I'd especially had my eye on—an A-line dress the color of the Atlantic. But that morning, I took what I'd been offered and I headed back to my room.

By the time I returned, the family was already in the kitchen, eating toast and eggs around the table. The kids all had on their Sunday best, the girls with bows in their hair and Michael Henry's combed better than I'd seen it thus far. Mr. Griffin, on the other hand, was sitting at the table in an undershirt and dress pants.

"Iron Mr. Griffin's shirt," Mrs. Griffin directed, before I could sit with the rest of the family and eat. She pointed to the ironing board in the corner of the kitchen. She seemed to think that pointing at the contraption was enough instruction for me to be able to actually use it. I walked over to it and stood staring at the shirt, board, and iron for a minute.

Being a lumberjack, Daddy had no need for fancy clothes. Flannel and denim suited him just fine. While he had summer and winter clothes, there was no reason to separate work and weekend attire. And since I could still go to school with a few wrinkles in my dress, we had no use for an iron.

I smoothed the shirt out on the board, took the iron in my hand and pressed it against the fabric.

"Do it like that and you're only gonna burn it," Mrs. Griffin instructed. When I didn't say anything, she held out a fist and moved it side to side. "Move it back and forth. Back and forth."

I began moving the iron from side to side, mimicking her motions. I must've been doing something right because she didn't say any more before she walked out of the kitchen with Mr. Griffin.

The wrinkles began to fade with each movement I made, and I had just started on the last sleeve, nearly done with my chore, when I heard the glass clang against the table and a splash of a mess cascade down to the floor.

The eldest two Griffin children jumped from their seats, trying to avoid the waterfall of milk tumbling onto the linoleum.

"Look what you've done!" Michael Henry said to his youngest sister.

"Jeez, butterfingers!" Eva Jane cried as she checked herself for signs of a spill.

Mary Ann stayed in her chair, crying, "I didn't mean to!"

"Don't just sit there. Do something!" her brother commanded.

But Mary Ann was too caught in the moment to know what to do. I hurried to the drawer that held the extra kitchen towels and grabbed a few, dropping one on top of the table before bending to the floor to mop up the mess as Mary Ann sat in her chair.

"Thank you," she whispered to me. I put my hand on her leg and squeezed.

With the mess contained, Michael Henry and Eva Jane sat back down to finish their breakfast as I rinsed out the towels in the sink.

"What's that smell?" Michael Henry's question pulled my focus from the towels and back to my original task, where a smoking iron sat on top of Mr. Griffin's shirt. Michael Henry stood from his chair so quickly that it crashed to the ground. He ran to the ironing board and lifted the iron off his dad's shirt quicker than I could do it myself. His eyes met mine, and we looked at each other for a moment, our faces separated by only a few inches, before we heard footsteps heading toward the kitchen.

"Is that shirt—" She didn't finish her sentence. She saw the mark. And that's when her puzzling turned to quiet anger. She walked to the board and grabbed the shirt, examining up close the black burn mark—like a dolphin's dorsal or perhaps more pointed like a shark's—on the sleeve.

"Mama, it was an accident," Mary Ann said from the breakfast table.

Mrs. Griffin opened her mouth, but shut it again. She took a deep breath and looked to the ceiling as her chest puffed full of air and then fell flat as it emptied. I stood frozen, unable to speak or move or blink. I waited to hear her anger, but someone else spoke first.

Still holding the iron in his hand, Michael Henry said, "It's my fault."

My eyes grew wide. He stared at his mama, who looked as confused as I was.

"Leah was cleaning up a mess, so I took over. I guess I left it on too long."

"What mess?" Mrs. Griffin growled.

"Mary Ann spilled her milk," Eva Jane said.

Mrs. Griffin whipped her head around to look at Mary Ann, who cowered in her chair.

"It's all cleaned up," I said, finally finding my voice. I walked to Mary Ann and put my hands on her shoulders. I could feel her body shivering.

Mrs. Griffin looked at all four of us, squinting as if trying to see who would break. Her cheeks flushed deep red, and then she exploded, "Get out. Now!" She pointed to the door. Her voice rang through the room. I shook and shivered. Never had I heard an adult raise their voice like that, except maybe when Daddy was trying to get the horses to mind him right. But not even the time I'd colored the rug on the floor had he gotten as loud as Mrs. Griffin did.

Eva Jane's eyebrows scrunched together. "Where're we supposed to go?"

Michael Henry reached for his sister and warned her to be quiet.

"To the car. For church!" Their mother's voice echoed in the kitchen.

The Griffin kids all ran to the back door, but I hesitated. Seeing the abandoned dishes on the table, I didn't know if I should clean up first or follow the others. When Mrs. Griffin barked, "I said now!" I figured I should also leave.

We rode to church in Mr. Griffin's car, a family all packed together inside. Mary Ann sat between her parents in the front seat, and me between Eva Jane and Michael Henry in the back. His leg pressed against mine and our shoulders brushed against one another's with every turn in the road.

That morning was the first time I had been outside the Griffins' house since I'd arrived. I watched out the car window as the houses went by, all of them overshadowed by a canopy different from the one in Brunswick County. There were more oaks here, reaching from side to side, and fewer pine trees growing tall toward the sky.

Mrs. Griffin sat in the front naming all the new things: the car that so-and-so had gotten, the flower boxes spilling with pansies in front of one house, the curtains in the window of another. Mr. Griffin only nodded as his wife pointed from one place to another.

As we walked into the church that morning, the comments continued about shoes and dresses, hairdos, and necklaces until we climbed the stone steps and walked through the wooden archway of the church. Then with so many around us, Mrs. Griffin's voice changed, lilting higher, annunciating without so much as a hint of a Southern drawl, a smile across her face as she shook hands and greeted other churchgoers.

The rest of us followed behind her, a row of ducklings of various sizes, waiting for her to lead the way into the sanctuary. But first she had to say her hellos, to hear women ask how her week had been, how the new girl was doing, how she was such a saint for taking in an orphan.

"Another jewel in your heavenly crown," one woman told her. Mrs. Griffin didn't respond with words, but she put her hand to her chest and sighed deeply. That was when Mr. Griffin took his wife by the arm and guided her into the sanctuary to a wooden pew where the family filed into place, as if they had assigned seats, each knowing where they needed to sit—first Eva Jane, then Michael Henry, followed by his mother with Mary Ann on her other side. Mr. Griffin stood in the aisle motioning for me to take a seat.

"Down here!" Eva Jane said, patting her hand on the wooden pew. "Sit by me!"

I scooted my way in front of the Griffin family, shuffling along, trying to make as little contact as possible, trying not to step on their feet.

"I didn't know you had a crown," I heard Mary Ann say as I sat down. No one answered her, so she said, "Mama, can I see your crown?"

"What crown?" Mrs. Griffin finally responded.

"That woman said you had a crown."

Mrs. Griffin didn't explain. She simply shushed Mary Ann and told her to be quiet.

Eva Jane turned to me and said in a low whisper, "Do you see what she is wearing today?"

I wasn't sure who "she" was, but I was afraid to say anything, wondering if I'd be shushed.

"Look!" Eva Jane pointed in the direction of a girl who looked about her age.

"Quit pointing!" Her brother smacked her arm down.

"Ow!" Eva Jane rubbed the spot where her brother's hand had made contact. "But look! Look at Sally's dress. I can't believe—" and then her sentence trailed off as the girl looked in her direction and waved. Eva Jane's scowl turned to a smile as she waved back, but once the girl took her seat, she continued, "I'd never wear that."

"And what you have on is so much better?" her brother asked.

"If you can't tell, then clearly you don't know fashion."

"SHH!" came a short, yet forceful, shush from Mrs. Griffin. With that, all conversation ended and the service began.

The organ music filled the room as if sliding up the wooden archways before falling down upon us. The Griffins looked at their paper programs as two kids walked to the front with fire on the ends of some sort of pole that each held in their hands. After the flame bearers lit candles and the music stopped, the pastor stood up and spoke for only a minute before the music started up again and everyone stood. All except for me until Eva Jane told me to.

I tried to follow along, to be a part of what everyone else somehow knew how to do, to be another member of the family. But my mind went wandering, my eyes caught by the colors that shone through the windows. The sun shined brightly through the stained glass that morning, covering the walls and ceiling in a disorganized rainbow of hues. I watched as the color slowly moved to new places as the service went on. What had started in one spot moved ever so slightly, yet somewhat noticeably, the longer we sat there.

Mary Ann started fidgeting and fussing about halfway through the service. Mrs. Griffin acted like she didn't notice, but I saw her jaw muscles clench. Finally she turned to her youngest and asked in a harsh whisper what the matter was.

"I have to go to the bathroom." She had tried to whisper, but her breathy response came out loud enough for the couple in front of us to giggle.

Mrs. Griffin motioned for me to take Mary Ann. The two of us shuffled out of the pew and walked together down the aisle. I had to follow her lead, not knowing where to find the restroom. As she sat in the stall, I could see her black patent leather Mary Jane's pointing down to the floor, swinging back and forth.

"Why does Mama yell?" she asked from behind the door.

That morning had been the first time I'd heard her raise her voice like that. "Does she do that a lot?"

"Mm-hm." Then she asked, "Does your mama yell?"

It was a question I wished I could answer. I wished I knew if my mama would yell. Would she get upset if I messed up the chores? Would she raise her voice if I didn't wake up on time? What would her voice even sound like?

When I didn't answer, she said, "Oh. I forgot." Mary Ann flushed the toilet and walked to the sink. Before turning on the faucet, she said, "Sometimes when Mama gets that way, I think of a balloon."

"A balloon?"

"Yeah!" She smiled at herself in the mirror. "I got one at the fair last spring. It floated on a string, and when I looked up, it made me smile."

Our eyes wandered upward as she said that, our lips curving into smiles because who couldn't find a bit of joy in a balloon dancing in the breeze even if it was only in our minds?

Inspired by her asking questions, I thought I'd ask a few of my own.

"Can you tell me about Alma?"

Mary Ann shook the water from her hands before wiping them onto the skirt of her dress.

"Mama says we shouldn't talk about her, but I miss her."

"Oh." I handed her a paper towel, but she preferred using her dress.

"It's okay. What do you want to know?" she said as she skipped toward the door.

I knew Mrs. Griffin was expecting us back, so I figured I'd get straight to the point.

"Did she have a mommy and a daddy?" I thought Mary Ann might understand that wording more than to ask if Alma was an orphan.

Mary Ann tilted her head to the side and looked toward the ceiling. And then she said what I had feared. "Don't suppose she did."

She reached for the door to leave, but I asked her to wait. "Where is she now?"

Mary Ann shrugged.

I hesitated to ask. "Did they send her to a home?"

She nodded her head. "Yeah! I think I heard Mama say that."

Mary Ann opened the door to leave, but I couldn't move. My feet felt like bricks, too heavy to budge, while my heart pumped in my chest. My body felt hot all over as I pictured Alma at that moment—alone on a thin mattress in a room full of beds, her hair greasy, her stomach rumbling with hunger, her cheeks dirty except where the tears had washed them clean.

"Come on!" Mary Ann held the door. I blinked hard, trying to get the image of Alma to wash out of my mind. As I stepped into the hallway, she grabbed ahold of my hand and led me back to the sanctuary.

After we took our seats, I watched the colors of the windows shift through the sanctuary. I thought about how Mary Ann reached for my hand, Michael Henry rested his leg against mine, and Eva Jane appreciated my listening each day after arriving home from school. I hadn't been there long, but I'd begun to be comfortable in their presence. We might not've played games or run through the yard like Jesse and I did, but I thought for a moment that maybe they thought I was okay. Maybe they saw me as more alike than different.

But then I thought of Alma. Had they treated her like family until they sent her away? Maeve's persistence showed Daddy that even a stray could be something to love. But as Mrs. Griffin shushed Mary Ann and told her to "be still," I wondered if Mrs. Griffin could ever love a stray.

CHAPTER TEN

I stopped spending as much time in the morning waiting for the birds to wake up. Instead, I started getting into the house before Mrs. Griffin made it to the kitchen and even had a chance to knock on the wall to wake me. I started the grits. Dusted a few end tables and knickknacks, even took a broom to the kitchen floor so it would be free of dirt and crumbs when the missus came down for her coffee in the morning. I didn't know what kind of a helpmate Alma had been, but I hoped my ambition would show the missus that I belonged.

I'd already discovered that she preferred to do some duties herself. Like the mail. One day I'd taken it upon myself to get it from the postman. I walked into the house, the pile in my hands, rifling through to count, but not read. That stack was bigger than any Daddy and I had ever gotten. Before I finished counting, Mrs. Griffin saw me. Again it was one of those moments when she took a deep breath before speaking.

"From now on," she had said, "I'll bring in the mail."

I looked at her, a smile already on my face, expecting to hear a thank you, thinking she'd be happy with what I'd done. I'm sure she saw my confusion. I was too busy being puzzled to respond to her stern expression as she reached out and grabbed the mail from my hands.

Every day I looked for a way to get Mrs. Griffin to smile at me like the rest of the family did. And I thought I'd found out how to do it the morning I heard her fussing on the phone about the price of getting her hair done. After saying she refused to pay that much, she slammed down the receiver.

Now, I didn't know much about hair. Daddy didn't even require me to brush my nest of curls each day. 'Course when I stayed at the Barnas, Tulla decided it was time I learned to be more presentable. So she showed me how to gather my hair in a ponytail at the base of my neck.

However, there had been a few rainy days at the Barnas when I'd sat and watched Tulla brush out Mrs. Barna's hair before setting it into pin curls. Tulla remarked that watching this was the only time I'd sit still.

Her hands worked quickly, applying some hair lotion then brushing a swath of hair three times before putting a pin into her mouth. She'd fold a piece of end paper around the tips before twisting and twirling the locks. Once tight enough, she'd grab the pin from her mouth and put it in place before crossing it in the opposite direction with another pin, crisscrossing the two until they made an X over the curled hair.

So that morning, I told Mrs. Griffin that she didn't need a hairdresser—I knew how to set curls. I hadn't ever done it for myself, but I didn't want to get into those details just then. Though reluctant at first, Mrs. Griffin relented and brought the basket of pins into the kitchen. Mary Ann was off playing outside, probably digging in the garden dirt and hoping her mama didn't see her. The house was quiet but for the movement of the newspaper that Mrs. Griffin held in front of herself.

I began by combing through her hair, slowly and steadily, careful not to pull on her. After getting it all smoothed out, I stepped back and looked over her hair. With it wet and straight, it stretched nearly to the back of the chair. I stopped for a moment, trying to remember where Tulla would start, what section of hair would be the first to be rolled up.

I chose a spot, gathered it into a section and began to comb it out straight before I remembered the lotion and the end papers. I looked to the table, but all that she had brought were the pins and comb.

"Where's the lotion?" I asked.

"What lotion?"

"For your hair. To help it set."

"We don't need it."

"And the papers?"

She simply shook her head no as she continued to look at the paper.

My moment to impress was quickly slipping away, so I decided to make do with what she had given me. I gathered a section and tried only doing three combs through like Tulla always did, but it still wasn't straight, so I combed through more. When I got it properly smoothed out, I reached for a pin, but as I stretched, I lost hold and had to start the section again. It was the third time of starting all over when I heard her let out an exhale.

I didn't have time to be perfect. I needed to get the job done, so I began twisting and pinning. Each section combed out a bit better than the one before, each pin a little bit tighter and less floppy than the one before. But it wasn't until Mrs. Griffin started talking that I fell into the rhythm.

She had turned to the next page in the paper and let out a groan, nearly a growl similar to the sound Maeve would make when a stray cat would wander onto her property. I glanced at the paper and saw the headline of the article that had caught her attention: FIRST-OF-ITS-KIND DANCE IN MATTHEWS.

"A dance sounds fun," I said, hoping to take her focus off what I was doing.

"What?"

"Dance? In the paper there."

Mrs. Griffin let out a sigh. "It's a ball. They were supposed to call it a ball."

As she shook her head back and forth, her hair slipped from my fingers and I had to start that section over again.

"Oh. You going to the ball?" I asked as I regathered the strands of hair and began combing them again.

"Yes, I'll be there. Of course I will. But the *ball* is for girls Eva Jane's age." She paused for a moment. "It's like a cotillion." And that's when she took off talking like Eva Jane. "It's about time Matthews hosted its own. I can't tell you how long I've been working on this, me and the other ladies. It's taken a lot of organizing, but it's finally going to happen, just in time for Eva Jane to be of the presenting age."

"The girls must be so excited," I said as soon as she paused for me to interject.

She sat up a little straighter and began to tell me how important it was.

Standing in the kitchen with her, I got lost in what I was doing and forgot where I was. As I combed her hair, twisted and twirled it into place, an excitement energized my entire body. So I started asking questions, carrying on a conversation, asking for a story, wishing I could do the same with my own mama.

"Did you have a ball like that when you were Eva Jane's age?"

Mrs. Griffin turned the page of the newspaper, growing stony, no longer sharing as much information. "We had one," she said. I expected her to continue on with details.

"What was it like?"

She shrugged her shoulders. "The night every little girl dreams of."

"Tell me about your dress!" I coaxed her to tell me more, but her talking mood must've passed.

"Yuh," she cleared her throat and started again, "You sure do ask a lot of questions." She flipped the newspaper to the next page.

Not satisfied, I pressed to know more. I wanted to hear the details of her dress, of that night. I wanted to imagine that my mama's own cotillion was just like that. Daddy didn't have any pictures of mama at the dance, nor memories since he hadn't been there. But he'd told me how mama had attended.

Mrs. Griffin huffed out a short answer, "Of course it was white. Fitted at the top, as was the fashion." Then she paused. When she continued, her voice had softened, her answer grew longer, as if she was carefully examining a past memory. "I know Eva Jane wouldn't like this, but back then, the skirts were full. They were thick with tulle that billowed." She put down the paper and moved her hands outward, away from her body to make her point clear. "They were so long, only the very tips of the girls' shoes showed when they walked."

I bet Mama looked beautiful. I wondered what it would've been like to get dressed up so fancy. As I pulled the comb through her hair at the base of her neck, it tugged on the string of pearls she wore each and every day. The missus startled out of her reminiscing. Her hand reached for her necklace, pulling it forward to protect the pearls.

"Watch what you're doing!" she warned.

"I'm sorry, ma'am," I said before she even finished speaking. I worried that the ease we'd shared while she was telling me about her cotillion had broken thanks to that simple mistake.

She exhaled loudly and went back to looking at the paper, not sharing any more of her past with me. So to find her good graces once more, I decided to tell my own story. I reminded myself of what Jesses had said. *Let them give you a chance.* I took a deep breath and tried to be myself.

"Those are beautiful pearls you have," I began. "You know, my daddy told me how pearls go about being made. Seems it happens when something small gets stuck inside an oyster, like a grain of sand." My hands worked as fast as the words escaped me, one flowing right after the other without any sort of interruption. "That little thing, so tiny, rubs on the inside. Now it seems like the oyster should just spit it out and get on with its own business, but instead, it turns that little grit into a pearl." I assumed the missus was listening. She kept on turning pages of the newspaper, but she didn't tell me I needed to stop talking. "It takes years, but over time, that tiny speck turns from something in the way to something beautiful."

By the time I finished, I had nearly gotten most of the curls pinned in place. They may not have been in neat rows like Tulla could make, but I stepped back for a moment and smiled at what I had accomplished. Surely she'd be proud of what I'd done, even as I'd gotten lost in storytelling.

Mrs. Griffin remained silent. I figured she intended for me to keep on talking, so I continued. "Men risk their lives diving deep to find pearls. Some hold their breath for so long that they die. Or sometimes a shark or something gets to them. Can you believe that? People dying for jewelry?"

"If one chooses such a line of work, why shouldn't others benefit from it?" Mrs. Griffin asked, her voice even and low.

The comb scraped the missus' scalp and caught in a tangle, causing her to grumble. But I didn't hear much of her moan because in that moment, I did what I'd been hoping I wouldn't do in front of this new family. Despite myself, I flashed. I stood motionless, vacant, and unseeing. Of course it had happened at the Griffins' house before that day, but it had always happened in my room, while standing at the sink, or in some other place where the others hadn't seen me.

Mrs. Griffin apparently felt the change as I stood behind her. She knew something had happened, because when I came to, she was calling my name and asking why I wasn't responding. But before I could offer an apology or an excuse, Mary Ann ran into the kitchen, the door flapping open, nearly hitting the cabinets as it swung with full force.

"Mama! Mama! Guess what I found!"

In her dirt-covered hands, an earthworm wiggled through her fingers.

As Mrs. Griffin stood from her chair, she pushed it into me, nearly knocking me to the ground.

"Get out of here with that!"

"But I wanted to show you. Look how big and juicy he is!"

"Out! Now!"

As her mama pointed at the door, Mary Ann shuffled back outside with less energy than when she'd entered.

"That child needs a bath."

"Curls are done," I said, as I stepped back to look at what I'd completed.

She put her hand to her head and felt around.

"This side is far too loose," she said before she eyed me suspiciously and walked out of the kitchen.

The back door hadn't closed all the way behind Mary Ann. As I went to close it, I could hear Mary Ann's sweet voice saying, "I'm sorry Mama didn't say hi to you, Mr. Worm. But I hope you have a nice day."

She put her newfound friend into the soil, brushed her hands back and forth, and then lay down on her back in the grass. I wanted to go out there with her. I wanted to lie on my back and look at the clouds as they shaped and shifted and moseyed on their way. As much as I wanted to share that moment with Mary Ann, what I wanted even more was to rest in the Barnas' lawn alongside Jesse and point out the clouds that looked like animals and those that looked like strange faces. I wanted to share in his imaginings and hear his laugh as we got lost in silliness. But that was for another time, or perhaps *in* another time.

The ball was all Eva Jane wanted to talk about that afternoon when she got home from school. I nodded along as usual, but I kept thinking about how little Mrs. Griffin had told me about her own dance. And I kept trying to picture Mama as a teenager, dressed in a gown at such a society event. What a different childhood hers was compared to mine.

I interrupted Eva Jane's monologue to say, "You must be excited to have a dance like your mama's."

She paused and thought for a minute, "Well, I guess. I mean I don't know much about Mama's. She hasn't told me about it. Not yet."

"Really?" I asked. "It seems like something she'd want to talk about."

"Mama's not one for saying much of anything about the past." Eva Jane shrugged her shoulders and changed the subject. "I wonder who I'll dance with," she said after spending a few minutes rattling on about her dress, shoes, and hair. "I'll tell you who I hope to dance with: Aiken."

I giggled a bit and Eva Jane took a breath.

"What's so funny?"

"Is that his name?"

"Why of course it's his name. What did you think it was?"

"I've just never heard that name before."

"Well, I like it. I think it's a wonderful name: Aiken Beaufort. Maybe someday I'll be Mrs. Beaufort." Eva Jane looked off in the distance for a minute, and I let her be. It didn't take long for her to continue, "Say! I know just how to tell if I'll be Mrs. Beaufort. Do you know the apple peel legend? Michael Henry says it's nothing more than nonsense, but what does he know?"

I wasn't sure which question she wanted me to answer, so I kept quiet. She continued, "I'm gonna run down to the kitchen to get some apples. I'll be right back."

While I waited for her to come back, I looked around her

room in a way I couldn't when she was there. I opened the jewelry box on the dresser, touching the gold necklace chains curled up inside. I picked up one of the earrings and held it to my ear, not certain that I had time to actually clip it in place. Then I ran my fingers over the matching brush and mirror set. I touched the paper and thumbed the envelopes of a stationery set, still so full that it didn't look like she'd so much as written a single letter. There was so much stuffed in that room, it made me wonder if this is what Daddy thought of when he was talking about *more*.

I walked over to her bed, felt the quilt on top of it before taking a seat. I'd always only sat in the window seat, never on her bed. I bounced a little as I sat, testing the springs, wanting to jump on top of it but deciding that sitting was already far enough. I wondered what it was like to lay under that quilt at night, feel that mattress beneath as the full pillows cradled my head. I didn't get too far with my imagining when I heard Eva Jane in the hallway. I stood up as she came through the door.

"Got 'em! Surely Mama won't miss two apples." As she began to explain, she pulled a knife out of her dress pocket. "So what you have to do is peel this apple in one, long, connected peel. Like this." I watched her as she took the knife in one hand and glided it just beneath the red skin of the apple. She rolled the apple in her other hand, slowly but firmly, so that its peel stayed together in one long curl. "Like that!" she said as she placed the naked apple upon her dresser and held up the peel for me to see. "Now it's your turn."

I took the knife from her and began to peel the other apple. I'd never peeled an apple like that before. I'd always done short swipes, taking off a bit of skin at a time. It took me a few starts and stops to get the feel for it, to not cut off a small section instead of continuing to make one cut. After a few short cuts, she said, "It's okay. I'm sure it will still tell your future."

As I cut more, the juice of the apple dripped along my hand and down to my elbow before dropping onto the floor. While she waited for me, Eva Jane picked up her apple and took a few bites, juice dripping down her own chin as she said with a mouth full of pulp, "Hurry! Before Mama comes!"

Once we both had our curly peels, she told me to stand beside her, shoulder to shoulder. "Now we say the rhyme. Then we toss the peels over our backs and whatever letter the peel makes when it lands, that's the first initial of the man we'll marry."

Maybe Michael Henry was right. Maybe this was all superstition and silliness, but Eva Jane's excitement swept me right along with her. I listened closely as she told me the rhyme.

> Pare this pipping round and round again,
> My sweetheart's name to flourish on the plain.
> I fling the unbroken paring o'er my head.
> My sweetheart's letter on the ground is read.

After speaking it in unison, we flung the peels behind us, so excited that they had barely touched the ground before we spun around to see what the future had to say.

"Look! Look!" Eva Jane said before I could get a good look at my own. "Do you see it?!"

I did see the peel. I saw it in a heap on the floor, partly curled, partly stretched, lying in a lump that didn't look like any letter from the alphabet that I knew. "I knew it! I knew it! It's an A!"

I tilted my head from side to side and squinted a bit as she danced with excitement. "You see it, right?" I knew what my response had to be, so I smiled, nodded, and reassured her that it was definitely an A. She picked up the peel, held it in her hands and kissed it. Then she looked at my peel.

I saw it there on the floor, in a different configuration than her own, a clearer one. Her excitement calmed for a moment as she said, "Shucks. I was hoping it'd be an M or even an H. Wouldn't it be great if you and Michael Henry got married and then you and I could be sisters? How amazing would that be?"

Just as she swept me into the superstition of an apple peel, she swept me away in the fantasy of being her sister. But clearly neither of us saw an M or an H. She never did tell me what letter she saw, but she didn't need to. It was obvious on the floor there. And she never asked me if I already knew a boy whose name started with the letter J. Eva Jane had a way of creating her own future, and she didn't need the details of my past to make it happen.

Our giggles and talk of the future ended as Michael Henry came into the room. The subject changed back to the ball, as the two of them began discussing people I still didn't much know. As usual, he made some comment about that girl Sally's dress being more impressive than anything Eva Jane would find.

"Where'd you hear that? From her? Of course she'd say that, but she has no taste, just like she has no brains."

"Hey, careful there, that's my future wife you're talking about."

"So you are in love with her?"

"Well, if Mama has her way."

"You know she always gets what she wants."

"Not always," Michael Henry said. "Say, how about we practice a bit more? The ball'll be here before we know it."

"Practice is all you've been wanting to do. 'Course you still need it."

This had become a typical afternoon occurrence. Most days after school, Michael Henry would insist he needed to practice his dancing. Of course his sister wanted nothing to do with being his dance partner, so he and I would two-step and dip our way around her room.

Eva Jane walked to the radio and turned the dial to locate some music. "Pretend you're dancing with someone else," she said to me, assuming I needed to be coaxed into dancing. She winked, smiled, and waited for her brother to retaliate, but instead he held out his hand to me.

Someone else. I hadn't necessarily minded dancing with Michael Henry, even if he did hold me close and sometimes step on my toes, but the thought of someone else immediately brought Jesse to mind.

No one spoke for a few minutes while the music played. If I looked to the side and couldn't see my dance partner, I could pretend Jesse held me tight, his arms wrapped around me. But as we'd dance and spin, the mirror or the window kept coming into view, and the reflection would do away with my imaginings.

Truth be told, I didn't mind dancing in that room with a girl who said she wanted to be my sister and a boy who didn't mind holding me close. At least on most afternoons, but after being reminded of Jesse, I couldn't dance and smile and act as the companion they expected me to be.

After one song, I made an excuse to leave, saying I needed

to get dinner started. First, I walked out the back door, took off my shoes, and stood in the grass. I wiggled my toes, feeling the blades brush against my skin, letting the low afternoon sun fall on my face even though the breeze chilled me. The Griffin children seemed to be accepting me okay, much more than their mother did. But as I stood grounded in nature, I questioned if I could accept who I needed to be for them, especially if that version of me was so different than who I'd always been. But as a girl with no parent, nor home, the question remained: Did I have a choice?

CHAPTER ELEVEN

Hosting wasn't something Daddy and I ever did. Having guests over meant needing to have food and drink to share and acquaintances to share it with. Seeing as how we kept mainly to ourselves, we never had a need to invite someone in and entertain them with conversation. Some afternoons, I would invite Maeve in for a special treat, when I had one to spare. As she'd purr beside me, I'd carry on a conversation, telling her about my day, pretending as though she also told me about her own, of chasing squirrels through the trees and finding wood roaches scurrying around the porch. Thinking of her made me wonder if she had anyone at the Barnas' caring for her while I was away. Tulla said not to worry, but I couldn't help but wonder how she felt when I hadn't come home.

I was with the Griffins a few weeks before I had to serve guests—a couple of ladies who were coming over for tea. Leading up to that morning, Mrs. Griffin had me cleaning the house more than usual. The night before, she'd told me that I'd need to be up early to help make finger sandwiches. She'd instructed me to say "yes, ma'am," to not speak directly to the guests unless spoken to, to make sure the tea was hot and ready, and to refill their cups before they even had to ask. It was a lot of rules for one day.

When I got to the kitchen the morning of the tea, Mrs. Griffin was in her housecoat, her hair still set in the pins I'd twisted the night before with a scarf tied around it. I knew talking to her before she finished her coffee or before she had on her pearls was best avoided, so I stood a few steps back and observed her as she pulled the ingredients out of the refrigerator and put them on the counter. She had her way of doing things, especially in the kitchen, so I let her go on with the mixing without interrupting her.

"And this is the secret ingredient, but don't you go telling no one about this." Her Southern accent always rolled off her tongue thicker and stronger first thing in the morning in the privacy of her own home. "I don't care how much Mrs. Wemberton begs, and she will, yuh don't tell her what makes my pimento cheese better'n all the rest. Yuh hear me?"

"Yes, ma'am."

She added a bit of mustard and handed me the wooden spoon to finish stirring the mixture. Then she gave me a loaf of the bagged bread with the bright circles on it.

"Cut off the crust and cut each sandwich into four triangles. Then keep 'em in the refrigerator to stay chilled." I nodded. "Now I'm going upstairs to get Eva Jane and Michael Henry up for school. But don't you go giving neither of them any of those sandwiches."

When she came back downstairs, she still had her hair in pins, but her pearls were strung around her neck and her accent was mostly gone. That was, until Mary Ann spotted the mouse. The youngest Griffin had been unusually quiet up until that moment, not too eager to eat her breakfast, her cheeks a rosier red than normal.

My back was to the table as I finished up organizing the sandwiches on the platter. I didn't see the furry thing scurry across the kitchen floor, but I heard Mary Ann's giggle and Mrs. Griffin's scream.

"Not today!" she yelled. "Of all days! Not today!" By the time I turned around, Mrs. Griffin was standing atop her chair, her one hand covering her wide-open mouth while her other held her hair in place. "Stop fussing with those sandwiches and kill it!" she yelled at me.

"How?" I asked.

"How should I know? I'm sure you had those critters living in your shack."

"We had a cat."

"'Course yuh did. Well, not in this house! Get it out!"

"I'll catch it, Mama!" Mary Ann said her first words since coming into the kitchen that morning. She scooted out of her chair and tiptoed in the direction of the mouse, who took one look at the little girl with outstretched arms and ran in the opposite direction.

"We aren't keeping it, Mary Ann! That vermin is no pet! Get it out!"

While Mary Ann circled the kitchen table, crouching low to the ground with her hands out in front of her, I went to the back door and opened it. The mouse scampered, circling the legs of the chairs before making a run for it only to bump against the kitchen cabinets. I stood still at the door, holding it open.

"Chase him in this direction," I said. Neither Mrs. Griffin nor I knew yet if Mary Ann was trying to get it out of the house or into her own hands. But she looked at me, nodded, and walked closer to the mouse, corralling it in my direction, and when the only escape route it had was the wide-open door, Mary Ann charged forward.

Now I can't be certain of what happened next. I do recall the little guy running to the open door. It looked as though he ran outside, especially from where Mrs. Griffin stood. She cried out for me to shut the door, and I did. As the other two celebrated, I can't be certain, but I think I might've seen a little brown tail sticking out from beneath the kitchen cupboard right next to the back door. I nearly said something, but then Mrs. Griffin took Mary Ann upstairs. I figured we'd had enough excitement for one morning.

Mrs. Wemberton arrived first and had to wait at the door for me to open it. I was busy in the kitchen brewing the tea when the doorbell rang. Mrs. Griffin hadn't told me that, along with serving, my duties also included answering the door. She stood in the front hall calling for me. As I walked past her, she scolded me for leaving her guest waiting.

"Elaine!" she said as the door opened and I stood to the side for the lady to walk into the house.

"Vivian! Is she here yet?" she asked, looking around, trying to peek into the parlor.

"Not yet. I'm glad you got here first. We apparently have some kinks to work out," she said with a glance in my direction.

"Are you going to make Mrs. Wemberton stay in her coat all day?" She motioned to me, and as I helped her guest remove her coat, she continued, "It's so hard to find good help these days."

"That it is," Mrs. Wemberton said.

Mrs. Wemberton was both shorter and skinnier than Mrs. Griffin. Even if they were the same height, she'd still be thinner. She didn't have lines beside her eyes and creases in her forehead either. And she didn't have a soft belly pushing against her dress, trying to bulge with each exhale if she wasn't careful. I saw all this in quick glances. I couldn't look for too long because she seemed to also be checking me out. As I turned my back to hang up her coat, she whispered, "How's it working out?"

"We're getting there," Mrs. Griffin responded. Then she turned her attention to me. "Don't you have things to attend to in the kitchen?"

In the time I'd been there, I'd never been relegated away from everyone else. I'd had my things to do, the rooms to clean, the meals to make, but I'd always done them near the others. On that morning, with a guest present and more on the way, I was told to hide, feeling like that chased mouse.

When Mrs. Foster arrived a few minutes later, thankfully I answered the door in a timelier manner. The three ladies stood in the foyer as I removed Mrs. Foster's coat. They all looked like they were going to church that morning, wearing their dresses, their hair all done and set, a bit of rouge on their cheeks.

"Mrs. Foster, I'm so glad you could join us today," Mrs. Griffin began. "Please, allow me to introduce you to Mrs. Wemberton."

"I'm so pleased to meet you," Mrs. Wemberton said. She was the shortest of the three women and could barely hide her excitement when she spoke. "Viv...Mrs. Griffin has told me about the great work your husband is doing. I'd love to know more."

"All in time, Mrs. Wemberton," Mrs. Griffin said with a wide smile. "But first, let's take a seat, shall we?"

Her smile quickly faded as they walked into the sitting room, each lady carefully smoothing out the backs of their dresses before they sat at the edge of their chairs, their ankles crossed and backs perfectly straight. By the time they were all situated, Mrs. Griffin was smiling again.

"Mrs. Griffin, your hair looks especially beautiful this morning. I suppose you went to that downtown hairdresser again?" Mrs. Wemberton asked.

I waited to hear Mrs. Griffin tell her how I'd done her hair. Instead she said, "Why thank you, Mrs. Wemberton." She touched her carefully coiffed curls, the hair spray holding them together so her hair moved all together when her hand touched it. "As a matter of fact, yes, I did. I spent yesterday there. You know sometimes a lady just needs to take some time to herself, that's what Mr. Griffin told me anyway, so I drove into Charlotte just yesterday. I'm so glad you like it."

I stood in the doorway to the dining room, waiting to announce that the tea and sandwiches were ready. If anyone had been looking at me just then, they would've seen my confusion. I didn't know why she had to put on such appearances for these two women, why she'd lie to her own friends. When I caught Mrs. Griffin's eye, her smile dropped and she sat up a bit straighter. She knew I'd heard the lie. But she also knew I wasn't going to say anything.

"Mrs. Griffin has a hairdresser in the city," Mrs. Wemberton said to Mrs. Foster, "but she refuses to tell me who this woman is. She always does such an extraordinary job. I do wish she'd tell."

"Well, I always say a lady never tells her secrets." The women all laughed behind their closed mouths before Mrs. Griffin said, "It seems that our tea is ready. Shall we move into the dining room?"

Mrs. Griffin directed Mrs. Foster to Mr. Griffin's seat at the head of the table. The other two ladies took a seat, one on each side of her. I served the head seat first, just like I had been told. At first she held up a hand to pass on the sandwiches.

"Oh, I'm so sorry. Do you not like pimento cheese? I considered cucumber sandwiches instead, but it's so difficult to find cucumbers this time of the year."

"It's not that," Mrs. Foster said. "I'm afraid I finished my breakfast not long ago."

"But you must try one," Mrs. Wemberton said. She sat at the edge of her seat, her back as stiff and straight as my mattress. She leaned toward the table, and if she didn't have such good manners, her elbows and arms would've been on the table so she could lean in even closer. "Mrs. Griffin has the best recipe for pimento cheese. It's been passed down for generations. Why we've been friends for years, and still she won't tell me what her secret ingredient is."

Mrs. Griffin chuckled behind closed teeth. "How kind of you, Mrs. Wemberton, but if Mrs. Foster doesn't want a sandwich, that's quite alright indeed." The coloring of her cheeks turned a deeper red, even darker than the rouge.

I don't know if Mrs. Foster suddenly felt hungry or if she wanted to end the discussion of sandwiches, but she took the tongs and chose the smallest one. The other two ladies leaned in and stayed quiet as the woman at the head of the table took a small bite. Even Maeve took bigger bites than that nibble. She put the sandwich back on her plate and wiped her mouth with her napkin, though there was nothing much to wipe away.

"Mmm. Yes, well, I do indeed see what all the fuss was about." The other two women looked across the table at one another and breathed out.

"One day, I'll figure out that secret ingredient," Mrs. Wemberton said.

After serving the sandwiches, I returned to the kitchen to grab the teapot. As I walked into the dining room again, Mrs. Wemberton looked at me and said, "Leah, is it?" Midstep, I paused and looked at Mrs. Griffin. She'd told me not to speak, so I nodded my head and gave a little smile. "How old are you, dear?"

I had been okay with not having to talk, with being able to blend in while still in plain sight. I'd learned how to do that in the comfort of my forest and even in the schoolyard. But standing in the dining room, I had no tree or swing set to hide behind. Mrs. Wemberton seemed kind enough, but I still began to shake and sweat as all three women turned their gaze toward me.

"Well, go on," Mrs. Griffin began. "Mrs. Wemberton asked you a question." I wondered if the others heard the sharp edge of her tone that hid beneath the smile.

My voice wavered as I said, "Fourteen." And then I remembered to add, "Ma'am."

"Apparently the cat had hold of her tongue," Mrs. Griffin joked, and the ladies all laughed.

"Fourteen!" Mrs. Wemberton finally stopped looking directly at me and said to the other ladies, "What an interesting age. I do remember it well. Where's she from?" she asked the missus.

"They lived off the coast." Mrs. Griffin waved her hand in the air, as if dismissing my birthplace.

Irritated by her disregard, I couldn't stop a further explanation from coming out of my mouth. "Supply, to be exact, in Brunswick County."

"I'll admit I don't quite know where that is. Is it close to

Raleigh?" Mrs. Wemberton leaned in close to the table and lowered her voice as if sharing a secret with the other ladies. "I've seen pictures of their cotillion and it's something—"

Too excited by a connection, my mouth continued talking, cutting off Mrs. Griffin's guest. "My mama was a debutante there!" Mrs. Wemberton's eyes grew big. She sat up a bit straighter and scooted to the edge of her chair. She looked like she wanted to hear more, and even though out of my periphery I could see Mrs. Griffin commanding me to stop, I kept on going. "She grew up in Raleigh. I don't know much about her, but my daddy said she went to her own ball. Like the one y'all are planning."

Mrs. Griffin's cold hand gripped my arm and squeezed. She cleared her throat and let out a chuckle before saying, "Sounds like the cat's let go of her tongue." As the three women laughed and nodded, Mrs. Griffin shot me a look and said, "Let's not keep the guests waiting any longer. It's time for the tea."

I knew she wanted me to be quiet, but I didn't know why I couldn't tell them a bit about mama, let them know she was more like them than they thought. Plus, Mrs. Wemberton seemed interested. But I stopped talking. I stepped toward Mrs. Foster, my body shaking from trying to stop the anger from bursting out. I knew I'd been asked to serve them tea and sandwiches, but I hadn't realized I would be made the butt of jokes and asked to hide who I was.

As I'd been instructed to do, I poured Mrs. Foster's tea first. The cup was near the edge of the table, so at least I didn't have to reach too far. But my arms were still shaking. I focused on pouring, filling the cup to the right amount.

But then Mrs. Wemberton said, "Perhaps I should ask Leah for the recipe."

Being asked another question brought on more trembling. I felt sweat begin to roll down my back, my forehead, my upper lip. My anger and nerves mixed together and gripped me so I couldn't even see what I was doing. And that's when what I had been trying to hide most came front and center.

I flashed there in the dining room, pausing as they went on talking. When I came back, the two guests were laughing. But Mrs. Griffin was yelling, "Girl! What has gotten into you?"

The tea splashed out of the cup and over the edge of the saucer. It dribbled into Mrs. Foster's lap and flowed onto the rug beneath the table. She waved her napkin like a flag back and forth, wiping at her skirt. Her face looked like Mrs. Barna's when she scolded Jesse.

"I'm so sorry!" I said as I grabbed a napkin from the table and began dabbing at Mrs. Foster's lap. She held her arms in the air, asking me to stop, saying she could do it herself. I stood up and backed away from the table, looking between Mrs. Foster, who was trying to clean her dress, and Mrs. Griffin, whose eyes danced with disgust when she looked at me.

"Don't just stand there," her voice started in a low growl. She paused and swallowed. As she continued, her voice came out higher, trying for chipper but not able to fully mask the anger. "Get something for Mrs. Foster. Now!"

I ran to get a towel and brought it to Mrs. Foster. I knelt on the floor beside her, once again trying to help clean up, apologizing for the mistake.

"I'll take care of it," Mrs. Foster said, but I kept trying to wipe her skirt clean. "Thank you, but I've got it."

I wiped more, trying to dry the mess on her skirt.

Then Mrs. Griffin's voice exploded with one word, "Leah!" I

jumped, nearly bumping into the table. "Step. Away." Her voice was quieter, but the rage still boiled.

I moved to the mess on the floor, blotting at the rug as Mrs. Wemberton tried to change the subject. "Mmm. I could simply eat these all day."

I crawled under the table, wiping up every last bit of tea.

"I do wish you'd tell us," Mrs. Wemberton went on, "what is that secret ingredient?"

I didn't know why the woman rattled on about those sandwiches. I don't know what made me say it. I suppose I was feeling a bit prickly, embarrassed at what I'd done, angry at how Mrs. Griffin had made a joke of me and then yelled at me in front of the others, and for what? Trying to clean up? Being positioned under the table, it seemed as though I wasn't in the room anyway. I felt that rush that I did sometimes, the one that usually got me into trouble. But I'd been holding it together so far. I'd been biting my tongue, smiling when I thought that's what they wanted. I thought I said it low and quiet.

"It's just mustard."

But when Mrs. Wemberton and Mrs. Griffin gasped, I knew I'd said it louder than I'd expected.

The room grew quiet. All movement stopped. Even breathing paused. Until Mrs. Griffin reached under the table and grabbed my arm.

She marched me to the kitchen and pulled out a chair from the table with her foot. "Sit. There." She pushed me onto the seat and then marched back to the dining room. By the time she sat down with her guests, her voice had returned to normal.

I sat at the table and looked out the window to the backyard.

Two birds—a red cardinal and a brown one with it—perched on a tree branch together, hopped around a bit, then flew off into the neighbor's yard. I found a cardinal nest in one of the Barnas' azalea bushes the spring before. Jesse and I had watched the nest together, each day checking to see if the mama had laid a new egg. There were three in there before they started hatching, the babies so ugly they were cute when they first broke free of their shells. They'd squawk and open their little beaks when we got near the nest, thinking we were their mama coming back to give them food. But when their eyes opened, they didn't squawk at us anymore.

While we looked at the babies, the mama would always stay nearby, not too far away, keeping an eye on her nest. She never flew at us, but I kept waiting for her to. Then one day, about a week or two after they had first hatched, we came back and the babies were all gone. A fat, little round bird sat in a different bush nearby, letting me get close, but watching me the whole time, just like that mama. Covered in brown, fluffy feathers, I couldn't be sure, but I thought maybe it was one of those babies who'd left the nest, staying close, wanting to be near his home even if the rest of his family had left already.

But the Griffins didn't have any azalea bushes in their back-yard. They had some out front, and I wondered what they'd look like come spring. Would they be as full of blooms as Mrs. Barna's? She always took such good care of them. Even as old as they were—Jesse told me that his grandmother had planted some of them—they weren't as tall as Mrs. Griffin's. Hers out front were taller than the porch rails, their branches darting off in different directions. Mrs. Barna said the mistake some people made when it comes to azaleas is trimming them like they were hedge bushes, making them all perfectly round or square. She said you had to let an azalea bush determine its own shape and trim only the stragglers that tried getting too tall too fast.

As I watched out the kitchen window, waiting for the birds to come back, longing to be home again, I could hear the conversation from the other room or at least most of it. I heard Mrs. Wemberton praise Mrs. Griffin by saying, "What a saint you are for taking in an orphan like that."

Ever since Daddy died, that seemed to be all anyone saw me as: an orphan. To others, it seemed to matter more than any other part of me. I was no longer a girl, but rather a problem needing a fix.

Thing is, if anyone had bothered asking me, I had a solution. I didn't want to be crashing tea parties. I didn't need to be trying to blend in with society. I'd give up the dream of a two-story house with pillars and a wide porch. I'd even surrender the beach cottage. All I wanted was Maeve and our little shack. I didn't care if the tree still crushed the front entrance. It didn't matter if the rain dripped in the ceiling or the wind blew through. I'd be most content in the only place that had ever been home with our forest waiting outside the back door. I wouldn't bother anyone. They wouldn't even need to know I existed.

I tried listening more, but the pounding of my heartbeat in my ears and the presence of another voice caught my attention.

"Where's Mama?" Mary Ann stood in the kitchen in her pajamas, her cheeks rosy and her eyes brimming with tears.

"Mary Ann!" I dared not stand and walk to her, though I wanted to take her by the hand and lead her back up the stairs to her room.

But Mrs. Griffin had told me not to move. The spot where she had grabbed my arm still stung. Mary Ann didn't speak at first. Big, fat tears the size of first raindrops before a summer afternoon storm started to roll down her freckled cheeks. "You feelin' okay?"

Mary Ann shook her head no and began to cry more. "Come here," I said.

She ran over to me, climbed into my lap, and curled up into a ball. Her tears soaked through my dress. I sat and held her, one arm wrapped around her small body, the other petting her hair. After a few minutes, I asked, "Does something hurt?"

The question made the tears start all over again. I could feel the heat of her body, the clammy sweat on her forehead. "It's okay. How about something to eat?" I could reach some of the extra pimento sandwiches from where I sat. I pulled the tray closer, but she shook her head no, so I scooted them away. "Some tea?"

"Can I just sit here with you?" she asked.

"Of course," I said. I tightened my arm around her and she relaxed into my body. After a few minutes more, her breathing slowed and became louder. I tried to hear the dining room conversation over her breaths. There were words I didn't understand so much. Those seemed to have more to do with Mrs. Foster's husband and his work. He was apparently a doctor of sorts, but I couldn't make out exactly what he did. These words seemed a bit more hushed, more important to Mrs. Griffin. Mrs. Wemberton spoke little. Mrs. Griffin seemed to be asking the most questions and Mrs. Foster giving the information, something about "cutting edge" and "breakthrough" and "the betterment of our society."

By the end, they were making plans to discuss this at the next society meeting "so all the ladies could hear about such an important topic." I hoped it wasn't going to be at Mrs. Griffin's or that she didn't expect me to serve the tea again. But I didn't realize at the time that that was the least of my concerns.

I could hear the chairs scooting on the dining room floor before Mrs. Griffin walked into the kitchen and saw Mary Ann asleep on my lap. "What is she doing here?"

"She isn't feeling well."

"Don't you think I know that? I told her to stay upstairs." Mrs. Griffin looked back and forth between us and the voices coming down the hallway. "Just stay here. I'll get the coats and see the ladies out. Then you can take her upstairs and put her to bed. Do not come out of this kitchen until they leave."

I don't know who she was madder at: me for spilling the tea and the secret, or Mary Ann for not listening and maybe spoiling her party. But it was okay with me if I stayed there. I didn't want to see those ladies and get the coats for them. While I sat in the kitchen, waiting for permission to take Mary Ann upstairs, I looked out the window again. The cardinals were still flying around the backyard, landing on one branch before flying off to another, around and around they went, never satisfied, always moving. And that's when, out of the corner of my eye, I saw the mouse scamper across the floor.

I thought Mary Ann was asleep, but she must've seen it too, because I heard a little giggle before her breathing settled back into a slow rhythm. To Mary Ann, that furry creature was a delight, but to her mother, it was a threat, a nuisance, something to be done away with. I hoped I could rescue it before it was destroyed.

CHAPTER TWELVE

There's a liturgy to each of our lives, whether we realize it or not. When the sun began warming the winds as the branches budded, my body reminded me of the ritual it ached for, the one I couldn't practice when I wasn't by the shore. How long had it been since I'd stood in the sand, watching for those sand fleas and counting all the whole conch shells I could find? But instead, I was in the Griffins' backyard, cursing the weeds that tried to choke out the lettuce and cabbage plants before they could fully take root.

A few weeks had passed since Mrs. Griffin's tea. I replayed that disaster of a day as I pulled and tugged on the weeds, the dirt packing tighter beneath my nails. I couldn't get Mrs. Griffin's words about my parents out of my mind, how angry she got with me for mentioning Mama. I had only been trying to relate, to show those women that she had been like them, but the missus didn't want them to know. Who did she want me to be? For a woman so fixated on the ball, she didn't seem to care that my mama was a debutante just like her. No matter how many weeds I pulled, none of them gave me clarity to figure out why.

Sweat began dripping from me, dropping onto the clay before seeping down into it. I went on like that for a while, not needing to rush back into the house because Mrs. Griffin and Mary Ann had headed out for errands. Without her here, I could take my time outside instead of needing to be confined within the walls of the house. I could listen to the birds and watch the clouds shapeshift overhead. I could lay on my back and pretend I was in the yard back home, not hearing the constant motors of cars going by, but instead hearing the leaves of our oak trees rustling in the wind.

But of course it only made me long for home even more.

I refused to let myself get too lost in those feelings, especially when I hadn't yet figured out a way to go back. Every time I had thoughts of trying to leave, I remembered how the Barnas said the state had a say in things, how they had no control over where I went. But I also remembered how Mr. Barna said that distance would do me good. Apparently the state felt the same way. Otherwise, why would they send me so far away?

Then I thought of what Jesse told me, "Let them get to know you." I'd been doing that. Some. The kids seemed to be catching on, but not Mrs. Griffin. I hadn't figured out how to crack her quite yet, and I wasn't sure I ever would. Or that I even wanted to. I couldn't quite put my finger on it, but it seemed like she was predisposed to hating me.

She seemed to have a notion that I was stupid. Maybe because she didn't permit me to go to school. She had no idea what I could do. So I thought I'd take the empty house as an opportunity to show her. I never was good about apologizing without prompting, and I hadn't told her I was sorry for spilling her secret about the mustard, but maybe I could do something to make things right.

I'd been hankering for one of Tulla's biscuits since the day I'd arrived. I never had helped her make them, but I figured I'd been around them enough to figure things out, plus the missus had a cookbook I could consult.

So I went inside and began pulling together the ingredients I needed. Mrs. Griffin still did most of the cooking, having a specific way of wanting things. She gave me tasks I could handle after I first proved my ability. Of course I made the morning grits. The first morning I made them, Mrs. Griffin wrinkled her nose and insisted that such low-country fare wasn't a part of their breakfast repertoire. When all three of her children took a liking to them, she permitted me to make them regularly.

I consulted the cookbook and scooped the dry ingredients out of the bags in the pantry before adding the refrigerated items. I did my best to roll out the sticky dough, sprinkling flour on it to help the rolling pin glide over it. Once I had them cut into circles, I decided to add my own touch, to sweeten the treat a bit by sprinkling them with sugar before I put them in the oven.

While I waited for the biscuits to bake, I sat down to my lunch. Mary Ann had introduced me to my new favorite food: peanut butter sandwiches. I had never heard of peanut butter before she pulled the jar from the cupboard, scooped out a spoonful, and demanded I try it. I wasn't sure what the brown stuff was, but as I tasted that rich cream, I fell in love. And then when she told me to spread it on top of that sliced bread, well, forget the pimento cheese.

The morning paper still lay on the table. I turned it to the front page and began to read. There weren't many books in the house, and I hadn't had much chance to practice my reading since I'd gotten there. The front page showed a big picture of Charlotte. I hadn't been into the city yet. Eva Jane loved going there and said she'd take me someday. She talked about the streetcars, the tall buildings, the department store with the lunch counter, "You can shop and have lunch without even leaving the building!"

Whenever I got the chance to read, I'd choose my story according to the picture beside it. If it didn't have a picture, I didn't bother with it. And if the picture looked too boring, I'd keep looking until I found one that seemed more interesting. That morning I found something on page two. It had a picture of a Ferris wheel. Now, I'd never seen one for myself before, but I knew that's what it was because Jesse used to tell me stories about the time he rode one at the county fair. He couldn't believe I'd never been on one before (I couldn't tell him I'd never even seen one), but I think when he realized I'd never been to a fair, he figured things out for himself.

The article was a short one—just a couple of paragraphs about how a fair was coming to Mecklenburg County in about a month. There would be rides and games, some bands playing on the main stage, and even a few wonders our eyes had never seen before. I wondered if Eva Jane had heard about the fair yet. I doubted she had since she'd said nothing about it yet. That girl couldn't keep anything quiet if she tried. I'd have to be sure to tell her about it when she got home from school later. Finally I'd have some news for her instead of the other way around.

It took me some time to work my way through the couple of paragraphs there. My reading was improving, or at least I thought so. I didn't have Miss Heniford to tell me if I was doing something wrong, so I made sense of what I could and filled in the blanks if I needed to.

As I read through the words, something caught the corner of

my eye. On top of the counter, next to the bag of bread that I had left open was the mouse. We looked at each other, neither of us moving, me wanting another bite of my sandwich and him wanting to get into that bag. Carefully and quietly, I tore a piece of bread from my sandwich and moved toward him, but he ran down the cupboard and into the space beneath it.

"It's okay," I said to him as I crouched on the floor, holding out the piece of my sandwich for him. "I won't hurt you." I couldn't see him, couldn't hear him, but I knew he was there, so I put the piece of bread on the floor and walked away, hoping he'd be brave enough to get it. By the time I had cleaned up my lunch stuff and put the bread away in the bread box, the piece of my sandwich was gone.

I guess Tulla was right about something: the quietest mice are the ones who go free.

The biscuits baked to a perfect golden brown. My mouth watered looking at them, but I told myself I had to wait for dinner. I scooped them into a bowl, covered them with a towel, and tucked them away into the back of the kitchen cupboard, waiting for dinner later that night to surprise the family with what I could do.

I opened the back door, encouraging the warm, buttery biscuit smell to leave the kitchen before Mrs. Griffin and Mary Ann arrived home. They didn't mention it, and Mrs. Griffin didn't say anything before Mary Ann asked me to put her down for a nap that afternoon.

"I don't know why Mama makes me nap," she said as we walked into her room. "Ain't I old enough to go without?" She asked an honest question, but I'd already gotten the impression that the rest time was more about peace and quiet than it was about needing more sleep.

"Say, can you keep a secret?" Mary Ann held her index finger to her lips, her eyes growing wide as she quieted for a minute.

"Sure," I said.

"Most days, I don't sleep none at all. Know what I do instead?" I shook my head no. Mary Ann tiptoed to the door, slowly opened it a few inches, and looked into the hallway. Then she closed it, walked to her bed, and climbed on top. "I bounce!" She began jumping up and down, the springs starting to squeak and creak. As they moaned louder, she began to giggle.

"Mary Ann!" The shout came through the floorboards. "Quit being naughty!"

Mary Ann threw her feet out in front of her, so when she came into contact with the bed again, she was sitting.

"She calls me that a lot."

"What's that?"

"Naughty. Did you ever get called that?"

I took a moment to think. "No."

Mary Ann's eyes grew wide again. "You never got in trouble?"

I thought of the crayons and the rug I drew the last time I saw Daddy look at me in a disappointed way. "Oh, sure I did."

"So you were naughty?"

I hadn't meant to be. "I suppose that sometimes I did things I shouldn't have."

"But you aren't naughty anymore?"

I thought of the tea and the secret I'd given away. "I'm trying to be better."

Knowing that if Mrs. Griffin came up the stairs and heard us talking we'd both get in trouble, I tried to remind Mary Ann of what she should be doing. "Now it's time for you to rest."

Mary Ann lay down on her bed, her head resting on her pillow. She reached out toward me and said, "Lay with me a few minutes?"

I supposed I could spare a few minutes. I hoped I could anyway. While I can't say I was being naughty, there were moments since I'd been with the Griffins when I'd gotten in trouble. Sometimes I didn't understand why. But naughty to me meant more. It was choosing to do what you knew not to be right. I chose to color that rug on the floor, but I didn't mean anything bad when I got the mail for Mrs. Griffin that one day. When it came down to it, I suppose I hadn't been naughty since I hadn't had Daddy there to show me how I was to act and then correct me when I got it wrong.

As I lay in bed with her that afternoon and her eyes began to get heavy, I kept my gaze straight ahead of me, looking over the items on Mary Ann's dresser. Between the doll and the bird's nest she had collected from outside, something caught my eye. A letter. My eyes worked hard to make out the name on the envelope. The longer I stared, the more and more it looked like my own name.

"Mary Ann," I whispered, testing to see if she was still awake.

"Yeah?" Though her voice was raspy, the volume was nearly as loud as her typical talking voice. She had been working on her whispering since before I'd arrived, but she still didn't understand the quiet part. She thought whispering meant adding a bit of breath to whatever volume she chose.

"What's that letter on your dresser?"

I didn't mean for her to get out bed, but before I could say anything, she rolled off the edge and sprang across her floor, grabbing the letter and bouncing her way back to bed.

"I found it in Mama's apron pocket when I was being naughty one time."

I took the envelope in my hand and read the two addresses on it. The big one in the center had my name at the top. The smaller one in the upper left corner had Jesse's name.

"Her apron pocket?" I said as my heart pounded, so I could feel it in my chest, throat, ears, thrumming all throughout my body.

Mary Ann nodded her head yes.

"Mm-hmm," she said as she snuggled in close to me and began to close her eyes. "Say, don't let Mama see that," she said in her attempt at a whisper. "She doesn't know I found it."

Mary Ann settled into her nap, her breathing growing slow and steady. Before she fully drifted off, I had to ask her one more thing.

"Can I keep this safe? So your mama doesn't find it? How about I put it in my room?"

Mary Ann opened her eyes, looked at me, her eyebrows showing her confusion. "It has your name on it."

Of course I could keep it. To Mary Ann, who else would have the right to have it? From her perspective, if my name was on it, then it rightfully belonged to me.

I lifted up my dress and tucked the letter into my underpants. Yes, my house dress had pockets, but not deep enough and certainly not hidden enough. I knew I had to sneak it to my room, past Mrs. Griffin. I waited for Mary Ann to be fully asleep before

I snuck out of her room down to my own, opened the envelope, and read the few sentences it held.

Dear Leah,

Maeve misses you. She nugs up against Tulla whenever she can. Drives Tulla crazy. I lay down in the grass the other night to look at the stars. I found your orange one. Maeve curled up beside me. We fell asleep out there. Mama yelled at me. Said I'd catch the death of me lying in the wet grass when it was so cold.

Write back when you can.—J

I remember the first time a wave swept me off my feet. I was little. Daddy was holding my hand, but he let go just as a wave crashed to shore. It wasn't a big wave but big enough to knock a child off her feet. My face fell beneath the water, the saltiness stinging my eyes, the taste catching in the back of my throat. I coughed and cried from the surprise.

As I sat on the bed, tears streamed down my cheek and landed on the letter, making marks that faded but never fully disappeared. Jesse wrote as if we were in the middle of a conversation, as if this letter was part of a series. But a conversation requires two people who are willing to respond. Until then, I hadn't known that someone was waiting to hear from me.

And somehow I needed to find a way to not keep him waiting any longer.

I sat on my bed alone with Jesse's letter for as long as I could until Mrs. Griffin pounded on the wall to help with dinner. I tucked the note away before going into the kitchen that evening, but I let the words replay in my mind as I went through the motions of prepping and cooking. Mrs. Griffin didn't converse, only speaking directions when necessary, but the supper that night was one I had learned to prepare on my own.

With the Griffins elsewhere in the house—Mary Ann most likely on her father's lap while the others busied themselves in other rooms—I got to imagine uninterrupted, but truth be told, I wouldn't have minded an interruption or a friend who would sit down at the table and strike up a bit of conversation. I couldn't help but wonder if Tulla had wished the same as Jesse and I spent our afternoons arranging the seashells outside and she cooked alone in the kitchen.

During dinner, Mrs. Griffin told her husband about the day's events. She waited for him to put down the newspaper, though he still didn't look at her much. If his head wasn't behind the day's headlines, his eyes were focused on his plate.

"I ran into Dr. Foster," Mrs. Griffin began.

"How's that?" Mr. Griffin asked. After being gone all week, he had arrived home shortly before dinner. He looked exhausted enough to fall asleep at the dinner table if he wasn't careful. "Wasn't the man working?"

"Well, yes, but I stopped by his office." Her husband looked up. "I just dropped in to say hi."

"You shouldn't go bothering people at their work."

"I wasn't bothering. He told me to stop by if I was in the neighborhood, and I was, so I did. We had the most fascinating conversation. Turns out he's got some cutting-edge things he's doing. Mrs. Foster told us some about it when she was here for tea. He gave me a pamphlet. You'll have to read it. He's coming to speak at the Women of Matthews meeting."

"Now don't go bothering that man when he has work to do."

"I'm no bother," Mrs. Griffin seethed. "He told me so himself. Says he needs someone like me to help get the word out."

"Well, he's come to the right lady then."

Mrs. Griffin changed the subject. "Mary Ann is registered for school in the fall."

Mr. Griffin gave a quiet "hmm."

"I squared it away with Mr. Hammond. He said of course he couldn't wait to have another Griffin in his school." She sat up a tad straighter when she said that.

"Wait till he sees that chatterbox," Michael Henry said between slurps of his mashed potatoes. "He might go changing his mind."

Mary Ann looked at her brother and stuck out her tongue. Michael Henry returned the gesture, but with a bit of mashed potato on the end of his tongue.

"I'd be careful what I say if I were you, seeing as how we had a nice little chat about your own grades while I was there." Michael Henry's cheeks reddened. "You better get your act together or no law school is going to want you."

"What if I don't want to go to law school?"

Mrs. Griffin's fork dropped to her plate, its clinking sounding like a start bell at a fight about to take place. "We've already talked about this."

"But what about Eva Jane?" He pointed his fork across the

table in the direction of his oldest sister, who looked up from her plate with eyes the size of saucers, as if she hadn't heard the discussion at all.

"What about me?"

"I'm smarter than her."

"This conversation isn't about her."

"Maybe it should be."

"She does fine. Besides, she's not going to law school."

"What if I want to go into sales like Dad?"

At the mention of his name, Mr. Griffin looked up from his plate, not ready to say anything quite yet, as if hoping he wouldn't have to.

But his wife continued, "We've discussed this. Your future is in law. It's what you've been preparing for."

"But—"

"Don't you sass me. Frank! Are you going to let him talk that way to me?"

Mr. Griffin paused a moment, holding a spoon full of mashed potatoes before saying, "Don't sass your mother. Eat your dinner."

Michael Henry slouched in his chair. He pushed the rest of his potatoes and roast around his plate. In the silence, Mary Ann asked a good question, "Why do I have to go to school and Leah doesn't?"

Without missing a beat, Mrs. Griffin said, "Because she has other things to do."

"But she's older than me."

"Yes, and she's had some schooling. Now she has work." Mrs. Griffin took a sip of her drink as Mary Ann continued.

"But what if she wants to be a lawyer?"

Mrs. Griffin coughed. A dribble of tea came out of her mouth and began to fall down her chin before she wiped it away with her napkin. She smiled as she said, "It doesn't work that way, dear."

"All I want's to live on the beach," I said before realizing I was saying anything. Everyone looked at me. I'd been so distracted by Jesse's letter that I hadn't spoken a word at dinner until that moment. And those words made everyone in the room go silent at the same time.

Mr. Griffin looked up from his plate and his wife let out a small laugh. "In whose house?" Another snicker escaped her. "Fisherman don't employ servants."

My chest tightened. I put down my own fork and looked at her, my breathing becoming fast. I could feel my cheeks begin to flame, but I couldn't put together words to challenge her thinking that all I'd ever be was someone's helpmate.

"Why can't she have a place of her own there?" Michael Henry asked. His words quenched me like cool water on a hot day. As I looked across the table at him, he winked at me and shrugged.

"The notions," Mrs. Griffin began to say, but her laughter interrupted the sentence so each word came out one at a time, "of a simpleminded girl."

My heart was beating so hard in my ears that I could hardly hear her snicker. I stood from the table, took my plate, and walked into the kitchen. I wanted to throw it into the sink, but stopped myself. I grabbed onto the back of the kitchen chair, hoping the squeeze of my fingers could replace the scream I felt bubbling up inside me.

I stood alone in the kitchen, wondering how she could sit there and laugh, how she could say whatever she wanted, especially after all I did for her, even after the biscuits I'd made for them.

That's when I remembered the biscuits. My first reaction was to pull them out of the cupboard and throw them into the dining room, but apparently I'd matured a bit since I'd arrived. I took a few deep breaths and wiped the couple of tears from my eyes and the sweat from my upper lip before I walked into the dining room with the bowl of homemade biscuits.

"I made these for you," I said as I placed them on the table.

The five Griffins all looked at the biscuits. Mary Ann was the first to speak, "You made those?" Her eyes lit up as her little hand reached for one.

"Yes, just this morning."

Each of the Griffins took a biscuit. Michael Henry smelled his first and then all of them took a bite as I stood and watched. It took only a few seconds for their expressions of amazement to turn to disgust.

"Ew! What is this?" Michael Henry asked first, before he spit the bite of biscuit onto his plate.

"What's wrong with it?" Eva Jane asked, as she spit hers into her napkin.

Until Mary Ann spoke, I thought they were playing a joke on me. Mary Ann's nose wrinkled and she whispered to her mother, "Do I have to eat this?"

I reached for a biscuit, smelled it for myself, and wondered what all of the fuss was about. I tore off a small bite, my mouth watering in anticipation. As I placed it on my tongue, Mrs. Griffin asked, "Exactly how much salt did you use?"

Salt. It's such a simple and necessary seasoning, but a little goes a long way. Since Mrs. Griffin had been the one to mix the ingredients and follow the recipes, she also knew what each unmarked bag on the kitchen cupboard held. The flour was obvious enough, but salt and sugar look quite similar, and when mixed up in a recipe, they result in very different tastes.

As I walked back into the kitchen, I heard Mrs. Griffin say, "So simple, she can't tell the salt from the sugar."

Once their laughter died down, they resumed their conversation. I caught snippets of it over the clang of washing up the dishes. With my fingertips turning to raisins in the sudsy water, I heard Mary Ann ask, "When will we go to the fair, Mama?"

I paused the washing and cleaning to hear the response.

"The first night, of course."

The three Griffin children all celebrated the answer, anticipating the big event a few weeks away. As they went on with their evening, I stood at the sink and worked things out in my mind. After the discovery of earlier that day, I longed for someone who already knew me. Someone I didn't have to try to impress. Someone who could laugh with me when I mistook the salt for the sugar. I had to write to Jesse.

I had tried my hardest, but every time Mrs. Griffin snickered, I knew better than to think she'd ever accept me. I needed to know if I stood a chance at making a home with the Barnas, especially if I promised to live quiet as a mouse next door, not bothering a single soul.

I couldn't ask him to write back, especially if Mrs. Griffin got to his response before I did. So, what better opportunity to see Jesse again, to get all my questions answered, than an event bringing people in from all over the state? But with the fair quickly approaching, I needed to get him a letter sooner rather than later. And I needed to do it without the missus knowing. Good thing I knew a thing or two about being a sneak.

CHAPTER THIRTEEN

While I had first longed to have a room behind one of those upstairs windows that looked out on the street that showed life outside the house, I began to find solitude in my room. The small window up top only let in faint streaks of daylight during the brightest moments of sunshine each day, though I spent most of those hours doing my daily chores. But I began to welcome the darkness of the den, let it wrap around me as I curled up under my quilt each night, willing myself to feel Daddy's presence in the darkness, sometimes putting my pillow beside me, imagining it to be someone.

And now with Jesse's letter too, I felt the presence of someone else I longed to be near to. Objects can't replace people any more than an essay with some scribbles of the beach can be a substitute for a future, but when all you have is your ability to imagine what you miss, you allow yourself to escape into a world of your own making.

I let myself imagine for a few nights before I decided it was time to act, but what could I do? I had nothing—no money, no transportation, no way of knowing how to phone him. I had his address, but that did me little good without so much as a stamp, let alone stationery. I considered asking Mary Ann to help, knowing she could find things, but I didn't yet trust how quiet she could be when I needed her silence most.

One day when Mrs. Griffin accidentally left an extra envelope on the kitchen table after she'd finished with her correspondence, I scooted it under the newspaper she'd already finished reading. And then I waited for her to leave the kitchen before I grabbed the newspaper with the envelope hidden beneath it and stowed them away in my room. The paper had an advertisement for the fair inside. I tore it out, folded it, and placed it inside the envelope. I tucked them beneath my mattress, waiting to figure out what to do next. The answer came that Saturday.

Mrs. Griffin was out. I don't know what it was, but everyone seemed to sense a change that day. Eva Jane and Michael Henry weren't bickering with one another quite so much. Mary Ann spoke with less whine in her voice. Even Mr. Griffin, who'd arrived home the evening before, seemed more relaxed as he sat out back and smoked a pipe.

I'd already washed Mary Ann's sheets that morning and hung them on the line to dry. That wasn't typical Saturday work, but I'd had to do it when Mary Ann had wet the bed again. Mrs. Griffin, disappointed in Mary Ann, had instructed us all to leave the girl be while she was away. Had no one else been home, and despite instructions to not give her anything, I would've snuck Mary Ann a small breakfast or snack of sorts, seeing as how she hadn't eaten anything yet that morning. But instead of helping, I spent my morning by Eva Jane's side.

We sat on the front porch; she was in the swing, coaxing it back and forth. I had been sitting beside her, but she said I made the swing go a bit sideways. So she asked me to move. Wanting to please her, I didn't argue. Thankfully, I'd swept the thick layer of yellow dust off the porch the day before, so I could sit on it. You could still see clumps of the pollen in the bushes on the outside of the railing. It had made such plumes as I swept that it tickled the inside of my nose and caused me to sneeze.

"I'm so happy Aiken finally asked me to the ball," Eva Jane said, looking off in the distance and not down at me on the porch floor. Her feet rolled from the tips of her toes to the edges of her heels as she pushed back and forth, causing the chain overhead to complain and creak in rhythm. The ball had been Eva Jane's topic of choice over the last few weeks, even more so than the fair—especially after Aiken had officially asked her to go. While the misses kept us all updated on the planning and progress of the event, she still hadn't shared any memories of her own.

"I hope Mama takes me shopping soon for a new dress. She said she'd take me into Charlotte." Eva Jane had a way of shortening, yet drawing out, the city name all at the same time. It rolled off her tongue as *Shah-let*. "Mama said we'll go to Belk. I hope we get to eat at the lunch counter there. Say, why don't you come along?" she said, finally looking down at me. Dust and dirt had resettled on the porch floor, and I was busy making lines and designs with my index finger.

"Really?" I asked, knowing that ultimately Mrs. Griffin would decide if I could go.

"Well, of course! I mean, why not? You've never been to Charlotte, or any city for that matter, which I still can't believe. And I need your help picking out a dress. I have to make sure it's just the one." Her gaze once again left me and drifted toward the street, but I don't think she was really seeing much of anything.

I went back to tracing the design on the floorboards, carving out the dust to make curls and swirls.

"Say," Eva Jane started pushing the swing again, words coming out in a faster pace than before, "how about we go on a little adventure right now?"

"Adventure?"

"Yes! How about we talk Daddy into letting us go to the soda fountain?"

I again stopped making designs. My eyes danced with excitement. She had asked me to do something, as a friend, to be out and about alongside her. And while I had been waiting for that moment, something else thrilled me more. We drove past the drug store with the soda fountain each Sunday on the way to church. Though I'd yet to be inside, I was certain it was exactly the place I needed to be, the place that could help me get one step closer to corresponding with Jesse.

"I'll talk Daddy into it," Eva Jane continued. "He's a pushover. I'll handle him."

"Who you handling?" Michael Henry walked around the side of the porch opposite the direction Eva Jane had been looking.

"You hiding in the bushes listening to us?"

Michael Henry laughed. "I was just wondering where you two had run off to, that's all."

"We're about to run off to the soda fountain if Daddy lets us go."

Michael Henry looked at me. I looked back down at the lines in the porch dust and continued drawing, trying to slow my breathing and act as normal as possible while plotting how I'd post the letter with them along with me.

"You better ask sooner than later, before Mama gets back."

That was all the motivation she needed. Eva Jane insisted that I go with her to ask Mr. Griffin. I didn't know how my presence would help. I still wasn't sure the man knew my name, and I honestly wondered if I walked out of the house just then if he'd even know that I had left. Or had ever lived there to begin with.

We were halfway around the side of the house when I first caught a whiff of Mr. Griffin's pipe. He only ever smoked it outside and when the missus was gone. As we walked around back, we found him sitting alone, staring up into the sky, a slight smile and complete contentment on his face.

"Daddy," Eva Jane began, in a voice much sweeter than she used with me and especially with Michael Henry, so sweet that it was like thick honey dripping off Tulla's biscuits. "I was just thinking it's such a beautiful day that maybe a walk would be nice."

"How's that?" he asked, as if he hadn't noticed us until Eva Jane spoke.

"A walk."

"Where you walking to?" He put the pipe to his lips, inhaled, held it for a minute, and then let a trail of smoke billow from his parted lips.

"I thought maybe we'd go to the soda fountain."

"I see," he said.

"It's only a few blocks away. And I promise it won't spoil our lunch."

"Our? Who all's going?"

"Me and Leah."

Mr. Griffin's eyes looked over the top of his spectacles. "Well, I don't know—"

"I'll go with them," Michael Henry said as he stepped closer to his father.

Mr. Griffin looked to the three of us, from one set of eyes to the next before answering Michael Henry. "Well, as long as you're going."

"Thank you!" Eva Jane leaped toward him and threw her arms around him. She squeezed him tightly. Then she let go, took a step back, and begged, "Do it, Daddy!"

I had no idea what she wanted him to do, but she kept saying it, demanding something from him. Mr. Griffin acted like he didn't hear her at first, but then he began to smile and asked, "You really want to see it?"

"Yes! Please! Leah," she said, turning to me. "Watch this! Watch!"

Mr. Griffin put the pipe to his mouth and inhaled again. When he exhaled, he rounded his lips and puffed out in short breaths, creating a line of smoke rings that floated into the air. They wobbled and faded the higher they got. Eva Jane giggled with delight, and for the first time, I saw her as more like Mary Ann than I had ever seen before.

Mr. Griffin laughed, proud of his accomplishment. Then he reached into his pocket and pulled out a handful of change. It seemed like more money than Daddy and I spent on half our week's groceries, especially those times when the woods would be too wet for him to work. Usually, Mr. Barna would try to give him some chores around the house or even ask him to stock up the store for him, but sometimes even those odd jobs weren't enough.

If only I could get one of those coins, I'd be able to purchase the stamp I needed. I stood still and watched, feeling my insides vibrate with anticipation. Mr. Griffin handed Michael Henry and Eva Jane a dime each. And then he called my name.

"Get yourself a treat," he said as he placed a silver dime into my hand.

My fingers closed into a tight fist, gripping that coin so it couldn't slip from me.

"Thank you," I said.

Before we left, I tucked the envelope into my dress pocket, folding it so it wouldn't poke out. My stomach danced with anticipation as I tried to figure out the rest of my plan, telling myself to not get my hopes up, knowing good and well that my mission had a higher chance of failure than it did success.

On the way to the soda fountain, Eva Jane and Michael Henry discussed what flavor of soda they'd get that day, as if they had been so many times they had tried all the options. Finally, they asked me what I wanted. I had no answer.

"You've never been?" Eva Jane asked. "Well, you're gonna love it! You should try the strawberry. It's the best!"

"I was thinking maybe ginger ale." I said the only flavor that came to mind right then.

"Ginger ale?" She laughed. "You got a tummy ache or something? Nah, you gotta try the strawberry."

"She doesn't have to do anything you tell her to," Michael Henry said.

"You think she should get chocolate, like you?"

The two spent the rest of the walk discussing why their own choices were the best. By the time Michael Henry opened the glass door to the Matthews Drug Company, I had decided that I'd listen to Eva Jane. She knew how to dress, so maybe she had good taste all around.

I stopped a few steps inside the drug store door, taking in all that was around me. The shelves full of bottles and tinctures. The bar with the stools. The mirror behind the glasses and soda machine. A man in a white apron and hat cocked to one side stood behind the bar. With a cloth in his hand, he scrubbed the wooden top clean.

He looked up as the bell above the door announced our arrival. "Mornin'," he said.

The Griffins ordered their drinks, but I waited.

"Go on and order," Michael Henry encouraged me. "Don't be shy."

"I'm still figurin' it out," I said. He seemed satisfied by my response, not pushing me to order when I wasn't ready.

What he didn't know was that I wasn't sure if I could afford a soda. Each drink cost the entire dime. If I ordered something then, I'd not have the three cents I needed for a stamp. Though I'd yet to taste a soda like that before, what I thirsted for more was to see Jesse again.

The soda jerk handed them their glasses full of fizzy drinks. A straw stuck out above smooth cream and a cherry the color of no cherry I'd ever seen before.

Eva Jane giggled as she sipped it. She wasted no time taking a long drink, the level of her red liquid dropping from the rim to beneath as I watched.

"Go on and taste it," she said, offering me a sip.

I put the straw to my tongue, closed my lips around it, and took a sip. The sweetness of it hit me first, and then the carbonation popped into my mouth, around my tongue, and bounced off the insides of my cheeks. I coughed as I swallowed.

"I told you it was the best."

I sat down on one of the stools near the end of the bar. It was about that time that the door opened, the bells jingled, and the laughter of two girls our age came tumbling into the soda fountain, bouncing off the walls just like the fizzy bubbles did in my mouth.

Eva Jane stood up, smoothed out her hair, and walked to the girls. One girl looked familiar. I'd seen her at church, but I'd also noticed she had a similar silhouette, shape, and coloring as someone I'd already met. Though this one was a younger version of the woman I'd served.

"Well, Sally Wemberton! I wasn't expecting to see you here," Eva Jane said as she walked toward them.

The girls became a cluster of three, moving around the drug store as one unit. Once they all had their drinks, they took up the table in the front window, their skirts flared like fans, their legs crossed at the ankles, their backs straight and stiff.

As I watched them in the mirror behind the bar, I caught bits of chatter, talk of the ball and their dresses, and what had been happening at school. Eva Jane had told me some of the stories already as I'd sat in her room on the window seat. I'd heard the tales, and maybe that's why she didn't call me over. Maybe that's why she hadn't introduced me to the girls I'd heard of but had yet to properly meet.

I kept my eyes on the mirror, my sweaty fist wrapped around the dime and my arm pushing against the letter to hold it in my pocket. I watched the girls sip their drinks, lean in, and whisper words that would make the others laugh. I also watched the men and women outside the window. The mothers holding the hands of the little ones like Daddy used to do for me. I watched the cars go by and slow for the stoplight. So many people on their way to someplace. So many people with somewhere to go.

I wondered where they were all headed. What they had to do. I made up stories of groceries they needed or new shoes for school. Maybe they had a watch that needed fixing or were seeking some extra seeds for their garden. Their faces began to blur, and I stopped seeing individuals but rather a sea of movement, of purpose, and places to be.

My mind got lost in that ebb and flow of people, and my imagination took over, playing a trick on me, showing me what I longed for. I saw a boy with sandy brown hair. It had a bit of a wave to it. He walked in that slow, lumbering way like his dad did. He could be fast when he tried—well, not as fast as me, at least not in the rain or even on the ice. But I didn't want to think about the ice just then. Or ever. And as that boy started to turn so I could see if he was Jesse, someone bumped into my leg.

"Whatcha think of the strawberry?" Michael Henry asked. He sat on the stool closest to mine, his leg touching my own. I sat up and answered by shrugging my shoulders.

"Yeah. Try this instead." He pushed his glass of brown liquid in my direction. "It's chocolate. You'll like it."

I wasn't sure I wanted to try it.

"Take a sip." He held the straw to my lips. I took a small sip and smiled.

"It's good, right?"

I nodded as sweetness once again overwhelmed my taste buds.

The girls' laughter died down, and I heard Sally ask, "Say, who's that girl Michael Henry's sitting with?"

I watched their reflections. I saw Eva Jane turn toward me

before looking back at her friends. "Her? Oh, no one. Just Mother's helpmate."

The girls nodded their heads as they sipped their drinks. Michael Henry sucked down the last of his soda before scooting his barstool back and walking toward the girls.

"Ladies," he said with a bow. "What a surprise to see you this morning." I couldn't see their expressions, but I could hear the giggles of the girls. I assumed Eva Jane was rolling her eyes while Sally was blushing. Then I saw Michael Henry take Sally's hand in his and bring it to his lips and kiss the top of it.

"I trust you're well?" he asked before letting go of her hand.

"I am now," she said.

For the first time in a long time, I didn't want an invitation to join the group. I wanted to be left alone. When I thought they were busy with one another, I motioned to the soda jerk.

"What can I getcha?" he asked.

I pulled the envelope from my pocket and placed it on the bar, my hand covering as much of it as it could. Not wanting the others to hear me, my eyes begged and my voice squeaked out my request so that only the soda jerk could hear. "One stamp. Please."

I slid the dime in his direction, and he slid back a stamp and change. I tucked the coins into my pocket. Then I gave the stamp a quick lick and placed it on the upper right corner, but something else was missing. The soda jerk must've noticed. He pulled a pen from behind his ear and slid it to me.

I checked the group in the mirror. Michael Henry was still making Sally laugh, but Eva Jane was beginning to look around. I knew I didn't have much time. So as quickly as I could, I scrawled all I knew onto the envelope.

Jesse Barna
Supply, NC

My handwriting had gotten shaky without use, but it would have to do. I nearly gave the letter to the soda jerk, but I thought I had another minute, so I slid the fair advertisement from the envelope and wrote:

Can you come? Friday night.—L

I began to fold up the newsprint, but I had one more thing I needed to say:

P.S. Say hi to Maeve.

"Leah!" I nearly jumped off the stool when I heard my name. "It's time to go!"

I shoved the advertisement into the envelope. "Coming!" I said with my back to him. I didn't have time to lick it closed. I didn't even have a chance to slide it to the soda jerk, but I caught his eye and we nodded to one another. As I stood, he reached for the envelope and put it out of sight before Michael Henry could call for me again.

I did my best not to smile too much on the way home, not to skip down the sidewalk. 'Course success depended on the soda jerk getting my letter in the mail, Jesse receiving it, and the Barnas deciding to go to the fair Friday night. Regardless, I allowed myself to feel something for the first time since the ice storm, something orphans instinctively know not to give much attention to. Hope.

CHAPTER FOURTEEN

Mary Ann had the most elaborate dreams, as if her imagination got fired up while her body slept. She'd race to tell me them each morning—Mrs. Griffin not caring to hear about the nonsense, doubting that she actually dreamed at all, but instead believing that she used it as an excuse to tell tales. But Mary Ann could pull me from the real world and into her dreamed one with her retellings of creatures and colors, joy and excitement, and sometimes a touch of fear. While she had an imagination, the details of her dreams could not have been created by her awake mind. They came from somewhere deep inside, or maybe somewhere far outside, like little gifts and picture shows for her own delight.

But me? I didn't dream while I was with the Griffins. Daddy always said, if he could, he'd pay admission to watch those nighttime picture shows that my mind created. But since he'd passed, they had seemed to shut off. Or maybe they'd been given to Mary Ann. Maybe I was too tired by the end of each day that my mind slumbered too deeply. Or maybe it was because I was afraid to peek into a different world, afraid of wanting something more.

So I don't think I was lost in a dream when Mrs. Griffin called for me to wake up the morning of the meeting. I heard the voice faint and off in the distance, kind of like in those moments when

I flashed, but there was no flashing. My body must've been holding me in a deep sleep as Mrs. Griffin's voice first echoed through
the wall. My room was still dark, the sun not yet fully over the
horizon, but when I didn't answer, Mrs. Griffin made her way
into my room. When I still didn't wake, she grabbed the quilt
and ripped it off the bed.

"Get up, now."

As sleep was letting go of me, not even a faint peek of daylight
made its way through the window.

"You've got chores to get to before the ladies get here. And no
grits this morning. There's too much to do."

I sat up so quickly my head spun with dizziness. I couldn't
believe I had overslept, especially on that day. Mrs. Griffin had
made clear the importance of hosting the meeting for all the
Women of Matthews, a bigger affair than the tea had been. Mrs.
Griffin always busied herself with those get-togethers, but that
was the first time she'd hosted one since I'd come to stay with
them. After mailing that letter, I'd been on my best behavior,
doing what I could to ensure I could also go to the fair with the
family. Oversleeping could wreck it all.

"Yes, ma'am." I bolted out of bed, my head spinning again.
Knowing Eva Jane and Mary Ann would be disappointed about
not having their usual breakfast, I continued, "I can make the
grits and still get the chores done."

"Not today. They can have toast."

She turned to walk out of the room, and as her eyes passed
over my dresser, she paused. I could only see her from the side,
but I knew what she was looking at. She never asked me about
the picture, nor did she ask about Mama and Daddy, as if all that

happened before I arrived was to be tucked inside a bottle and lost at sea.

"Get yourself presentable."

She left the room, and I reached beneath my pillow to pull out Jesse's letter. Thankfully, I hadn't left it lying in the open overnight.

By the time I got to the kitchen, Mrs. Griffin was buttering a piece of nearly burnt toast before putting it on a plate and setting it at Michael Henry's place. Seeing as how the sun still wasn't fully up, there was time before the kids would be making their way down the stairs, time for that toast to get cold, but Mrs. Griffin seemed too busy to care.

As the knife scratched its way across the top of another piece of darkened bread, Mrs. Griffin asked, "Is the sunroom all set?" Her hair was still in pin curls, housecoat still wrapped around her, and slippers upon her feet.

"Yes, ma'am," I said.

I'd spent a good portion of the previous day getting it ready. In the few months I'd been in that house, I'd never stepped foot in that room. It was on the other side of the dining room, opposite the kitchen, but the doors had been closed since the day I'd arrived. Judging from the layer of dust and cobwebs, no one had been out there in even longer.

I saw why they called it the sunroom. Rows of windows made up three whole walls, with a door to the wraparound porch on one of them. I'd tried to open it to let some air in, but it hadn't budged until I used all my strength, planting my feet on the floor and tugging with all the muscles God had given me. I guessed they didn't use the door much, which I suppose made sense because they never used the big wraparound porch much either.

It'd taken me till lunchtime to clear out all the dust, bat down the cobwebs, and sweep up the floors. By the end, I was sweating as if I'd been racing Jesse to the schoolhouse.

The sunroom looked good that morning, if I did say so myself. The folding chairs were all in lined up rows. Mary Ann agreed that the room looked nice.

Once I finished handing the children their toast and tidying things up, I poufed, teased, and curled Mrs. Griffin's hair, just like she wanted, just like the magazine picture she'd shown me. I had to rush to do it. I think we spent as much time tightening up that corset of hers. She hadn't even had her toast and hardly any coffee either. Good thing, because not even that amount of food was fitting inside the boning. Welcoming Mrs. Wemberton that morning, I noticed their waists had inched a bit closer to being the same size, though Mrs. Wemberton looked more at ease without sweat forming on her face that she'd have to wipe away when she thought no one was looking.

"I'd like to officially call today's meeting of the Women of Matthews to order. Thank you all for joining us, and a special thank you to Dr. Foster for taking time out of your busy schedule to honor us with your presence." I had been in the kitchen, stirring up the lemonade, and I had missed his arrival. I tried to get a good look at this man the missus talked so much about, but I couldn't see him through the room full of women. The missus continued, "Ladies, I can't wait for you to hear what he's doing for the future of our country."

I wanted to hear too. It was all Mrs. Griffin had been talking to her husband about (well, that or the ball, of course) for about as long as I'd been in the house, though I still couldn't understand what exactly any of it meant.

I stood in the dining room, just outside the threshold of the sunroom. All the ladies had arrived and taken their seats, their dresses fanned out, the ends draping down the sides of the borrowed folding chairs, their ankles crossed, and gloved hands folded in their laps. Mary Ann had wanted to see them all, but her mama said children weren't to be a part of such a grown-up discussion, so she was in her room playing with her doll. I'd check on her later, maybe sneak her up some fresh-squeezed lemonade that she'd helped me stir up that morning, but for now I stood in the shadows of the dining room.

"With thanks to Mrs. Griffin, the ball is right on schedule." Mrs. Wemberton bounced as she gave her report, and I noticed several of the other ladies turned to one another and smiled. "We are weeks away from the big day. The first ever Matthews junior ball is going to be here before we know it! So, ladies, it's time for all your girls to find that special dress and for the men to press their suits. I don't think I have to tell you how special this is. For any of you who," she held her right hand to her chest, "like me, had the honor of being a debutante, this is more than a cotillion. This is our daughters' moment to be presented to the community for the women they are becoming."

The ladies clapped a muffled applause. I watched Mrs. Griffin, who stared out the windows behind Mrs. Wemberton. While the other women smiled and cheered, the missus looked into the distance, as if caught in a memory. But not something worth smiling about. A moment later, Mrs. Griffin straightened her posture and walked to the front of the room to thank Mrs. Wemberton for the update and for all her hard work.

"Ladies, let's remember this isn't an official debutante ball, but this could be the beginning—"

"Well, if Charlotte's society wouldn't be so exclusive—" a woman in the second row began.

"Yes, Mrs. Brant, we're all aware of that, but now we have our own to look forward to. One that we hope will become a tradition in its own right." Again, muffled applause. "Now if there's no other business to attend to, without further ado, I'd like to introduce Dr. Foster."

I have to say that the doctor didn't look as I'd expected. He was rather short. Mrs. Griffin had picked out her lowest heels to wear that day and, even still, she stood a few inches taller than him. He had puffy black hair with a sprinkling of some white, though his beard showed even more white than the top of his head did. His wire-rimmed glasses cut into his nose so that the skin on the top and the bottom curled around the wire, as did his cheeks to the arms of his glasses. I never once saw him have to push them back in place. It seemed as though his folds kept them from moving.

"My name is Dr. Foster," he began. Instead of taking her seat in the front row, Mrs. Griffin walked to the dining room, blocking me from seeing the doctor. "For the past decade I've been studying genetics. What I have to say today could have great impact on your children and especially their children and their children's children. What I speak about is for the good of our town, our state, and our country as a whole. It is about planning for the betterment of our future and our society."

That was as much as I heard before Mrs. Griffin told me to go pour the drinks.

"I thought that was for after the meeting."

"Yes," she said, moving into position so I couldn't see the doctor. "But it's best to be prepared, now, isn't it? So, run along and pour the drinks. Make sure the snacks are all set." She knew they were. She had been fussing with them around the table up until the doorbell rang, moving each tray and platter to a different spot until they looked the same as when she'd started. "Oh, and close the doors behind me."

She walked back into the sunroom, taking a seat in the back row. I closed each door, one at a time, slowly so they wouldn't creak, but also so I could keep listening. But once they shut, there was no hearing. There were only muffles, sometimes gasps and murmurs, and then finally applause before the doors opened and the women came out to partake of their refreshments.

I stood behind the table, refilling drinks and smiling at the ladies who came to choose a cookie or a spoonful of nuts, though no one really looked at me.

Mrs. Wemberton followed Dr. Foster to the table. As he got closer, I realized I could look him straight in the eyes, not looking up, nor down, but straight ahead.

"You have a very uncommon hair color," he said.

My hand reflexively reached to my curls, as if protecting what I had. He looked at me, not meeting my eyes, but as if I was some strange object that needed closer examination. I wrapped my arms around myself and leaned toward the wall. I rarely felt comfortable in the presence of others, but this man made my insides shiver. "Not abnormal, but certainly not common."

"For the life of me," Mrs. Wemberton began, "I can't recall how you say the name of what you study."

She looked down at a pamphlet she had in her hand. All the ladies had left the sunroom with that same brochure. "For you to share with your husbands" were the words I'd heard as the doors had swung open.

His eyes finally let go of my curls. He took a sip of the lemonade. A few droplets clung to his salt-and-pepper mustache. "Eugenics." He slurped another drink. Sighed. Held the glass up as if to examine the color and then sipped again.

Mrs. Griffin walked to the snack table, her hand extended for Dr. Foster to take. "Again, I can't thank you enough," she said. He looked at his lemonade. "Is everything alright?" she asked.

"Yes." He continued looking at his drink. "It's just, I haven't had lemonade this refreshing since I was a boy. My grandmother used to make some that tasted exactly like this." He sat his cup on the edge of the snack table and removed his glasses. He cleaned them with a handkerchief that he tucked into his vest pocket before putting his glasses back on. And then he looked at me again.

"I was just remarking on her hair," he said, staring at me, but not talking to me. "What's her name again?"

"Leah. This is the girl I was telling you about."

"Right. Right. Yes." And now my face was starting to sweat like Mrs. Griffin's had before everyone arrived. *What would Mrs. Griffin have to tell this doctor about me?*

"Leah, I'm Dr. Foster." He held out his hand to me, and as

our fingers were about to touch, a woman from across the room let out a scream.

"MOUSE!"

Mrs. Griffin and Dr. Foster both turned to see. The women who had been chatting in the sunroom flowed out in a quick and steady stream, their carefully honed Southern manners preventing them from fleeing as quickly as their pumping hearts wanted them to. They gathered their pocketbooks and headed out the front door with only a wave of their hands to signify their departure. A few of the ladies dawdled on the front porch, watching the commotion through the windows at what they thought was a safe distance.

Mrs. Griffin called after the ladies, attempting to reassure them, not wanting the gathering to break up quite so soon. "Leah!" She spoke through clenched teeth and forced smile. Her voice was measured, holding in both a scream and embarrassment, "Get the broom. Now!"

I didn't bother with manners. I ran into the kitchen and grabbed the broom. I could tell right where the mouse was by the movement of the ladies who had been brave enough to stay inside the house. They huddled in the front parlor and pointed to the sunroom.

As I walked into the room, Mrs. Griffin closed the doors behind me.

"It's okay, ladies!" Through the closed doors, I could hear her muffled instructions as I stood still, looking for the mouse. "We have everything under control. Please, have more snacks and stay for a while. No need to rush off!"

Mrs. Griffin couldn't see me anymore, so I put the broom

down. I got onto the floor and crawled around. I'd watched Maeve catch mice enough to know that being quiet was going to get me further than crashing about. I saw him sitting on the floor, facing the chairs as if he had something to say, if only he could catch his breath. His little stomach moved in and out, up and down. He saw me. He was watching me like I was watching him. If only I had a piece of peanut butter sandwich in my pocket.

"It's okay," I told him, sticking my hand out in front of me, hoping I could trick him into thinking I had something for him. But he wasn't moving. Then I remembered the other exit. I moved to my left and opened the porch door, again having to tug with most of my weight to get it to budge. I hoped the movement didn't scare him too much and send him into the dining room.

Thankfully, he stayed in the room with me, so I got my broom, walked around the other side, and chased him to the opening. He saw his escape and he took it, pumping those tiny little feet of his so they were a blur of motion. I followed him onto the porch, not taking any chances of losing him in the house again. I pulled the sunroom door closed behind me and watched him scamper around the side. But instead of taking off for the bushes, he headed for the turn in the porch to right where the ladies were standing, trying to see the action through the windows.

I took off after him, broom in my hand, hoping to show him his way to the bushes, but he had a head start. Those scurrying feet were taking him faster than I could go. As he rounded that corner, those peeping ladies screamed and jumped off the porch. And as I came around after, I saw Mrs. Griffin and Dr. Foster standing outside the front door. The mouse must've seen them too because he stopped and ran back in my direction. But when he saw me, he zigged and he zagged and he headed to the wood siding of the house, seeking protection, but stopping in his tracks when he realized the overlap of the siding didn't give him an exit.

"What are you doing? Kill him!"

I looked at Mrs. Griffin and at the mouse. I raised the broom in my hand.

"Do it now! Before he gets away!"

Living close to nature, I'd seen plenty of creatures die. But until I brought that broom down to the ground, I hadn't ever had a hand in ending one's life. I'll never forget that thud, nor the look of the lifeless body when I lifted the broom to show Mrs. Griffin that I had been a good girl. I had done what she had asked of me, hoping I could earn an evening at the fair. Mrs. Griffin smiled at me, but I looked away. I'd promised Daddy I wouldn't go forgetting who I was. My desperation caused destruction. And truth be told, I'd do it again if it meant a few moments with Jesse.

CHAPTER FIFTEEN

From the moment he arrived home the day of the fair, Mr. Griffin had been locked away with Mrs. Griffin in their room, their voices moving in waves, growing louder before receding to quiet and then crescendoing once more. I had done nearly all my chores and more: dusting, sweeping, washing windows, straightening knickknacks, avoiding the mail though every part of me thirsted to know if Jesse had sent me another letter. The last thing to do was to knock down the cobwebs that had gathered in the corners of Mary Ann's room.

I crept up the stairs, avoiding all the squeaky floorboards. I meant to go back downstairs immediately, but as I left her room, I couldn't help but overhear. I tiptoed to their bedroom door and quieted myself to listen.

"I don't know why you insist on telling me these things," Mrs. Griffin hissed. I leaned in closer, trying to hear what Mrs. Griffin didn't want to be told.

"I thought you'd want to know that a lot has changed since you left." Mr. Griffin sounded tired, which was typical after spending all week traveling, spending nights away from his family.

Mrs. Griffin snapped back, "Why do you insist on going back there?"

"'Cause that's where the work is!" Mr. Griffin's voice rose, coming through the door loud and clear. "And the work is what pays for this sort of life!" I looked around the landing to see if the outburst would bring one of the children, but Eva Jane remained in her room while the other two seemed to be staying downstairs.

"Fine!" The volume of her voice matched her husband's, and her accent came out of hiding. "Go on if yuh have to, but don't come back tellin' me all about how this store's changed, that buildin's goin' up, this one's comin' down, that road's bein' constructed where the field once was. Why do I care?"

"Because," Mr. Griffin quieted. I leaned in, trying to steady myself so I wouldn't make a sound. "It's part of your past. Not everything that happened in Raleigh was bad."

Raleigh? Mama's birthplace?

I teetered back and forth, struggling to maintain my balance. I wobbled and bumped up against the door despite myself. I held my breath and didn't twitch a muscle, hoping they hadn't heard me. Then the voices in the room stopped, and I knew I needed to flee before they opened the door and found me eavesdropping. If the missus sounded angry before, I could only imagine what she'd sound like if she caught me with an ear pressed against their door. Quick as a mouse, I scurried across the landing and flew down the stairs as questions raced through my mind.

Mrs. Griffin and Mama lived in the same town?

I wasn't good at estimating age, but best I could tell, they could've grown up at the same time. Could they have known one another?

I ran into the kitchen, hoping to hear more through the ceiling. Mary Ann sat at the table, drawing pictures of birds and bugs she'd seen earlier that day when she had helped me in the garden.

"Why're you out of breath?" she asked.

I paused to hear more of the discussion overhead but could only make out mumbles.

I finally responded to Mary Ann, though I changed the subject. "That's a colorful one." My voice was breathless, but I tried to act normal as I pointed at her picture, hoping she would put her focus on her paper instead of me in a fluster and her parents arguing.

Mr. Griffin's voice rose and came crashing into the kitchen, "Will you ever be pleased?"

Mary Ann looked up. No child needed to hear her parents argue like that.

"Let's get some fresh air," I suggested.

Once we stepped outside, we couldn't hear their shouts anymore. As much as I wanted to stay inside and listen—figure out why Mrs. Griffin disliked Raleigh so much, learn if I'd be going to the fair with the family or if I'd have to sneak there myself—I needed to distract Mary Ann. Just like me, the outdoors always seemed to lift her mood.

Since we were alone, I decided to see if Mary Ann could answer something for me.

"Do you know where your mama grew up?" Mary Ann shrugged but didn't have an answer. So I pressed on, "Have you ever heard her talk about Raleigh?"

She shrugged again before saying, "Not really. Though she did tell me once about a friend she had growing up. She was kind of like you."

My breath caught. My eyes widened. My heart started thumping in my throat. "Me?"

"Yeah! Mama didn't say much, but she said she had red hair. Like you!"

"What was her name?"

"Don't know. Mama never said."

Could they have been friends? Best friends? Could they have gone to the cotillion together? Shared secrets and maybe even crushes?

Before I could ask more, the back door opened and out walked Mr. Griffin. His shoulders slumped and eyelids drooped. He put his hands in his pocket and took a deep breath. Mary Ann and I watched him, neither of us saying a word. Like I used to, Mary Ann gave her father a minute to be quiet. After he stared at the trees and collected himself, he offered us a smile, his mood and manner appearing as usual.

Then he asked me if we could have a light dinner, perhaps some sandwiches. "We can get some treats at the fair tonight," he said. "Have you ever had cotton candy?"

"I love cotton candy!" Mary Ann jumped up to her daddy. He grabbed her and pulled her into an embrace as she wrapped her legs around his waist and hugged him around his neck.

"I know you do," he laughed and spun in a circle. "Leah, you want to try some tonight?"

I hadn't been the one spinning, but I felt dizzy. Surely him asking me that meant I would be going along with them.

"Mm-hmm." I nodded my head so my curls bounced.

For the rest of the afternoon, I tried not to get too excited. I knew there were lots of reasons Jesse might not show up: the soda jerk never mailed the letter, the postman couldn't read my writing, the Barnas weren't going to drive that far for one night. I could barely eat my dinner that evening, or any food that whole day, anticipating what we'd say to one another when we saw each other again, *if* we saw each other again. Plus I was still trying to figure out if somehow Mrs. Griffin had known my mama. And if so, why she hadn't told me.

Later, the six of us walked down the sidewalk as if a family on our way to spending an evening together. When I first heard the music, I thought it was coming from inside my head, but once Mary Ann picked up her skipping, I knew it wasn't just me. All those trees that lined the streets kept the spectacle out of sight until we rounded the corner and walked onto the fairgrounds. There were striped tents, clowns, and jugglers. Booths with games, balloons flying high. Kids ran around with faces sticky and glittering with sugar. And behind it all was the Ferris wheel I'd been waiting for.

We walked to the ticket booth, and Mr. Griffin took out his wallet before turning to us to hand out tickets. First, he gave some to Michael Henry, then Eva Jane, and finally Mary Ann. I kept watching the Ferris wheel turn, the lights blink off and on, the people wave from the top. I didn't pay attention to Mr. Griffin, but then I heard him say, "These are for you."

I didn't take them at first. Though the carnival surrounded me, in that moment I wanted a reunion more than I did a ride. But when Mr. Griffin said, "Go on and take them," I did.

"Let's go," Eva Jane said, already walking ahead of me. Mary Ann grabbed my hand and pulled me into the crowd.

We joined the line of people waiting to get onto the Ferris wheel, inching forward every time the ride stopped. The three of us stood together until Eva Jane spotted Sally across the way. Sally stood beside a boy, shoulder to shoulder, their hands nearly touching. "I knew he liked her," Eva Jane said. I looked over to discover Michael Henry standing beside Sally, whispering into her ear, making her laugh.

"I'll be right back," Eva Jane said.

"We're not holding your place," Mary Ann said.

Eva Jane turned to her little sister and said, "Fine." And off she ran.

The line in front of us began to move. I kept looking back and around, as Mary Ann pulled me forward.

"It's nearly our turn! What're you looking at?"

My eyes scanned the crowd again before looking down at her, her face lit up with joy and anticipation. "Nothing," I said. "Let's go!"

Mary Ann and I handed our tickets to the man, who directed us to a carriage. As we sat down, it swung back and forth. He closed a bar across us and then hit a button that made us lurch upward, so the couple behind us could get into their carriage. One couple after another, we rose higher and higher into the air. The fairgrounds came into view and then all the town of Matthews. The trees and the green canopy that covered us all, surrounded our homes and our lives, the sun starting to lower toward the horizon, it all opened up in front of us as our carriage rounded the top of the ride. I saw Michael Henry with his arm around Sally. She laughed and he smiled at her. Neither of them seemed to notice anyone else around them. But I didn't see the boy I was hoping to.

As the wheel picked up speed and its motion became a steady

measure, Mary Ann scooted in closer to me, the wind catching her hair, the lights making her eyes dance. And she began to giggle. It started quiet, a belly laugh from within, and got louder.

"Isn't this the best?" she yelled, thinking I couldn't hear her over the breeze that blew across our faces and through our hair. The lights of the ride flashed, reflecting off her soft round cheeks. "Don't you wish every day was just like this?"

Her hands that had been bracing the bar across our laps let go of their hold and lifted into the air as her fingers danced. "Look! I'm touching the sky!"

She continued to giggle, to wiggle her fingers, and then she said, "Let go, Leah! Let go!" I shook my head, but she wouldn't stop asking until finally she took one of my wrists and pulled my arm into the air. I still held on with one hand, clinging to the safety of what I thought I knew, but with that one arm free, my heart and breath quickened as a smile widened across my face. I began to giggle.

With Mary Ann still holding onto me, the ride began to slow and the carriages all stopped one at a time at the bottom so the passengers could step off.

"Let's go again!" Mary Ann said before the bar fully lifted.

And I nearly said yes. I wanted to stay there with her and rise into the air again and again as we held our arms in the air and let go.

But then I saw him.

I'm not sure who saw the other one first. Maybe it happened at the same time. I told Mary Ann to go on without me. Then I stood frozen in time, not in a flash, but in full presence of the sandy-haired boy who I used to race to school, the author of the letter, the boy who had given me a star.

"Leah," he said. To this day, I try to recall how he said it. Was it with question or exclamation? I know it wasn't a simple statement. There was more rolled into that one word, my name, as he said it.

"Jesse!"

I can't say we'd ever hugged before, but in front of that magical wheel as people streamed by us, walking to the next ride or sight or carnival game, we grabbed each other and held on. The lights blinked, the rides turned, but we stood there, lingering in an embrace before stepping back and examining one another, though not knowing what words to say next. And we didn't say another word until someone bumped into me, pushing me back into Jesse's arms.

"You okay?" he asked as he steadied me.

"Yeah," I said. "Let's go sit down."

We walked toward a group of benches that sat across the way from the Ferris wheel. The benches had been positioned so that the people sitting would look in the direction of the displays, but we angled our legs toward one another, looking at each other instead of the fair lights all around.

"You came," I said.

"Of course. I got your letter. It was short, and when you didn't write me back, I wanted to make sure you were okay," he said. His voice had changed since we'd been apart, a deeper sound hiding beneath the one I knew.

"I'm glad you got it. I wanted to write more, but—" I hadn't thought of how to explain the short letter. "I suppose I was short on time on that day, but I wanted to get it to you before it was too late."

"That's okay," he said. "You must have a lot of schoolwork." I looked at him, my eyes squinting into a question.

"No," I said. "I'm not going anymore."

"Lucky you," Jesse said. "You wouldn't believe the themes Miss Heniford has us writing now, about one a week, I'd say. And the math quizzes. You'd hate it."

I smiled because I figured that's what he wanted me to do. When he'd known me, I would've hated it, but now I found myself missing it, wishing I could trade in the chores for the classroom, even if I had to see Jean-Louise. Well, maybe not her.

"Your hair's gotten longer," Jesse said.

"And you've gotten so much taller." It was true. We had both changed in the months since I'd left, his shoulders having broadened, his fingers longer.

I don't think either of us knew what more to say, so when we heard the man start talking from the stage in front of us, we both looked toward him, and I saw someone else I recognized.

"Ladies and gentlemen, thank you for coming out tonight," Dr. Foster said from the stage. "I have a rather special presentation to offer you. It's an important topic that needs to be heard. I think you'll all agree that what I have to say to you tonight is for all of our good, for the betterment of our society as a whole. It's what will make our town, our state, our nation one to be admired by others."

As he continued using a few phrases that I'd heard him say at the meeting, I noticed the poster boards behind him. "Some people are born to be a burden on the rest" one said in big letters with even larger letters above it all that said "American Eugenics."

I strained to make out one board in particular that had

something on it. Jesse tried talking again. He didn't care to listen to Dr. Foster. But I did. I pointed to the board and asked Jesse, "What's on that?"

"On what?"

"That board right up there. What are those black-and-white things?" They looked like rolled-up somethings. Soft and squishy. At the top it said, "Genetic Inheritance."

We both leaned forward, squinting our eyes. Jesse figured it out first. "Rats. I think they're rats. But what are they trying to say?"

Then Dr. Foster began to explain. "When you take a pure white and a pure white, what are the results? Pure white, of course. No tainted abnormalities. But mix in a black with a pure white, and you're not guaranteed what you'll get. Any impure abnormality can result."

And then he said, "How many generations of abnormalities is too many? Especially when we have the ability to do something about it? To stop it. To sterilize the offender—the feebleminded, the promiscuous—so future generations don't have to suffer. Sterilization is a simple procedure that will ensure that those people won't have future generations who will drain our society."

The people who had gathered on the benches looked at one another and shook their heads in agreement.

"Leah! Leah!" I'd forgotten all about Mary Ann, but now she stood beside me, bouncing and calling for my attention. "Did you see me? I was waving from the top!"

I couldn't gather my thoughts, free myself from the distraction of what Dr. Foster was saying, long enough to respond to Mary Ann. I stood from the bench, looking for a way out, yet feeling as though I couldn't leave.

"Leah? What's wrong?" Jesse asked.

"Nothing, it's just, it's so loud here, maybe we should go somewhere else."

I couldn't stand to hear anymore of Dr. Foster's words. I didn't understand all he said—surgeries of sorts for the sake of making life better. *But for who?* The talk filled me with that dread I felt the day of the meeting. And it distracted from my reunion with Jesse.

"Did you see me, Leah? Did you?" Mary Ann stood there, still ambling for my attention.

"Oh, I missed you. I'm so sorry. I ran into an old friend of mine," I said, looking into her eyes and getting caught up in her excitement for a moment. "Mary Ann, this is Jesse."

"Nice to meet you," she said, extending her hand to shake his before she returned to her excitement. "I'm gonna go again! Will you come? You can come too, Jesse!"

Jesse and I looked at one another, the lights of the midway reflecting in his eyes. Oh, how I had missed those eyes. We could've joined her. We could've sat three-wide on the Ferris wheel, but instead we said no. We let Mary Ann run off into the crowd to stand in line again as he and I searched for a quiet place to talk.

Together we walked across the midway. The farther I got from those benches, the more air I could breathe. We wove through the crowds of people, which grew larger as the sun dipped deeper into the horizon. We walked past clowns and jugglers, all too focused on their own performances to notice us.

I didn't know where we were going, but I wanted to go some-place alone, away from the lights and the sounds, the movement, and the people. Finally I had something of my own, and at the moment, I didn't want to share him with others. I wanted to find the quiet we once knew and sit in that together.

We sat down on the ground behind a tent, his shoulder pressing against mine. The lights of the fair shone on the treetops in front of us, flashing color changes as we sat in the tent's shadow. Only one star was bright enough to be visible from where we sat.

"Look. It's your star." Jesse pointed upward to the orange light in the sky.

"I remember."

We sat in silence for a few minutes, our eyes focused skyward, my body expecting to feel Maeve rub against it. In all the time I'd been in Matthews, I hadn't spent enough time gazing at the stars, remembering how, even though we were separated by distance, he and I were still under the same night sky.

"Since you've been gone, Tulla's been caring for Maeve, sneaking her scraps, giving her belly rubs, letting her curl up on her lap when she sits on the porch. Even Mama's taken a liking to her."

"No!"

"It's true!" His voice cracked as he spoke, as if the boy and the man fought to speak at the same time. He cleared his throat and started picking at the grass as he told me more tales. I got lost in his stories, soaking up the normalcy, delighting in what used to be typical. "You'd be surprised at what's different since you left." He paused for a minute before continuing. "But you haven't changed."

"Me?" I asked.

"Yeah, you. I mean your hair's longer, but you're still the same Leah you've always been."

I couldn't tell him about my time there, being a helpmate, trying to blend in but not sure I really wanted to and how, in my desperation to see him, I'd taken the life of that helpless mouse. "I don't feel that way."

"Well you are. I can see it. And who knows you better?" He had a point. "You see that oak there? I bet you could climb it just like you always could at home."

"It's been a while since I've climbed a tree."

"But you still could, couldn't you?"

I leaned in even closer to him until my head rested on his shoulder. He shook my body every time he laughed, as he told about Maeve dropping a living skink on his mama's feet and how she screamed and ran inside the house, locking the door behind her like the lizard knew how to open a door.

When his stories and rememberings quieted, I asked what had been burning on my mind. "Do you know anything about the Griffins?"

Jesse thought for a minute and then said, "Nah. Like what?"

"Just wondered if your parents said anything about them."

"Daddy said he'd heard Mr. Griffin was respectable. But they don't know them. Why?"

"No reason."

Jesse chuckled deep in his chest and shook my body as I rested beside him. "Don't act like I don't know you," he said. "There's a reason you're asking."

"I don't know." I pulled at some grass on the ground, trying to figure out how much to say. "I've overheard some things. And Mrs. Griffin, she's so quiet, but it seems like maybe—I know this sounds crazy, but I think she knew my mama."

"What?" Jesse's body jerked upright, the surprise erasing his ease.

"I know. It turns out they both grew up in Raleigh. They were both debutants and just today Mary Ann said her mama's childhood friend had hair like mine." I said the last part slowly, still wondering if it could be true, "I think they were friends."

"What?" he asked and then paused for a moment. He seemed to be having as hard a time figuring out this situation as I did. "What does that mean? Do you think they chose to have you?"

I let out my own chuckle and two words tumbled out before I could stop them, "Not likely."

Jesse sat up straighter. "What's that mean?"

"Nothing."

"Leah—" he started, but I didn't want to get into explaining things just then. He didn't need to know how the missus was treating me or that if they'd chosen me it had been as a servant, not a family member. Before he could say more, I took a few deep breaths and asked the question that had been getting heavier and heavier ever since I arrived in Matthews. My stomach twisted. I remembered what his parents had said: that I needed to get out of Supply, that Mrs. Barna couldn't look at me. But I needed to know if that had changed, if they might see things differently now. If maybe I could go home.

"Do you think I could come back?"

"Sure!" Jesse didn't take even a second to consider his response.

I knew he hadn't heard what his parents had said that day in the barnyard, so I needed more information before I got too hopeful.

"It'd be alright with your parents?" I closed my eyes and sucked in a breath, not letting it go until I heard his answer.

"Of course!"

I exhaled and turned to look at him.

Even in the shadows of the tent, I could see his eyes dance with the thought of a reunion. "They'd love for you to"—and then he said the word that made me realize he didn't yet understand—"visit. They'd like to have the Griffins, get to know them, have y'all for supper. Tulla could—"

He didn't get to finish his sentence. And I didn't get to correct him, tell him what I really meant by coming back. Of course Jesse thought my life in Matthews had to be fine. I lived with a family, a respectable one in town, with a large house and a steady income. By all accounts, all had to be well. To a boy like Jesse, given the life that he'd had for those fourteen years, he had no reason to think otherwise.

"Here you are! We've been looking everywhere for you," Mrs. Griffin interrupted us, her voice heavy with exasperation as she walked around the side of the tent. "It's time to—" And that must've been when her eyes finally adjusted to the darkness, when she saw two friends side by side, finding quiet away from the carnival.

"What is this?!" Her eyes narrowed. She looked me up and down. "We've been here how long and you've already found yourself a boy?"

Jesse and I scrambled to our feet.

"I'm sorry, Mrs. Griffin," Jesse tried to explain. "We were just talking. Leah's my friend, my family of sorts."

"You're mistaken," Mrs. Griffin said. "She has no family." With her gaze focused only on me and a low growl climbing out of her, she said, "Go back to the house. Now."

I wanted to grab Jesse, to hold on to him for at least a few more minutes. I wanted to give him a hug, to say good-bye. Actually, I wanted to cling to him, like those sand fleas scratching for safety as the tide washed in and out. But I didn't. From the sound of things, the Barnas would only take me for a visit. I had no doubt that, even if I found Mr. Barna at the fair that night, he'd return me to my guardian, not take me back with him.

Mrs. Griffin positioned herself between us and pointed her finger in the direction of her home, and I obeyed. What choice did I have in that moment? I walked away instead of fighting, even after Jesse had reminded me of who I was. I guess he was wrong; apparently I had changed. And despite my promise to Daddy, I'd already started forgetting who I was.

CHAPTER SIXTEEN

After seeing Jesse, I ached for home even more: our back porch with Maeve curled up beside me, the Barnas' kitchen table with Tulla's biscuits, even the schoolhouse, the ocean, the smell of the salt water that the breeze would blow even as far as our house. I longed to hear the caw of the gulls, see them gliding, dipping, and diving overhead. But what I missed most of all was the oak path and the mounds covered with shells.

I could go about most days in the rhythm required, distracting myself with chores or Mary Ann or tending to the garden, but after my reunion with Jesse, in the quiet times—late at night, early in the morning, or when the house was so silent that I could hear its aging creaks—the memories lay heavier, tugging on my heart and distracting my mind, fueling it to find a way home.

Even if Mrs. Griffin knew my mama, it didn't mean she wanted me, and there was no use staying where I was. No matter how much silver I polished or how many shirts I ironed, I never seemed to please her. And I wasn't going to give her a chance to get so upset that she'd send me to the children's home like Alma. I stood a better chance of starting over in a place I knew with a few friends who might sneak me a little help if I needed it.

It took some calculating, but I thought I might have an answer: Michael Henry. His own discontent with his mother and his kindness toward me might be what I needed. Perhaps I could convince him of an adventure, one bigger than the soda fountain. Maybe I could talk him into driving me back home. I couldn't tell him all the details, that he'd be the only one returning back to Matthews. But I could sell it as a day of fun, relaxing by the sea, soaking up the sun. I needed some time alone to convince him, not with his sisters around; they talked too much. But with some time in the quiet, we could make a plan.

My life had been full of waiting, so that's what I vowed to do until the time was right, wait until I could finally run. I continued with my days like I had all the others. Doing my duties, smiling when I knew they expected it, biding my time until the plan could come together.

'Course when daylight breaks, there's no way of knowing how it will all unfold. The day of the ice storm started like most any other day. I may have woken with a fright, but I didn't know at that early hour how that one day's events would forever change me. The same holds true for the best of days. I suppose that's the way of time; we don't know if it's normal or something else until we're caught in it.

I should've thought it odd the morning Mrs. Griffin answered the door. She always made me answer it, but when the doorbell rang a few days after the fair, she rushed to get it, her hair already combed; her dress, pearls, and heels on earlier than a typical day. I stayed with Mary Ann in the kitchen. She was finishing up her breakfast as I was doing the dishes. I paused the washing for a minute to hear who it was.

"Dr. Foster!" Mrs. Griffin's voice was an octave higher than usual. "Thank you so much for stopping by."

Figuring this visit had nothing to do with me, I went back to my washing. But soon their voices got closer, and before I knew it, they were standing in the kitchen.

"Good morning, Leah," the doctor said.

"Good morning," I said, twisting around from the sink to offer him a smile despite the chill I felt in his presence.

Then he went back to talking to Mrs. Griffin. "Do you have a private place we can go?"

Of course, I thought they were talking about themselves, but again I was wrong.

"I believe the parlor would do."

"Someplace more private, perhaps?"

"Certainly. We can go to the sun porch," she motioned to the French doors that hadn't been opened since the ladies' meeting.

"That'll do just fine."

"Leah," her voice was back to the usual octave. "Dr. Foster wants to speak with you for a few minutes. Dry your hands and let's go. Let's not keep the good doctor waiting."

I reached for the hand towel I kept tucked in my apron and dried them as I walked toward the doctor.

"Please excuse her manners, Doctor." Mrs. Griffin's cheeks began to blush, but when she turned to me, I saw anger, not embarrassment. "Take off your apron. Dr. Foster doesn't need to see your filth."

For the last few days, I'd been trying to imagine my mama and her together, being friends. By all accounts, my mother had been good-hearted, determined yet just as sweet as nectar. I know people don't like to speak poorly of the dead, but I truly believed what Daddy, Tulla, and Mrs. Barna said of her. But I couldn't for the life of me understand how a woman like her could have been friends with someone who would grow to be as crotchety as the missus.

I reached around and pulled the strings of my apron loose. I draped it over the back of a kitchen chair and smoothed out my dress. I'm not sure it was much cleaner than the apron.

"Shall we?" The high pitch returned as the three of us walked to the sun porch. "Please excuse the mess. I'm not sure what state the porch is in at the moment."

"I'm sure it will be just fine," the doctor assured her as she opened the doors and began to walk in.

"I beg your pardon, Mrs. Griffin, but if you don't mind excusing us for a few moments."

"Oh, I thought—"

"I think it's best if you leave Leah and me to talk. We can discuss it all later."

I know she wanted to push back. Had he been her husband, she would've told him otherwise, but she stopped, straightened her drooping shoulders, and said, "Yes, of course. I'll be in the kitchen if you need me. Can I get you some tea while I'm there?"

"No, thank you."

"Some coffee, perhaps?"

"No, thank you."

"Water?"

"Thank you for your hospitality, Mrs. Griffin, but if you don't mind. Oh, and please close the doors behind you."

She did as she was told. I stood in the middle of the sun porch, waiting to hear what I'd be told.

"Please, have a seat." He motioned to the wicker couch. "Mrs. Griffin asked me to come give you an exam."

Dr. Foster put his black bag on the floor beside my feet and opened it. He removed instruments of all sorts that he used to look at my eyes, ears, throat. He listened to my heart and my breathing. I wasn't sure what he was looking for or what all Mrs. Griffin had told him. He had me lay down so he could push on my belly, kneading it kind of like Maeve would do when she'd get into one of her purring moods.

He asked me about my flashes, though he called them my absences. I wondered how he knew. Of course Mrs. Griffin had to've told him. I knew she'd spotted a couple in my months with them, but apparently she'd seen more than I'd realized.

"When did they first start?" he asked.

It was like asking when you took your first breath. Though you know you did it at some point, there is no way of recalling when the first one happened. And there's no way of knowing when the next one will come.

"When I was young," I said. "After a fever." At least that's all Daddy ever told me, and that was all I'd ever known anyway. I couldn't remember an age without them. If it were up to me, I'd be done with the lot.

"How often would you say they occur?"

Was I supposed to keep track? Daddy always pointed them out when they happened, more to make sure I was okay than to count them.

"Not too often," I said.

"Would you say you know what causes them? Do they seem to happen, say, when you're tired or have a headache or something along those lines?"

"I can't say that they do."

"Very good then. There's just one more thing I'd like to do."

He reached into his black satchel on the floor and pulled out a picture book. The cover had a boy and a girl on it. They looked like brother and sister, like Eva Jane and Michael Henry, but younger. And they were smiling together. Dr. Foster opened the book and turned to the first page of the story.

"I'd like to ask you to read the first few pages of this book."

I wasn't sure what a child's book had to do with my flashes, but he seemed like he really wanted me to tell him that story. It was a shame Mary Ann wasn't in the room so she could hear it too. I started reading about the boy and the girl; their pet, Spot; and their neighborhood. It was a nice enough story, but I didn't give him my best reading. My breath was short, full of nerves. As he sat so close to me, I could hear his nose whistle with every breath. I didn't get to finish it because Dr. Foster asked me to stop before the end.

"Thank you, Leah. I think that's all for today."

He packed up his satchel and walked out of the room. I figured that meant I could also leave, but he didn't say anything. He didn't tell me if I was okay, didn't tell me if I was sick or if he found whatever it was that Mrs. Griffin was concerned about.

I followed him to the kitchen, where Mrs. Griffin told Mary Ann to run along upstairs and get dressed. Then she told me I could finish my chores while she saw Dr. Foster out.

I didn't have any dishes left to do, so I headed out the back door for some fresh air. That's when I heard the voices from the front porch. I walked closer, staying to the side, hidden behind an azalea bush.

"What do you think?" Mrs. Griffin asked.

"From my examination of her, there's clearly something wrong. Not having seen one of her episodes for myself, I have to take your word for them, but I'm inclined to say she's suffering from absence seizures."

"Seizures!" Mrs. Griffin gasped. "I thought those were convulsions." She shook her body to emphasize her point.

"That's one form of seizures. This is different. This is a sort of neurological episode where the afflicted black out but without passing out. It typically lasts only a few seconds, but the frequency can vary."

Mrs. Griffin put her hand to her mouth and looked off into the distance for a minute before saying, "And her intelligence?"

"It's clear that she is not as mentally astute as others her age," the doctor replied. "I had her read a children's book. She did okay, but of course it was a few levels below where someone of her age should be. While I didn't conduct an IQ test, I agree with your assessment that the girl appears to be simpleminded."

Mrs. Griffin nodded her head in agreement, showing no surprise at what he had said.

I didn't understand all he said, but I gathered enough to know that he was calling me stupid. My heart beat fast, and I wanted to run out of hiding and set them straight. But I bit my tongue and stayed put.

"And the promiscuity." Mrs. Griffin's eyebrows raised and her head shook side to side as she told Dr. Griffin, "Just the other day at the fair, I caught her behind a tent with a boy who isn't from around here. I can't even imagine what would've happened had I not found them then."

I couldn't believe she was mentioning Jesse, that our friendship unsettled her, that she seemed to be suggesting something unsavory between us.

"Well, thankfully we do have a procedure to help with this sort of situation."

A procedure. I leaned in closer, holding my breath to listen better, but all I heard was Mary Ann calling for me. She came around the side of the house, singsonging my name.

"Leeee-uuuuh. Leeee-uuuuh."

I looked back to see if Mrs. Griffin and Dr. Foster heard her. They didn't seem to. I darted out of the bush and ran toward Mary Ann.

"There you are!" Her face lit up as she saw me running toward her. She held her arms out wide and wrapped them around me in a firm hug. She always had a way of making me feel wanted.

As much as I wished I could go on listening to Mrs. Griffin and the doctor, I couldn't walk away from Mary Ann. Together we searched the backyard for dandelions. She plucked one at a time and rubbed them on her cheeks until the pollen turned them orange, like wearing rouge the color of sunshine.

Daddy always said those in the wild had another sense about them, one that most folks had long forgotten, like how the horses seemed restless in the hours before an earthquake trembled our small town. As Mary Ann searched the yard for more yellow flowers, I played the conversation over in my mind, wondering what procedure they had meant. Though I didn't know much of what Dr. Foster ever talked about, that sixth sense of mine made me restless, as though a quake was coming for me.

Mrs. Griffin didn't ask me anything about Dr. Foster's exam. We went on with our day without a word about the doctor. Dinner started fine that evening, though not long after the "amen," Mrs. Griffin told her son about the call she'd received. Soon enough the mood changed.

"Your teacher says you failed another exam."

Michael Henry didn't respond but kept on eating his meal.

"She says your graduation is on the line if you don't start passing these tests. What are you going to do about this?"

Had Mr. Griffin been home, she would've asked him to help her get their son to respond. Instead she pounded her fists on the table and said, "Answer me!"

"Study harder," Michael Henry finally said.

That's when Mrs. Griffin dropped her fork onto her plate. The clang and clatter caused us girls to jump. Mrs. Griffin wiped her mouth with her napkin, placed her hands on the table, and leaned in. "Don't get smart with me," she said to her son.

"Don't know how I can get smart," Michael Henry looked at his mother as he continued, "when you just called me stupid."

Mary Ann's shoulders shook when she heard that last word. I shot her a glance, my eyes telling her not to laugh, and thankfully she seemed to understand.

"I did no such thing!" Mrs. Griffin retorted.

"You did, saying if I can't pass a test, then I won't graduate!"

The two went back and forth, their voices raising, the tension in the room filling the air like the pressure changing before a hurricane would barrel in off the coast.

I'd say we all stopped eating at about that time, as the accusations of stupidity and lack of responsibility and no hope for the future continued. Mary Ann began to move things around on her plate, wincing as the voices grew louder. She finally looked at me, and I gave her a nod that told her she could be excused from the table. We all knew that Mrs. Griffin didn't like waste, that she preferred clean plates, but she was too distracted then to pay any attention to what her youngest still had left on her plate.

I walked to the kitchen with Mary Ann and disposed of the leftovers, pushing them low into the trash can.

"Why don't you run along upstairs and get ready for bed?" I said to her. She nodded and then hugged me before running out of the kitchen.

I cleared the table myself that night as the conversation continued. Then I hurried to the backyard for some peace and quiet, a sanctuary of my own. I stepped out on the back porch, thinking I might need a jacket or a shawl or some sort of covering, but the air already gave hints of humidity, foreshadowing the heat that would be there soon enough.

The crickets sang their songs loud that evening as if celebrating an early peek at summer. I'd started hearing them through the thin walls of my room. Standing on the back porch, I could hear their full concert.

I walked into the grass, the blades tickling my toes, which had become accustomed to shoes. It'd take time for my feet to readjust to walking and running across pebbles and rocks and sticks without even noticing. I stood in the darkness of the moonless sky, looking up at the stars, finding the orange one right away, and when I heard the voices from inside getting louder, I decided to lie down in the grass and enjoy the view.

Lulled by the chirps and hums, I didn't notice when the

hollering stopped, but I realized it was gone when the door opened and a flood of light shone into the backyard and onto the ground where I lay. I could tell who it was from the outline, taller than Mrs. Griffin but not as broad shouldered as his father. Michael Henry closed the door, stepped off the porch, and came to stand over me.

"What're you doing in the grass?" he asked.

"Looking at the stars."

On a normal night, I'd have expected him to make some comment, some joke, but instead he sat down beside me and stayed silent for a few minutes.

"It's quiet out here," he finally said.

I responded with a simple "mm-hmm."

He repositioned himself from sitting to lying down. He was close enough that I could feel his warmth radiating off his body and onto mine. I didn't have much to say and very little I could offer, but I could give him a story, a distraction, something that could take his mind off his frustrations.

"See that up there? See those stars?" I pointed my hand above him, trying to get in his line of vision, so he could make out the shape I wanted to draw his attention to. "That there, looks kinda like a pan? That's the Big Dipper."

"Right there?" he asked, leaning his head closer to mine, trying to see exactly what I saw.

"Yeah, right there. And that over there, that's the Little Dipper. Or some people say they are bears."

"Don't look like bears to me."

"Me neither. But some say that's the mama bear and the baby bear, say they were put there by Zeus for protecting."

"Protecting from what?"

"Jealousy." Despite myself wanting some quiet, I began to turn a tale, one Daddy used to tell me when we'd stay at the shore long enough for the stars to start shining. "Story goes that Zeus was about to be married to Hera, but one day he saw a beautiful woman named Callisto. She was a widow and had a son named Arcus. Well, Zeus went about courting her, but Callisto didn't know about Hera."

"So what happened?"

"Hera saw them together and got so mad that she turned Callisto into a bear. Poor Arcus was left alone without his mama. He didn't know what happened to her, didn't know she was a bear."

"Why would he even think that?" We both kind of laughed.

"As he got older, he became a hunter, and one day he happened upon his mama in the woods."

"But she was still a bear, right?"

"Right. So he took aim, about to shoot her, but then Zeus came along. He knew that the bear was Callisto and that Arcus was about to kill his own mother. He tried to tell Arcus, but he wasn't listening to reason—not that any of this sounded reasonable. So to save Callisto, he turned Arcus into a bear too."

"Then what?"

"Once they were both bears, Arcus recognized his mother, but then Hera came along. She saw what was happening. She was about to kill them both, and to save them, Zeus put them among the stars."

He stayed quiet for a while before saying, "That's quite a story."

He seemed to be settled, calmer, just as I needed him to be before asking a big favor.

"Do you ever want to get out of here?"

"What?" he asked.

I rolled to my side and put my hand under my ear so I could sit up a little bit. "How about we get away?"

He turned toward me. "What do you mean?"

"Remember my first night here? How we talked about the ocean?"

"Yeah."

"What do you think about taking a drive out there? Get away for a day?"

He looked back at the sky.

"It sounds fun, but—"

I interrupted before he could think too much about what might come after the "but."

"I know you have a lot going on with school, the dance, your mother." He let out a breath of frustration. "I just thought a day away would do you some good. Plus, it's an easy drive." I'd heard adults say that sort of thing before. "Come on!" I put my hand on his arm and shook it, "It'll be fun!"

"I'd have to ask—"

"Wouldn't it be more fun if you didn't? She'll think you're at school. We can be back by dinner."

"But what about you? How would we explain you being gone?"

He brought up a good point, but what I needed now was to know he would do it. The rest of the details could come over time.

"Let me figure that out," I said.

We lay in the silence, side by side underneath the stars until he said, "Getting away does sound good, especially if it gives me a day off school."

"Really?"

"Yeah! Let's do it!" I nearly grabbed him and hugged him. "It'll take some time to figure out the right day, see how I can borrow the car and all. Say, don't tell Eva Jane, okay?" I hadn't planned to. "This'll be our secret."

I'd had plenty of secrets in my life, but few that I actually got to share with others. I looked up at that pan in the sky—the mama bear, as some chose to see it—and that's when a streak of something caught my eye. As the bright light darted away from the mama bear and fell through the darkness, a silver tail shooting out from behind it, my eyes traced that falling star as long as they could, but it was only a moment in time before it dashed away and disappeared. I hoped to be like that star soon enough— dashing away as if I'd never been there. I just needed to hang on a little bit longer as we got the plans in place.

CHAPTER SEVENTEEN

I began spending more time in my room, the garden—any place other than where Mrs. Griffin happened to be. With the thought that I could soon be returning home, I thought more about Daddy, gazing at the photo of him and Mama. I'd long since memorized the picture, how Mama's hair was curly and wild, how Daddy's smile was broad and bright, his arms wrapped around her waist with the waves behind them, a chunk of her curls blowing against his cheek. I'd run my fingers across the photograph, trying to feel something other than the flat, smooth surface.

One morning after I'd spent as much time in my room as I knew I could, I finger-combed my long curls, tucked them behind my ears, and headed out to do some gardening. The spring air was the perfect amount of cool with a warm breeze. The birds seemed to agree, filling the backyard with their song. I worked there for as long as I could, but I wish I had stayed even longer.

The garden had become my work, or the place where I preferred to work, since it was outside and away from Mrs. Griffin, whose conversations with me had only grown shorter since the night of the fair. Mrs. Griffin thought I spent too much time out there, but I know she liked the idea of having our own produce that didn't come from the grocer. So she let me do my digging and arranging. Sometimes she'd even let Mary Ann come dig with me. If dirt had purpose, she didn't seem to mind so much that it was messy. It got so that my hands itched to feel the dirt, let it slip through my fingers as my mind recollected the times Jesse and I knelt side by side, moving earth and shells and making patterns beside one another.

By the time I got into the house, Mrs. Griffin was sitting at the table sipping another cup of coffee. As I washed my hands at the kitchen sink, picking at the dirt beneath my nails that the gloves didn't prevent from getting to them, I looked out at the garden. Everything was small and in a row. The tomato plants were about the size of Mr. Griffin's hands. The bean seeds beneath the soil, a few weeks from sprouting any sort of green, right along with the cucumbers and zucchini. I'd noticed a few onion tails when I was out there that morning and even radishes starting to poke through.

The missus took a sip of her coffee and sat it on the table. "I'm still not convinced your piddling around out there's gonna matter. I told yuh nothing likes to grow in that soil, and don't get me started on the rabbits."

"With all the coffee grounds and egg shells I've been putting out there," I said, "I think we'll get a good yield." Then I said something I'd heard Mrs. Barna say as we'd knelt in her garden together. "Sometimes things just need a bit of attention and care to see what they're made of."

Mrs. Griffin raised her eyebrows but said nothing. I think she would've been surprised to see our tree grove and what it had become over the last fourteen years. All had started at various sizes of medium or small, and yet they grew and reached farther each year. All except for Four. I filled the silence with a quiet, final thought, "Maybe you'll be surprised."

Mrs. Griffin laughed, and a dribble of coffee rolled down her chin. "Not much surprises me anymore." She wiped away the coffee dribble, stood from her chair, and told me to sit down.

"I need to run a bit of water out to the garden," I told her.

"That can wait."

She pointed at the chair. As I sat down, she draped a towel around my shoulders and began pulling a comb through my curls. In the time I'd been there, she'd never combed my hair before. I thought she was just going to wash my hair, really scrub it clean as Tulla had done. Maybe she'd set it like she did Eva Jane's, twisting sections of hair before wrapping them around rags and pinning them in place. Maybe for once my curls would have purpose and shape instead of minds of their own. And maybe, with some of that work done, I could go to school. Or the ball. Maybe that's what all of this was about. Maybe she just needed me to get cleaned up a bit. Then maybe I'd be one of the Griffin children.

As she began to comb, her words took on a slow cadence. "You've been with us a while now. In that time, I've been watching, learning, seeing as to your character." I began to sit up a little taller, a smile coming across my face as I anticipated what she'd say next. Maybe she was moving me out of the closet and into Eva Jane's room after all. "We've given you a lot since you've been here. And that's why I can't for the life of me understand why you'd feel the need to take from us."

The smile fell from my face. As she struggled through the tangles, my head jerked back, my neck bending from the force.

"Hold still," she said to me. She put one hand on my head and pulled the comb through. Once it broke free of the tangles, she continued. "It's one thing to deal with those spells of yours. And then to find you with that boy at the fair, and now, just this morning, I find you've stolen from us?"

I began to shake my head from side to side. "Ma'am, I didn't take nothing. I promise."

"Nothing?" She pulled through another tangle, taking a few hairs from my head in the process. "Then what do you call that?"

With the comb, she pointed at the table and the seven cents of change that lay in the middle of it.

"No! You're mistaken."

"You're calling me a liar?"

"No, it's just, Mr. Griffin, he gave us all dimes to get a soda the Saturday you were gone. That's the change. Ask him! When he gets home!"

"I will." She pulled the comb through another tangle. "But a soda costs a dime. If you got one, then why is there money left at all? And why didn't you see fit to give it back?" She didn't give me time to answer before continuing, "Let me be clear: the things in this house aren't yours. That includes spare change."

Mary Ann skipped into the kitchen. She paused as she entered and asked what was happening.

Her mother responded, "Sometimes we have to be reminded of our place."

"What?" Mary Ann asked.

"Nothing," her mother dismissed her. "Run along now."

Mary Ann shrugged her shoulders and skipped out of the room. I stayed quiet and as still as I could, and even when I heard the scissors make their first cut, I stayed put. I thought maybe she was cutting rags to curl my hair. But then I saw whole sections of my ginger hair on the floor, lying limp like washed-up seaweed on the shore, no longer living or purposeful.

My hand jerked back, trying to hang on to my hair, protect it from the scissors, but Mrs. Griffin smacked it away.

"Girl, that's how you lose a finger! Fold your hands in your lap and be still."

My eyes began to tear as the sting of that slap tingled the back of my hand. But those tears were as much for the loss as they were for the hurt. Just that morning I'd looked again at the picture of Mama and her hair blowing in the ocean breeze. The shore had been taken from me months ago, and now my hair that looked like hers was also being ripped from me.

"Stop!" Spittle dropped from my mouth as I begged her to let me be.

"Do you know what it means for me to be your guardian?" she asked. I shook my head no. "It means I make the decisions concerning you."

"But," my words struggled to break free of my fury, "you're not my mother!"

"Never said I was or would be." She put her hand back on my head, pushed it down, and began cutting again. "Now hold still or you might lose the tip of your ear."

The cold metal of the shears brushed over the top of my ear. Tears dropped from my eyes and anger heated my cheeks while a shudder threatened to move my body. But I stayed still as a rock, certain she'd take more than just my hair, even if by accident.

A few minutes later, Mrs. Griffin unwrapped the towel from

around me and shook it over the floor. She told me to sweep up and put the mess in the garden, that it'd help keep the bugs away. Then she walked out of the kitchen. My hands reached for my hair, but they had to journey farther than normal to find it. Moments ago, it had reached to my shoulder blades, but now it barely touched my ears.

I got onto my knees and used my hands to gather the hair in front of me, making a pile of curled clippings, the same color as Daddy always said Mama's was. I had to take his word for it. I couldn't tell from the picture, but with the way Daddy had looked at me sometimes, I knew he'd told the truth.

Now I wondered if he'd recognize me at all. Of course he would. He'd still know my freckles. He'd never forget my eyes. But how much different would I look to him now? It wasn't just the loss of my hair but how much I'd grown—taller and thinner with arms longer than the last time I'd wrapped them around him and he reminded me that he was my home.

As I sprinkled my curls around the garden plot, a few strands blew away in the breeze, riding the movements of the wind. How I wished I could follow.

"I like your hair." Mary Ann walked up to me, circling me so she could see my cut from all sides. "I want Mama to do that to me," she said.

"Are you sure about that?" I asked as the wind chilled me in ways it hadn't been able to before.

"Yeah! Then maybe it wouldn't hurt when she combed my hair." She looked down at my apron, which held the last of the trimmings. "You sure did have a lot of hair." I wanted to answer, but there was a lump in my throat. Plus as I had come to learn, Mary Ann didn't need conversation. She just needed someone willing to listen. "Can I help?"

Before I could answer, she reached into my apron and gathered a handful of hair. She then walked straight into the garden and sprinkled it atop the dirt before getting down on her hands and knees to push it into the soil. She crawled around the plot, pushing hair deeper, the dirt catching under her fingernails.

"Mama says dirt ain't becoming of a lady." She stopped to look at me for a second. "Do you know what that means?"

"Not sure I do."

"Me neither." Mary Ann shrugged her shoulders and looked back at the work she was doing, her curls falling beside her cheeks, covering her face, and bouncing in the breeze.

"You know," I said, as I squatted down closer to the ground, "when I was a girl—"

"Wait!" She looked me square in the eyes. "Ain't you still a girl?"

"Yes, I mean when I was younger—"

"Ain't you still young?"

"I suppose."

"Michael Henry's older than you, and Mama still calls him boy."

"You're right—"

"And Eva Jane, Mama says, has the sense of a child younger than me sometimes." Mary Ann looked at me, her eyes serious, leaning in as if to tell me a secret. "She thinks I don't listen sometimes, but I do. I know what she says." We were both quiet for a moment before Mary Ann continued, "I like gardening with you. Alma never did this."

I winced at the name, wondering how she was doing in the orphanage, if another family had come for her.

"You still miss her?" I asked.

Mary Ann's cheeks rounded as she smiled wide. "She smelled like roses. And she made the best peanut butter sandwiches."

I held my hand to my chest in fake offense. "I thought you liked mine."

"Oh yours are good, but Alma cut off the crust." Without taking a breath, she moved on. "Mama didn't like it when I called her Gran Alma."

Confused, I stopped digging.

"Gran?" I couldn't imagine why Mary Ann would call a girl that name.

"She had gray hair like a grandma, wrinkles too."

"How old was she?" I asked, hoping more information would help this make sense.

"Really old. Probably forty or so." Of course Mary Ann's assessment of age probably wasn't accurate, but it at least let me know that I had been mistaken. Alma hadn't been an orphan like me. She wasn't a child. She was an adult, hired as a helpmate. Perhaps she didn't have parents any longer, but her situation was not mine. Her situation wouldn't send her to a children's home.

"Why'd she leave?"

"Mama said another home needed her. That's what she told me. But I heard her telling Daddy it was because she was disobedient. So I guess she was naughty."

"What did she do?"

"Mama yelled at her a lot, but the time she got the maddest

was when Alma brought a snack to my room. Said she was underlining her."

"Undermining?"

Mary Ann nodded yes. "When Mama saw, Alma said she thought I was hungry. I hadn't eaten all day. Besides, I didn't mean to wet the bed."

I saw her eyes begin to moisten. "I know you don't mean it," I said.

"I'm not trying to be naughty."

"I know. So why doesn't anyone talk about her anymore?"

"Mama said we couldn't. Said she wasn't part of our lives no more and we needed to move on."

I couldn't bring myself to tell her that, just because people are no longer present in our lives, it doesn't mean moving on happens—or at least not in the way we'd like it to. I'd spent my life trying to move on from Mama, aching for someone I didn't know except for a few minutes the first day of my life. And now there was Daddy. And Jesse. And Tulla and the Barnas. There was so much moving on I was supposed to be doing, but how could I move forward when each one of them threaded through me in a way that, to let go of them, would unravel parts of me?

Just then a tuft of curls caught her eye as it floated on the breeze. She jumped to her feet and chased after it, and she nearly had it when we heard the screen door screech open.

"Mary Ann, what on earth? Is that dirt on your knees? How many times do I have to tell you to stop acting like her? Get in this house right now!"

I'd spent a lot of my time in that house trying to be like them, trying to fit in, trying to say and do what they expected of me.

I'd never been good at doing what others wanted or expected, but when I had a Daddy and a friend who loved me nonetheless, I could be me. Daddy always told me to be myself. It might could be that Mrs. Griffin wanted the same for her daughter, but I'd come to see that Mrs. Griffin had ideals for everyone in her family. She had a picture of what she wanted, and she did her best to mold them into the picture she had in mind. Trouble is, molding yourself is hard enough; molding others is even harder.

CHAPTER EIGHTEEN

The Sunday after she cut my hair, I thought would be a typical Sunday with all of us lining up in the pew at church, the organ and recitation of prayers distracting me from reminiscing. But when I woke that morning, I didn't know that Mrs. Griffin wasn't going to require me to attend church with them. I didn't know that I'd be left alone with the wanderings of time past and people missed.

I didn't know that would be the case until I'd gotten up and dressed and had served breakfast that morning. As I dished out the grits, the steam still curling high as the tan mush plopped heavy into the bowls, I heard a banging coming down the stairs.

Michael Henry and Eva Jane already sat around the table drinking juice as they waited for their breakfast. Michael Henry had grabbed the morning paper off the cupboard counter, flipping through it faster than he could read a whole article. He stopped his flipping and looked across the table to his sister when the noise started up.

Silently glancing around, we all looked to one another, wondering if someone else knew what the noise was. The banging from the steps changed into a clip-clop through the front hall. Eva Jane and I had it figured out before Mary Ann walked into the kitchen, dressed for church and standing a few inches higher, thanks to a pair of her mama's heels.

Eva Jane let out a laugh as her little sister wobbled into the kitchen, a proud look on her face being replaced with a moment of fright as her ankles wobbled and she nearly toppled to the side.

"Better not let Mama catch you in those," Eva Jane said as she grabbed her freshly poured bowl of grits and stirred before bringing a spoonful to her mouth.

"Better not burn your tongue," Mary Ann shot back before sticking her tongue out at her sister. Eva Jane returned the gesture and then took a big bite of grits, which she immediately spit back into her bowl as she huffed and puffed with pain. "Told you so," Mary Ann said. She sat down at the table, crossing her legs at the knee as she'd seen her mother do, the shoes dangling from her toes threatening to fall to the ground at any second.

"She's right," Michael Henry said, the newspaper now tossed onto the counter as he began to blow on his grits to cool them. "Mama sees you with those, you know you're in trouble."

Mary Ann shrugged her shoulders, trying her best to remain proud, but the smile had since faded from her face. As we all heard the heavy feet of Mrs. Griffin landing in the front entry, Mary Ann jumped from the table and tossed her mother's shoes beneath the cupboard where the mouse had scurried for safe hiding. She made it back to her seat before her mother walked into the kitchen.

"Why y'all still eating?" Mrs. Griffin said without a hint of good morning first. "It's time to go."

With a mouth full, Eva Jane said, "Still. Hot." She huffed and puffed through her open mouth, trying to get her breakfast to cool before swallowing.

"I don't care. Your father's ushering this morning, so the three of you need to finish up. Now."

The Griffin children began stirring and blowing, trying to cool the grits quickly. I reached for my own bowl to eat before we needed to leave. As I sat down and began blowing, Mrs. Griffin said, "Get the ham in the oven before you clean up the breakfast dishes. Make sure dinner's on the table when we get back."

I stopped blowing on my grits and looked to her, but Michael Henry asked the question before I could. "Ain't she going too?"

"No. Too much to do," she said as she pointed her fingers and pulled on a glove, carefully positioning it and adjusting the seams to be just so.

Michael Henry dropped his spoon into his bowl, the metal clanging against the porcelain. "So I can stay home too?"

My heart began to race, wondering if that could be our chance to leave, to take off to the beach. Could I convince Michael Henry to leave then, knowing he wouldn't make it back before church ended?

Mrs. Griffin reached for the second glove and slid it into place, answering Michael Henry without looking at him. "You know we go as a family. Unless you're equating yourself with the help?"

Michael Henry's mouth opened, struggling to say something, but Mary Ann beat him to it, "Mama, can't Leah come along?"

"No. The matter's been settled."

Mr. Griffin walked into the kitchen, having arrived after the conversation and the questions and assuming all were ready. "Good, let's go," he said before taking a long drink of coffee.

With gloves in place, Mrs. Griffin grabbed her handbag and slid her arm through the beaded handle before telling the kids to get in the car. Mary Ann heard the order and planned to obey, but first she hugged me around the waist, holding the squeeze for a minute before letting go and racing out.

Mrs. Griffin probably meant to hurt me by leaving me behind. I figured she didn't want to be seen with me—the stupid girl with the spells and the hair so short it flew in all directions. I don't think she had it in her to consider whether or not I wanted to be seen with her. Truth be told, her presence was punishment. Being alone was a gift.

As soon as the Griffins left, I made sure to prepare the ham and place it in the oven before cleaning up the breakfast table and spotting the heap of the Sunday paper piled on the counter. I tried to keep that space organized, free of clutter and papers and random items the Griffins seemed to plop down there, but the pile always grew. I grabbed the paper and straightened it out, stacking it and folding it back into shape. After I moved the paper, I saw the mess beneath it: Eva Jane's math test with the C, Mary Ann's drawing of a bird she'd seen out back, the mail she had brought in from the box yesterday that Mrs. Griffin hadn't put away yet.

I started stacking and dividing, trying to make neat piles if I didn't know where to put things, leaving them for Mrs. Griffin or someone else to put away later. And in the stack of mail was an envelope, a color, size, and shape I recognized before I even saw the handwriting and names upon it—my own name being one and Jesse's the other.

He'd written me again!

I grabbed the letter and held it close, looking around the house, making sure no one had seen me, but of course no one was home to see. I wanted to tear into the unopened envelope right then, pull out the letter, and drink up every word he had writ-ten, but what if the Griffins came back? What if Eva Jane forgot something or Michael Henry caused enough of a stink that his mother let him walk home? I could go into my room, but the air was warm that morning and I wanted to get out from between those walls, from underneath their roof, so I headed out the back door and decided to take a walk, to put some distance between myself and the empty house.

The only direction I'd ever walked from the Griffins' house was toward town for the grocery store or the soda fountain. But that morning, I headed out the backyard and onto a street I'd yet to walk down, though it looked like the other streets I'd seen already. Houses in a row, green lawns and picket fences, window boxes spilling yellow and white winter pansies yet to be replaced with spring flowers.

The trees stretched above the sidewalk, creating a canopy that rustled and swayed with the breeze. I didn't know my destination that morning, but I kept on walking until I sensed that I had arrived. I stopped in front of the large iron gates of the town cemetery. They stood wide open that morning. I wondered if they ever really closed. What purpose did they have in closing anyway? It's not like they needed to keep anyone locked inside. Those who were there had no way of leaving.

I walked through the gates, careful to stay along the winding path, not wanting to trod upon the ground and what lay beneath it. But the longer I wound my way through the cemetery, from the places with the large markers to the sites with small, nearly hidden ones, the more I felt the pull to step off that path.

I looked around me, wondering if anyone would notice me

step onto the grass. Surely it wasn't forbidden. How else would loved ones place flowers and memorials on the graves of the deceased? But since these souls hadn't belonged to me, I felt like an intruder of sorts. Of course, no one was there at that time except for me. Most of the town sat in their services, whichever they belonged to. The birds that chirped overhead didn't care where I went. The squirrels watched me more, darting up trees if I got too close to them, their tails switching with anxiety, their paws taking them higher and faster in their escape.

I stepped off the path and walked along the headstones, reading the names and inscriptions:

Beloved on earth and in heaven.

A true light in life and death.

Wife, mother, daughter.

As I read each one, I began to wonder what Mama's would've said if she had had a headstone. What words would Daddy have chosen had he had the means to build a stone monument to his wife? What words would I have for Daddy's?

Then I saw the stone with the first and last dates far too close to one another, not enough life lived in the dash between:

Taken too soon.

Somehow that seemed right. Even though my parents' dashes held more years, they still had more to give, more to share, more time to spend with their daughter. But no one gets to choose the length of their dash.

I had no shell to offer that child's site, but I found a small rock nearby. I placed it beside the headstone, carefully wiggling it into the dirt so it wouldn't slide away in the next rain storm. As I put it into place, my body recalled the motion, the placement of a tribute, and as the breeze rustled the leaves overhead, my body shook with a longing—a longing for Mama and Daddy and the boy who knelt in the dirt beside me, who worked alongside me and never questioned the purpose in it all.

I chose a bench, the farthest from the gate, to sit down on before I reached into my apron pocket and pulled out the letter. I looked around for good measure before I unfolded the letter and began to read:

Dear Leah,

I'm glad I saw you at the fair. Wish we could've had more time together. If you want to visit, write me and I'll arrange it.

Hope to see you soon.

Yours—J

I sat on the bench, my heart pounding in my chest. I hoped that when I walked away from Michael Henry at the beach, they'd welcome me for more than a visit. I sat there thinking about words and conversations, considering what I'd write back to Jesse. Wondering if I could once again figure out a way to send it to him. Since Mrs. Griffin had taken the change, I had no means to buy more postage.

But what would I say to him? Should I tell him that we'd be coming to the shore but I didn't know when? Should I say that Mrs. Griffin had cut off all my hair? Should I mention how hard it would be to leave Mary Ann?

It was the deep, bone-chattering sound of the train rumbling along its tracks that startled me from my imagining. The tracks ran along the back side of the cemetery, quite near where I sat still holding the letter in my hand as I tried to think of how I'd respond if I could. The passing trains could be heard at our old house, but the proximity in that cemetery made the roar louder, more intrusive. And as the train barreled by, the vibration pounded deep within me, loosening up the memory of Jesse and the shoelace and the day that nearly ended quite differently.

I spent more time inside the iron gates of the cemetery than I'd planned to, but with the train's rumble, I decided it was time to leave before the reminiscing wouldn't let go and the tears would start flowing.

The Griffins still weren't home when I got back to the house. A good thing since I had the potatoes to peel and green beans to cook. The meal tasks busied my mind for a bit, but once the table was set, the ham was still roasting, and the potatoes were softening in a boil, my mind began to wander back to the long-ings of the past, trying to recall the smells, the touches, the voices. Through all the work, Jesse filled my thoughts and, in the silence of the house, I couldn't quiet the rememberings.

I pictured the letters he'd written—the one in my pocket and the one beneath my mattress that remained in my room, hidden and only brought out when the house quieted at night. I had to tuck away this new one before they got home. But more so, I needed to respond.

I didn't have long. The potatoes would soon be done and the Griffins would be walking through the door shortly, expecting to find a warm and complete meal set out for them. I had only a few moments to gather what I needed. My legs moved quickly, but my hands even faster. I rifled through the stack of papers I'd organized earlier that morning, searching for Mary Ann's drawing. Finding it near the bottom, I flipped it to the backside and wrote:

Jesse—

I'm coming home. Forever. I'm not sure when, but I am. Promise.

L

I had no time for salutations or pleasantries. I tried to write as calmly and steadily as possible, but I had only a few minutes to finish doing what I needed to, if I had any hope of getting it to him. I folded up the bird drawing with my message on the inside. Then I looked around, hoping to find an envelope in the stack, but none was there. Then I remembered the stationery set on Eva Jane's dresser. She'd received it for Christmas, but from the looks of it, she had never so much as used it.

I flew to the stairs, taking two at a time, racing into her room. I glanced out the window in the direction of the church, searching for signs of their car. The street was still nearly empty. Apparently churches hadn't let out yet.

I walked across dresses she had discarded on the floor, probably in her fit to choose her outfit that morning. I found the stationery, pulled out an envelope, and with it, came a stamp that had been tucked inside the set. My hands shook with the discovery. After placing the letter inside and licking the flap so it would seal, I took the pen that matched the blue flowers on the envelope and I scrawled *Jesse Barna, Supply, NC* on the outside. I glanced out the window again. With no sign of the Griffins, I raced down the stairs, out the back door, and into my room. I lifted the mattress and placed the letters beside the other one. I'd have to figure out when and how to mail it, but I couldn't be caught in my room with a boiling pot on the stove, so I ran back inside.

I didn't have much time to catch my breath before the front door creaked open and the voices tumbled into the house.

I heard Eva Jane say, "Mama, I'm starved."

"We all are," her mother replied before turning to me and saying, "No more dillydallying."

The potatoes had cooked, and the ham also appeared to be done. I pulled the roasting pan from the oven to let the meat rest on the counter as I carried the beans to the table as the last beads of sweat trickled down my back. As hungry as the family was, no one offered to help.

I drained most of the liquid from the potatoes, leaving a small amount in the bottom to help with the mashing. I also dropped in some salt and pepper. Mrs. Griffin preferred her potatoes with more pepper than Tulla typically added. She liked enough for a bit of bite in the back of the throat. I had grown accustomed to being able to eat them without much of a coughing fit. I found that a well-timed drink usually helped the potatoes go down better.

With potato masher in my hand, I began smashing the potatoes, forcing them flat against the bottom of the pan, squeezing them until each cube formed into a blob with the rest of the potatoes in the pot. As I worked out the final lumps, I heard Michael Henry and his mother talking in the dining room.

"Mrs. Wemberton tells me that you haven't asked Sally to the ball yet."

"I know, Mama."

"If you know, then why haven't you done it?" Mrs. Griffin would ask Mary Ann the same question when she hadn't properly made her bed.

"There's time."

"Not much. Besides you shouldn't keep her waiting. What would happen if you waited too long? You know how important this is."

In a voice so quiet I could barely hear him, he said, "How important it is to you."

"What does that mean?" Michael Henry didn't answer before Mrs. Griffin continued. "The Wembertons are a good family. Don't go messing this up."

"Messing up what, Mama?"

And that's when Mrs. Griffin's voice changed. She got even quieter, but not in a whisper. In a deep, low tone she said, "Do you know how hard it has been to start over? To make a name for this family? It's time I don't have to do it alone."

No one spoke. No one made a sound other than Mr. Griffin whistling in his bedroom overhead. I kept working in the kitchen, pretending like I hadn't heard. This woman seemed more guarded than a hornet's nest with secrets buzzing about her. This business about starting over. The past she never spoke of. The possibility that she knew my mama. Her accent she couldn't always hide. She even lied about who did her hair. I wondered what Michael Henry thought of her, but by nature, children are supposed to love their parents. Mary Ann was proof of that. Even still, maybe

Michael Henry's pushing back was because he knew something wasn't right.

While I didn't know what she had meant by starting over, I could understand. I hadn't wanted to start over. I hadn't wanted to leave the only home I'd known to be put into a house of strangers. But here I was with a haircut I hadn't chosen and a desperate letter tucked beneath my mattress, my hope for a return to the life I wanted, if only I could figure out how to see it through.

CHAPTER NINETEEN

It was one of those perfect Carolina days with the sky blue and the clouds white and puffy before the summer heat got started. The leaves were nearly full on the branches. As much as I loved seeing their return, I couldn't help but think of my own trees. They stayed whole and displayed golden tinges right before their new leaves opened and populated their branches, never fully leaving their tree to stand naked and barren. Daddy said I was too impatient each spring, anticipating too much when the leaves would transition, the old dropping to make way for the new. All seemed right when the limbs transformed into new, lush green again.

I'd already worked it out in my mind that, after Mrs. Griffin and Eva Jane left to go dress shopping, I'd make my way the few blocks to the drug store and hope the same soda jerk could assist me again. The letter lay folded and tucked inside my apron pocket as I prepared the breakfast that morning, careful not to splash water, coffee, or milk on myself and risk damaging the letter.

When they had discussed the morning's plans at dinner the night before, I assumed only Mrs. Griffin and Eva Jane would make the trip into the city. I didn't expect to see Mary Ann in a Sunday dress and bow in her hair at that hour of the morning.

"Don't you look fancy?" I said to Mary Ann as she hopped into her chair.

"It's for our shopping!" Her smile grew wide, as her legs swung. "Aren't you putting on your Sunday dress?"

I laughed and said, "Surely I don't need to dress up to clean the house."

"No, but Mama says we need to look right and nice when we go into the city."

I was about to tell her that I hadn't been invited to come along, but Eva Jane walked into the kitchen and spoke before I could. "Leah! You're not dressed yet? Mother! Don't we have to leave soon?"

Mrs. Griffin entered behind her, putting a few things into her pocketbook as she walked in. "Yes, as soon as Mary Ann's eaten."

"But look at Leah. She's not fit to go."

All eyes looked to me.

Mrs. Griffin sighed. "It'll be fine. She'll at least take off the apron."

My arm pressed against my apron, pushing the letter close to my hip.

"I...I—" I started to say.

Mrs. Griffin paused her fussing with her pocketbook to look at me. "You're not having another one of those spells, are you?"

"No. It's just, I thought, I didn't know, I thought I needed to stay here and get things done around the house."

"Well," Mrs. Griffin went back to her fussing as she talked, "I thought so too, but Eva Jane insisted on bringing you along. We don't have time now for you to change. Take off your apron and let's get going."

"I'm not done yet," Mary Ann said.

"Close enough. Let's get along now."

My arm continued to press the letter into my body. Mrs. Griffin expected me to leave my apron, but I couldn't leave the letter behind and there was no time to run back and stash it in my room. I walked to Mary Ann, grabbed a napkin, and helped her wipe her mouth as I figured out my next move.

"Come on, now!" Mrs. Griffin chimed.

"Let me get this bowl soaking and I'll be right there," I said. I helped Mary Ann out of her chair and walked to the sink with her bowl. As the others walked to the front hall, I slid the letter from my apron pocket and into my narrower dress pocket. I pushed against it, hoping the pressure would smooth the fold even more so it wouldn't bulge out.

In my flurry to transfer the letter, I hadn't realized that someone had come back into the kitchen until I felt a hand upon me. I jumped with fright, still uncertain of who stood behind me until I heard Mary Ann's giggle. "Come on, silly goose! It's time to go!"

She grabbed my hand, and together we walked to the car.

It was the funniest thing that we couldn't even see Charlotte until we were in it. I should know; I was watching out the window the whole time. The trees were thick, their budding branches contrasting with the blue skies above them. Then the trees moved apart and the buildings came into view. There were more buildings in one place than I'd ever seen before. I'm not sure all of Brunswick County back home had as many buildings as Charlotte did all right there together, and certainly none as tall as some of the ones there in that city.

Mary Ann sat in my lap in the back seat, both of us with our noses to the window, watching the buildings go by. She'd seen it all before. As had Eva Jane, who was in the seat in front of us. She perked up a bit when she saw the railway.

"There it is!" she said.

"There what is?" the missus asked.

"The place where it happened. Remember me telling you about it, Leah?" she turned around in her seat to look back at me. "That accident where the train went off the track and crashed into the building?"

"Is another train gonna crash?" I could feel Mary Ann's body shiver in my lap.

"I bet one will. Right when you're standing there on the sidewalk."

Mary Ann let out a cry.

"That's enough," Mrs. Griffin said. "You know we don't talk about the dead. And you know to stay quiet while I'm concentrating on driving."

Eva Jane turned back around in her seat, and I held Mary Ann tighter. I kissed her cheek and whispered in her ear that it was all a story, no use in getting worked up.

"Mama," Eva Jane's voice had changed. "Tell me about your cotillion."

"I'm concentrating right now."

"Please," she drew out the word into a long plea. "You promised you'd tell me. I want to hear all the details!" As much as she talked about the ball, I couldn't believe she hadn't told Eva Jane about her own yet. "Tell me about your dress."

"And who you danced with!" Mary Ann piped up.

"And the friends you went with," I added.

Mrs. Griffin's eyes darted to the rearview mirror. She looked at me for a second before shutting down all conversation. "Quiet! I'm parking!"

When I thought about it, Mrs. Griffin had told me very little as I twisted her hair into pin curls that morning that now seemed so long ago. Apparently she hadn't told her daughters much either. But clearly we weren't going to get to the bottom of the mystery as long as she had to concentrate on parking.

By the time Mrs. Griffin put the car in park, Eva Jane had forgotten about the dress discrepancy, too excited to find her own. And I was too distracted scanning the nearby sidewalk for a blue mailbox to try to get to the bottom of it.

I kept my hand in my pocket as I got out, not letting that letter slip from me. We crossed the street and walked to the entrance of the building. As the others looked at the window displays, I found what I had been searching for. It stood at the corner, not even a half block away. The problem was that the store entrance was before the box.

Eva Jane walked into the store first. Mrs. Griffin motioned for me to go before her, but I hesitated.

"You go on ahead," I said. "I'm going to get a little more fresh air first."

Mrs. Griffin began pulling off her gloves, one finger at a time. She stacked them in her hands and said, "Don't be ridiculous," and she waved for me to go ahead of her.

I walked into the department store with my head down and my hand holding firmly to the letter inside my pocket, trying to figure out how and when to sneak away. But it took only a minute until the store and all it held delighted and distracted me. If I thought all those buildings were something to see, I couldn't have guessed what it'd be like to walk into a place with so much stuff. We walked by glass cases full of jewelry, more than I could imagine being in all of Matthews. Eva Jane tried to get her mother to stop and look at some of the pieces.

"You'll borrow something of mine," was all she'd say.

There were gloves, hats, scarves, pocketbooks, and wallets. Any accessory imaginable in so many styles to choose from. Even handkerchiefs had their own glass cases. But we kept on walking through it all, past all the women patiently smiling from behind the displays.

We walked to a wall and stood at a doorway until it slid open to reveal a box within the wall. The other three walked into the box.

"Come on!" Mary Ann said, grabbing hold of my hand and pulling me inside. "Haven't you ever ridden an alligator?"

"Elevator," Eva Jane and Mrs. Griffin said at the same time.

I held on to Mary Ann's hand as the doors slid closed and a person inside the box lifted a lever. My belly dropped to my knees, and my head felt a weird spinning motion. When the doors slid open not even a minute later, the room outside the box looked different than the one we had left. It was full of clothes.

Eva Jane's closet was full of more clothes than I'd ever seen before until I walked out of the elevator and into the store.

Eva Jane walked from rack to rack, sliding hangers back and forth, adding to the pile of dresses I held in my arms before moving onto the next rack. Mary Ann wanted to help hold the dresses, but they dragged on the ground when they were in her arms, so I had to take over the task.

Every few minutes Mrs. Griffin would hold up a dress for Eva Jane to look at, but each time the younger Griffin woman would shake her head.

"White satin, Mama. Remember?" Eva Jane had decided white satin was the only style she wanted for this occasion. "I need to look like a woman, not a little girl."

"Mrs. Wemberton says Sally's dress has a tulle skirt."

Eva Jane simply said, "To each their own."

Finally, Mrs. Griffin gave up trying to find any. She walked to me and began going through the pile of dresses I held in my arms. She'd take one at a time, hold it at arm's length, and check the front and the back before looking at the tag.

"Are you sure you have the right size?" she asked.

"I think I know what size I am."

Mrs. Griffin piled all the dresses onto my arms again, the stack of satin weighing about as much as my quilt did on washing day.

When a woman who looked to be barely older than Eva Jane took the pile of dresses from me to put them in a dressing room, my arms fell to my side with relief.

On our way to the dressing room, I spotted a dress that looked like the one I'd seen in my mind as Mrs. Griffin had told me about her cotillion. "Does that dress look like yours, Mrs. Griffin?"

Instead of answering, she pushed us toward the dressing rooms. "Who can remember all the details?"

It seemed to me that such a detail is exactly what Mrs. Griffin would remember for the rest of her life, as a day that marked her, that welcomed her into the society she longed to be a part of.

The three of us waited in anticipation as Eva Jane opened the door to the dressing room and stepped out into the waiting area. She walked to the pedestal in the middle, stepped up and admired herself in the surrounding mirrors.

"You look so pretty," Mary Ann said.

Eva Jane did look beautiful—older, even—in that white gown that hung to the floor and covered her toes. She looked fancier than my mama did on her wedding day when she wore what she had on hand before she and Daddy met with the Justice of the Peace.

Mrs. Griffin stepped onto the pedestal. She looked at Eva Jane in the mirror. She attempted to grab the satin in different places—the sides, the hips, the shoulders. She tugged and pulled and pursed her lips before saying, "I think we need a bigger size."

"It's fine, Mama." But then she began tugging and pulling in the same places. "Maybe it needs a few alterations."

"Alterations aren't going to help this one," Mrs. Griffin said. "Go try on the next one."

With each dress came a similar conversation, the same tugs and pulls, the same call for something that fit better and that would hang like it should.

The store clerk, who had been standing in the corner for most of the conversation, disappeared without us noticing. She walked into the room with a dress very similar to the first one and asked Eva Jane to try it on.

As we waited for her to step out and show us the dress, Mrs. Griffin spotted someone across the department store. She looked between the woman and the dressing room that still hadn't opened.

"You about done in there?" she called to Eva Jane, who said she needed another minute. The zipper of the dress she was taking off had gotten stuck.

"Don't go breaking anything. I'm not buying two dresses."

Mrs. Griffin grew more impatient as the woman she recognized stepped toward the elevator. She told us she'd be right back; she needed to ask Mrs. Brant something. Then she reminded Eva Jane to be careful before she left us in the dressing room area, hurrying across the way, her hair bobbing and her heels scooting quickly but not quite running. After all, ladies hurried, but they didn't run.

Eva Jane pulled back the curtain to the dressing room and stepped out. She smiled even bigger than she had first thing that morning when she'd come to the breakfast table excited about the day's adventure. She walked to the platform, grabbing hold of the satin to pull the length up before stepping up. She looked at herself straight on and then turned. Standing on her tiptoes, she twirled around, twisting her body and her head to check all sides and angles. Then she said, "This is it!"

"You look beautiful!" the clerk said. It was the first time anyone other than Mary Ann had said those words that morning.

"What do you think?" Eva Jane asked me.

"It's perfect. Just like in the magazine," I told her. And I meant it.

Standing in that gown, she could've looked older. And in some ways, she did. She could've looked like a bride, waiting for her groom. But then she giggled, and her feet pranced like a giddy schoolgirl and we were all reminded of her age.

"You try one on!" she said.

"Me?"

"Yeah! Why not?"

I looked at the clerk, who walked to the rack of dresses Eva Jane, and especially Mrs. Griffin, had decided weren't just right. She chose one and hung it in a dressing room for me.

It took me only a minute to take off my dress, toss it to the floor, and slip the satin over my head, my body moving as quickly as Maeve used to when I'd sneak her a piece of shrimp, wanting to scarf down the beauty before it disappeared.

The dress fell over my body like a crashing wave rippling along the shore, spilling over itself as it fell into place. I ran my fingers over the fabric, petting my own body as my fingertips felt the rich smoothness.

I walked into the waiting area. Eva Jane still stood atop the platform. She reached for my hand and pulled me up beside her. I looked into the mirrors. Before me, beside me, and all around me was a girl with my hair and my freckles, but with a body I didn't recognize, a height that had happened sometime in my sleep.

Eva Jane put a hand around my shoulder, hugging me from the side. As I looked at the two of us in the full-length mirror, I wondered how much we looked like Mama and Mrs. Griffin. Had they worn similar, yet different, dresses the night of their cotillion? Had they transformed from giggling girls to sophisticated ladies as society accepted them into their fold? But the bigger question was what had happened next. What came after that night, after my parents fell in love and Mrs. Griffin became bitter?

Eva Jane and I stood side by side, two girls in similar gowns, for once more alike than different. She opened her mouth to speak, but I didn't hear anything she said. It must've happened again. I flashed there, on the pedestal in front of the mirrors, reminding each one of us that I was different, as if either of us needed that reminder.

Mrs. Griffin's words cut through the air as I came to. "Take that off before you ruin it."

As Eva Jane told her mama that she'd found it, she'd found the one, I walked to the dressing room. I took off the gown, tossed it onto the floor, and hurried into my dress. I waited until I heard Eva Jane come out of her dressing room clothed and ready to go. I didn't have time to sulk. I needed to get to that postbox. I figured that while the clerk rang up the dress, I could sneak down the elevator, out the door, to the box, and back. But I had no time to spare.

I slid back the curtain and crept to the edge of the dressing room area. Mrs. Griffin stood at the register, distracted by checking out. I took a deep breath and hurried out only to hear Mary Ann behind me. "You looked so pretty." She grabbed my hand and asked if I was ready to ride the alligator again.

"How about just the two of us ride it right now?" I said.

"What about Mama and Eva Jane?"

"We'll come back for them, don't worry." Mary Ann didn't seem sure. "It'll be like the Ferris wheel. Remember?"

With that recollection, Mary Ann's face lit up and together we sprinted toward the elevator. The door stood open, the operator waiting to be called to a floor. He smiled at us as we walked into the box, his hand on the lever, waiting to take us to our destination. My heart beat so fast that I thought maybe Mary Ann could hear it. I know she heard the gasp I let out when Mrs. Griffin's voice called out, "Hold the elevator!" before the operator closed the doors.

"We were gonna take an extra ride!" Mary Ann told her mother. "Can we still?"

"Not today," her mother replied.

I backed into the corner of the elevator, thinking that maybe I could still separate from them, run to the box and then back to the car. I'd have to be quick about it. I plunged my hand into my pocket to grab on to the letter and have it ready to drop into the box. But it was empty. I put my other hand in my other pocket. It was also empty. Again, I checked both pockets before patting my body, as if the letter could've moved to a different spot.

"What're you doing?" Eva Jane asked as the elevator doors opened.

"I, uh, I think I forgot something upstairs. I'll be right back." I made no move to leave the elevator as the other three stepped off, but Mrs. Griffin turned back and looked at me.

"What could you've forgotten?"

She stared at me and waited for a reply, but I had none to give. Of course there was nothing that I could've forgotten, because what would I have ever had on me to begin with?

I stepped off the elevator and followed the Griffin family out of the store. I couldn't bring myself to look in the direction of the blue box when we walked outside, but Mary Ann was already distracting my attention anyways.

"Look how tall that building is, Leah!"

She didn't know what had happened, but there she was reminding me again to look up. I'd fallen for her optimism before, at the fair, on the Ferris wheel. I wanted to wrap myself in her joy again, but I couldn't just then. The words I'd written to Jesse wouldn't make it to him, not yet. I'd lost them somewhere along the way. If I wanted to be able to look up again, I'd have to figure out another way of getting my message to him.

CHAPTER TWENTY

As the day of the ball got closer, Mrs. Griffin got more into a tizzy. We still had a couple of weeks until the big day, but that didn't stop the stress from coming, the stress she shared with me more than the others. She moved through the house as if she'd drunk a pot of coffee, but the caffeine never seemed to wear off.

One morning, before she and Mary Ann left to run errands, she told me to put the laundry away and to press Michael Henry's suit.

"And don't think I don't know what you've been doing," she said. "Shoving Michael Henry's laundry into his dresser drawers and squeezing them shut. Why I walked in there the other day, and it was all such a mess!"

While it was true that I did have to squeeze his clothes into his drawers, I didn't cause the overall state of his room. 'Course, I do admit I'd hurry through that chore every time I had to complete it. I never much liked being inside that dark room that had an odor reminiscent of the barnyard.

The phone rang before they could walk out the door. Mrs. Griffin answered it, leaving Mary Ann and me alone in the kitchen.

"Did you hear I get to play at Jane's next week?" She skipped around the kitchen table.

"You do?"

"Yeah, Mama got it settled. During her meeting next week, she's leaving me at Jane's." Mary Ann stepped close to me, leaned in, and said, "She's got a dollhouse."

The missus walked back into the kitchen and asked, "Who's got what?"

"Jane's got a dollhouse, and she says we can play with it when I'm there!"

"Oh, yes," Mrs. Griffin pulled on her gloves, grabbed her pocketbook, and said, "Right. Tuesday morning. We'll need to be up bright and early." This was the first I'd heard any of this news, but with the ball approaching, it made sense that she'd have a meeting to get to. She changed the subject without even taking a breath, "And find my missing shoes, while I'm gone. For the life of me, I don't know where they are."

Mary Ann looked to me with wide eyes before shifting her gaze to the space beneath the kitchen cupboard. I gave a little nod, big enough for only her to see.

"I'll find them, ma'am. Don't worry."

I waited for the door to close and then peeked out the parlor window to see them walking in the direction of town. With the coast clear, I went back into the kitchen.

Tuesday.

That would be the day I'd finally go home. I needed to talk to Michael Henry. We'd have to figure out a way to make it work. By the time Mrs. Griffin got home from her meeting to discover we weren't there, we'd be a few hours gone, and they'd be clueless as to where we were. I would've liked to have stuck around for the ball, to see everyone dressed up, but I had to leave when I could.

I wanted to get excited, but I told myself to calm down, keep going through the motions, and do what I needed to each day.

I got down on my hands and knees and spotted Mrs. Griffin's shoes exactly where Mary Ann had tossed them those weeks ago. When the laundry was done, I put the shoes on top of the basket and headed up the stairs. I stopped in the girls' rooms first and put away their clothes before straightening up Mary Ann's bedspread. Mrs. Griffin insisted she make her bed each morning, and she let the child know if it wasn't done to her standards. I don't think she understood how hard that might be for a child her age, so I sometimes touched it up before her mother could make an inspection.

Next, I went to Mrs. Griffin's room. I put her undergarments in their drawer, Mr. Griffin's undershirts in his, and then opened the closet to hang his freshly pressed work shirts. I reached for a hanger, placed the shoulders just right and buttoned the top button, so it'd stay neat until Mr. Griffin needed it for work. I had gotten pretty good at getting between those buttons, smoothing out all the wrinkles, taking something crumply and making it look like new.

Stacks of shoe boxes created towers of various sizes along the closet floor. I figured I'd help out by not just finding the missing shoes, but putting them back inside their personal box. First, I had to find the right one.

I sat down on the floor in front of the open closet doors, my legs crisscrossed. I opened one box after another, looking for the right empty one, finding pairs of black and brown, flats and heels. I stopped opening and began shaking, knowing the weight of a box and the sound of shuffling from inside would tell me if I'd found the right one.

After a few shakes, I heard something different. It wasn't an empty sound, but a softer, quieter one. When I lifted the lid, I didn't find an empty space for the missing shoes. I found a stack of secret things.

My name caught my attention immediately. There it was, on top of a stack of letters. I reached in and pulled them out, fanning them as my eyes saw my name in Jesse's penmanship printed on each one of them. My hands grabbed for the one on top. I slid the letter out of the already-opened envelope, my mind thirsting to drink up the words that had been waiting for me:

Dear Leah,

I know you haven't responded to any of my letters yet. That's okay. Maybe you haven't been getting them. Maybe you're too busy. Tulla said she thinks it's because you're so busy with school that you don't have time. (Tulla says hi.)

I'll keep writing even if you don't respond.

Yours,
Jesse

I read the letter a few times, tracing each curve and line with my mind, committing it all to memory. I read the words again and again before I folded it, slid it into the envelope, put it back into the box and grabbed the next letter:

Dearest Leah,

We had a strong rain storm the other day. I was worried the shell I put together wouldn't hold up, but I checked on it and it's fine. I thought about asking Daddy to take me to the beach to find a new one, but I figured it's best to leave the arrangement as you had it. You can change it, should you come back someday. I'll keep an eye on it until then.

Yours—J

I opened letter after letter, taking my time, reading the few words he offered and letting my mind fill in with other details and stories. Stories about my old school, how Maeve was doing since I'd been gone, how many mice she'd caught. How Jean-Louise still brownnosed. How he hoped to come to Matthews with his daddy if he ever came into town on business.

I wanted to stay on that floor in that room and devour every word Jesse had to share with me (and a few that I made up for myself).

But then I heard the front door open.

I still hadn't put away Michael Henry's laundry. I placed the letters back inside the box and put the lid on before tossing it on top of the laundry basket. Everything happening too fast for me to think or consider the consequences if Mrs. Griffin discovered that someone had taken it from her room.

I scrambled to find the empty box for the shoes Mary Ann had taken. My hurry didn't make the effort any easier, and soon enough the tower fell, bringing down a few boxes from the stack beside it. Shoes spilled into a heap, and I hurried to match left and right and put them back where they belonged. I tried listening for footsteps, but my frenzied movements and pounding heart made it too noisy for me to hear anything.

As I stood, I saw an empty shoebox beside the dresser. It hadn't even been in the closet in that tower after all. It had been on the floor in plain sight the entire time. I dropped the shoes next to it, not taking the time to position them carefully before I tiptoed across the upstairs foyer, missing every squeaky floorboard on my way.

I had to get in and out of Michael Henry's room before Mrs. Griffin came up those stairs. In the hurry, my mind couldn't recall where to put the laundry. I pulled open a drawer and pushed it closed, not finding what I needed within it. After many trials and errors, I had nearly all of his clothes put away. Where did his socks go? That's all I needed—a place to put his socks.

The door squeaked shut behind me, and I know I heard it, but my eyes were too busy searching and my mind was too busy making sense of Jesse's words. Why had they all been hidden from me? But a voice pulled me back from my distraction and into the present.

My body startled when he said my name.

"Did I scare you?" he asked through a giggle of a laugh.

"A little," I said, hoping that the startle would explain my panic. In that moment, I was thankful that Michael Henry was there, thankful that it wasn't his mother who had found me, thankful that I could tell him the good news, set our plan in motion.

"Where's Mama?"

"Running errands," I said. "Where's Eva Jane?" We didn't need her overhearing the plans of our adventure, my departure.

"At Sally's."

He walked toward his bed, the opposite direction from the laundry basket that held the box of letters. I didn't want him finding them, asking questions, needing to hide one more thing from his mother. To divert his attention, I walked closer to him, lowering my voice. "How about we take our adventure on Tuesday?" I know I smiled big. I was surprised when he didn't seem as excited. "Your mama has a meeting that morning. We can leave after she does."

Michael Henry sat down on his bed. He brushed back his hair and looked down at his lap. "Tuesday?" I nodded so hard that I shook the bed. "But how will we get there?"

"Drive!"

"Daddy'll have his car, and won't Mama use hers for the meeting?"

"If it's a warm day, she'll walk."

He kept looking at me. The longer he looked at me, the softer his brown eyes got and the more he started to smile. "I like the idea, but...I'm not sure... Do you really think it will work?"

It had to.

"Mm-hmm." I leaned in close, putting a hand on his. "Come on, Michael Henry. Don't you want to feel the sand between your toes, the wind in your hair? Smell the ocean breeze?"

"You had me until that. The ocean smells," he wrinkled his nose, "fishy."

We both laughed.

"Your mama will be too distracted with the ball to even notice."

With the mention of the dance, the smile faded from his face and he rolled his eyes. "I can't wait for it to be over. It's all she seems to care about." He took in a deep breath and said, "Okay. Let's do it!"

I nearly leaped into his lap. "Really?"

"Really!"

I couldn't help myself. I jumped toward him and hugged him tight.

"You know," he said, "the problem with the ball being over is then we won't get to practice anymore."

"Well, we better do it while we can."

Michael Henry stood up and held a hand in my direction.

"Now?" I asked. "There's no music." I walked toward the laundry basket, assuming I was about to leave.

"I'll hum it."

"But I really should finish a few things first." Like putting away the letters.

"That can wait." He grabbed the basket from my hands and dropped it to the floor. It landed on its side, the box falling open and the letters spilling all over.

Michael Henry saw the box open and the insides spill out onto the bedroom floor. He walked over and looked down at them.

"What're these?"

I had to think quickly. I had to say something. I had to find something else to distract him and get his attention away from the letters. So, I stepped between him and the basket and said, "Let's dance!"

He grabbed ahold of me, and we began to sway. With only the two of us in his room and no music playing, it should've felt odd, like the quiet before a storm, when the birds stop singing and nature seems to go into hiding. But the happiness of celebrating with a friend made it all seem right.

Michael Henry began to hum. He pulled me closer and rested his cheek against my temple. The vibrations of his humming rolled down my face, my neck, and shoulders, and gave me gooseflesh. I couldn't help but laugh.

"Is the song not to your liking?" he asked.

"It's not that," I said between giggles. "It tickles."

"Then let's try another one."

He began humming a different tune and when I continued to laugh, he moved on to the next. He hummed a variety of soft and slow, loud and quick songs. As his voice raised, our dancing picked up speed. Soon he began to dip and twirl me. The room began to spin as my cheeks hurt with laughter and tears trickled down my face.

"Stop! Michael Henry! Stop!" I pleaded, but I continued to laugh, he continued to hum, and we danced on.

It was the happiest I had seen him in the time I had been with them, and maybe it was the happiest I had felt too. In that moment, I wasn't thinking about anything: not my flashes or chores, letters or home, Mrs. Griffin or Jesse. I existed in that moment in time in carefree joy, my body moving around the room, twisting and twirling, jumping and shaking with a boy who had accepted me exactly as I was.

Then the door swung open.

The humming stopped.

Mrs. Griffin burst into the room. Mary Ann tried to follow her, but she quickly pushed her away and told her to go to her room.

"What is the meaning of this?" Mrs. Griffin looked at each of us, her crazed eyes trying to make sense of what she had walked into, at why her helpmate was speechless, standing in only the presence of her son.

"Mama!" Michael Henry's cheeks blushed red.

I inched to the basket, the box, and tried to put the letters back inside.

"What is this? Why were you alone? Why was the door closed?" She walked toward me and grabbed my arm, pulling me up off the floor and away from the letters.

"First the boy at the fair? And now my son?" And then she saw what I had been scrambling to hide. Her eyes grew wide as the words raged out of her, "You go through my closet, my things, while I'm away?" She paused to catch her breath before she continued. "You, you—" she searched for the words she wanted to say and finally spit out, "you thief!"

But she didn't end there. Her voice raised so I was certain the neighbors could hear her anger burst into their homes as a word I didn't even understand at the time exploded from her, "and whore!"

That was the last thing I heard before she lifted her hand and brought it with all her force across my cheek. My cheek and eye exploded in a pain that continued throbbing as she grabbed the box of letters, and stomped out of the room and into her own.

Somehow I found the strength to make it down the stairs, out the back door, and into my room, careful to lock my door from the inside. I crawled beneath my quilt, burrowing under as many layers as I could find before I screamed into my pillow, my body crying out with shivers that rattled deep inside me. But my eyes remained dry, free of tears that were too confused to fall.

I huddled in the darkness under the quilt, anticipating that at some point someone would knock on the door. Someone would check on me. Someone would at least tell me to make dinner. Though I heard movement during the dinner hour, no knock sounded. No voices called for me. No help ever came. I lay bound in my quilt, willing myself to hold on until Tuesday.

CHAPTER TWENTY-ONE

Whenever Daddy would take me to the ocean, I'd see it in its beauty—the blues and turquoises of the water, the ripples and movements that drenched my ears in soothing sounds. But Daddy never took me there during the storms. We didn't go to shore when a hurricane came or the waves crashed high and hard onto the sand. What Daddy had come to know was the dichotomy, the mixing of the beauty and destruction, the awe and devastation that the force of nature could unleash.

Maybe that's what fascinated me about the story Daddy told me about a woman he'd seen on the beach one day. Maybe that's why I thought of her when Daddy wasn't there anymore to guard my innocence, to save me from being stripped of seeing the beauty separate from the dangers beneath.

As Daddy recalled, it had been a typical day, fishermen casting out in hopes of a good catch. Daddy had finished clearing the trees he'd needed to, so before heading home, he'd gone to the shore. He remembered thinking there was something peculiar about the woman when he'd first seen her. Most people then had full outfits on, being there for work and not so much recreation. But what caught his eye was the way this woman walked out into the water, paying no mind to the salt water that encompassed the bottom of her dress and crept up higher and higher onto her body. Daddy said she walked with her eyes on the horizon, her hands at her sides even when the cold waves crashed at her chest and splashed into her face.

A few of the fishermen yelled to her. A couple dropped their poles and ran into the waves after her when they realized she wasn't going to listen to their warnings. They all saw her go under. Daddy said she resurfaced a couple of times, but then bobbed back beneath. Like the waves rolling to shore in their own rhythm, she continued to go under and up, her face always in the direction of the sea and never back to shore.

And then the bobbing stopped.

None of the fishermen made it to her in time. A boat recovered her body a few days later, by then her dress tattered by the relentless waves and ripped by a few curious sea creatures. Stories told that more of her had been taken by the creatures, the ones that lurked beneath in the unknown, the ones that made even grown men shudder, including Daddy. He'd talked to enough fishermen to know the stories of the things they'd seen on the open waters, the monsters they'd reeled in by accident. Daddy always warned me about them when I wanted to swim. That's why he only ever let me go so far out, not as far as I'd liked to.

"You don't ever know what lies beneath," he said. And he was right; the murky waters of the Carolina coast kept hidden their secrets.

Tuesday finally came.

Until it did, we all acted like the afternoon in Michael Henry's room never happened. Instead we fell into the usual rhythm of things. Mrs. Griffin never commented on the bruise that covered my cheek nor offered an apology. I'm not even certain if she told Mr. Griffin when he got home that weekend. Michael Henry kept his eyes hidden from me when the others were around.

He came to me once in the quiet of the backyard to say he didn't care how mad his mother got; he needed a day away. He'd worked it out, asking to borrow a friend's car. He said he was sorry for what she'd done to me. I didn't say it, but in my mind, I apologized for what she'd do to him when she found out he'd helped me run away. But I couldn't think that way. I couldn't let myself go on like that or I'd never escape. I just hoped he'd find a way to forgive me.

On Tuesday morning, Mrs. Griffin knocked on the wall bright and early. 'Course I'd been awake for hours, my nerves dancing with excitement and uncertainty, my stomach a knot that wouldn't uncoil. I walked into the kitchen, blinking at the light, my cheek still yellow and green from the slap. I served breakfast. Eva Jane walked Mary Ann to Jane's house. Michael Henry left for school, though I knew he was actually in the cemetery waiting for me. It was all as we had planned until Mrs. Griffin said, "It's time to get in the car."

I thought I'd misheard her.

"Have a good meeting," I said. I stood at the sink with my back to her, finishing up the breakfast dishes, the last chore I planned to ever do for the Griffin family.

But she said, "Dry your hands and let's get going."

I turned from the sink.

"Come on now. Let's not dillydally."

"I…I…didn't know I was needed at the meeting."

Mrs. Griffin started to say something, but must've thought better of it. She paused and started over. "Yes, you're needed. Now let's go."

My mind raced. Michael Henry was waiting for me. I needed to get to him. "But—"

Her eyes narrowed, and her voice raised. "No, buts. Let's go."

"But I'm feeling a bit sickly today," I put my hands on my stomach and faked a grimace. "I better stay home."

Mrs. Griffin stomped toward me. She grabbed the dish towel and wiped my hands before untying my apron and tossing it onto the table. She then grabbed me by the arm and marched me to the car, pushed me into the front seat, and slammed the door shut. I leaned close to the window, feeling the door handle in my side, giving as much space across that front bench seat as possible.

As we drove through town, I hatched a new plan. I'd leave the meeting as soon as I could, walk to the cemetery, and hope Michael Henry hadn't given up on me. I might have to wait for the meeting to start, for the ladies to all be distracted before I could sneak out, but there was still a chance.

That's what I told myself before I realized where we were going.

Mrs. Griffin didn't drive us to a friend's house. She pulled into the parking lot of Dr. Foster's office. I sat up straight. I took a deep breath, letting it flood my body. The fine hairs on my arms stood up in anticipation.

Even as Mrs. Griffin pulled me through the front door, I didn't know what she had planned. I still thought that, perhaps, the women's meeting was happening there. But then she dragged me through the waiting room and down a hall. A nurse opened the door to a room with a bed in it. She told me to remove all of my clothes and change into a gown she handed me.

"What is this?" I asked, my stomach now so tight, yet fluttering, as if it was full of both cement and butterflies.

"You said yourself you weren't feeling well," Mrs. Griffin said, finally letting go of me.

"I'm feeling much better now," I stumbled over my words. "We can go. I don't want you to be late for your meeting."

The missus smirked and then said, "Do what the nurse told you to."

Like a trapped animal, I cowered in the corner, not sure whether fight or flight would be better, not seeing a way to escape. I decided to play along, do as she said until I could figure a way out.

I took off my clothes and put on the gown; all the while Mrs. Griffin blocked the door. The gown hung large and loose, the neckline dipping low and the back flapping open. I pulled it tight, trying to reach behind me to gather it together, hoping to hide any indecencies. The two of us remained alone in the room until Dr. Foster and the nurse came in.

"Good morning, Leah," the doctor said without looking at me. "Take a seat on the table and lie back."

I reached to close the gap behind me as I walked slowly to the bed, which now I realized did look more like a table, less comfortable. I used the step stool to give me a boost so I could sit down, still gathering the gown behind me, trying to cover my back and legs, still trying to figure out a way to make it out the door.

Before lying down, I wanted to know more. "What's going on?" I asked.

"Lie down," Mrs. Griffin said from the side of the room. I hesitated. The nurse stood at a table covered in tools and pans, needles and vials. I watched her move things around as Mrs. Griffin warned me, "You heard Dr. Foster."

A cool breeze blew through the vent overhead. My body shivered as I waited to know why we were there.

"My nurse here is about to administer something that is going to make you sleepy," Dr. Foster said. "It's nothing to be concerned about, so please, lie down."

"What's this for?" I asked.

With a syringe in one hand, the nurse walked toward me. With her free hand, she took ahold of my shoulder, trying to guide me down, but I pushed back against her. She pushed harder, and I did the same.

"It's okay," Dr. Foster said. "We're trying to help you. You're going to fall asleep and then we'll do a little procedure, and when you wake up, you'll be fine."

"What kind of procedure?" I asked.

The nurse looked to the doctor.

"An appendectomy. To help with your appendicitis," he said.

Now, I remembered in second grade, there was a little boy named John. His family lived in a house much like mine, one that wasn't their own. He didn't talk much, but one day he was more quiet than usual and he kept his hand on his side. He fell asleep during class, and when the teacher made him wake up, she asked him what the meaning of it was. He started to cry and pointed at his side. The teacher walked him out of the class, and that was the last time we saw him. Apparently, a few days later, his appendix burst, and since his family couldn't afford the doctor, he died in his bed.

I remember how he held his side and cried when he wasn't a kid who was prone to crying. If it had been Jean-Louise trying to get attention, that was to be expected. But not John. And while I had some hurts to heal, my side wasn't one of them.

"But I don't have an appendicitis."

I saw the look he and Mrs. Griffin exchanged, the words not spoken, yet shared between them. "You said for yourself you weren't feeling well. Now lie back," she warned.

But I had seen the way they had looked at one another. My body tried to protect itself, to find a way to flee. Both Dr. Foster and the nurse put their hands on me. I fought harder. I did my best to resist. But they had more strength than a fourteen-year-old girl. I longed for a distraction. Still I resisted, pushing against them, flailing from side to side.

"I don't have an appendicitis!" I shouted.

"They can't help you unless you cooperate." Mrs. Griffin stepped forward, squeezing in beside the doctor. She put her arm across my chest and pushed against me.

I pushed back, trying to defend myself when no one else would.

Dr. Foster's face had grown red, his eyebrows angled toward the bridge of his nose, the fat pinching his glasses even harder. "Listen to your aunt!"

And then the room paused.

There are moments in life that speed up too fast, go by more quickly than we want—the last moments of a painted sky at sunset before darkness comes, the final purr of a cat drifting off to sleep, the contagious laugh of a loved one. But then there are moments that slow down despite us wanting them to go away.

It happened at the kitchen table at the Barnas' when Mrs. Barna told me about the accident. It happened standing on the front porch of the Griffins' house that first day. It happened in Michael Henry's bedroom when Mrs. Griffin slapped me.

This moment in the doctor's office paused like those. One word hung in the air, so I couldn't hear anything else going on at the time. I didn't hear any other commands they wanted me to obey. I couldn't see anything other than Mrs. Griffin's face, which was so close to mine. I couldn't feel anything more than her arm across me. Our eyes held each other's, and neither of us looked away.

I saw the fright in hers. But then her surprise changed to resolve, as the world around me trudged through a thickness too heavy for normal time.

"Aunt?" I said, the word heavy with a question, struggling to come out because it didn't make any sense to me. For that to be right, my mother and Mrs. Griffin had to be sisters. That couldn't be. Even for them to have been friends seemed like a stretch, but relation was too much. All this time, I'd thought I'd had no family, so how could that name be true?

Mrs. Griffin used my moment of disbelief to catch me unaware and push me down onto the table. Time sped up again as she threw her arm across my body and nodded to the nurse to do what she needed to get done.

I tried to wiggle myself free, but the prick of the shot stopped me, as did the words that Mrs. Griffin whispered into my ear, "Did you really not know?"

Questions tried to jump out of me, but my tongue lay thick within my mouth, my mind becoming more distant as it faded away, my eyes too weighted to hold open. With the drugs racing through me, no questions came out. No other information came in.

My body drifted to sleep, and whatever else happened in that room, I don't know. I have the scars to show, but I wasn't present to see it. I wasn't awake to hear what other conversations happened, if they did at all. From the sound of things, this had been figured out, planned, prepared for over time while I had been at home, cleaning and cooking and finding boxes of secrets tucked away inside closets.

But I didn't get to think about those things as I lay on the table. If only the anesthesia had dulled the pain of that day for the years to come.

I don't recall how I got home, nor into my own bed. But that's where I was when Mary Ann brought me some soda crackers later that evening.

"Don't tell Mama," she whispered to me, more quietly than I'd ever heard her do. "Mama always gives me these when I have a sore tummy."

My eyes were still heavy from whatever that nurse had given me, but I remember seeing the smile across her face and her eyes full of care.

"Mary Ann," I started. I needed a moment to breathe before saying more, a moment to figure out what to say, how much to say just then.

In my pause, she said, "I know. Don't let Mama catch me."

I looked at her smile, her spirit shining through. I looked for a physical resemblance, searched for her to look like my mother. It's funny how you can see what you want to when you look hard enough.

I could've told her then that we were relations. I would've loved to have seen her surprise, her smile and glee. I wanted to tell her, but I thought better of it. I still needed to make sense of things before I told Mary Ann anything. I still wanted her to see the beauty and not the things hidden underneath. So I said something to make her smile even more, a truth she could hear and understand, "You've got a special spirit."

"You think so?" Her voice was a little louder this time.

"I know so." I shifted just enough in my bed to feel pain I hadn't had that morning. I stopped moving and took a deep breath. My mind still thick with leftover drugs, I couldn't focus too long or too hard on trying to figure out anything, including why Daddy never told me about this kin.

"I almost forgot," Mary Ann said. She wiggled and moved, reaching up into her dress before pulling out a letter. "This came for you today."

Despite the pain, I grabbed the letter, too hungry to devour its contents to worry about any physical discomfort.

"Mama doesn't know I took it from the mail," she snickered.

I tore the envelope—ripped out the letter and unfolded it.

Dearest Leah,

I'm so happy you're coming home! Can't wait to show you how Daddy fixed your old place, got rid of the tree, and patched it up. You won't believe how fat Maeve's gotten since Tulla's been feeding her. You'd think she's about to have another litter. I got a lot to tell you about school, but I'll save that for when I see you.

I've been tending your trees. Heavy rain nearly drowned 14, but I staked her up and she's doing just fine now.

Come quickly. Stay as long as you want.

Yours,

Jesse

I read the letter a few times, confused by how he seemed to be responding to the one I'd lost. I looked at Mary Ann, who sat smiling beside me. Before I could ask, she said, "I didn't tell no one! I found your letter in the dressing room, and I saw the stamp and figured you needed it mailed. So I tucked it away and gave it to the postman the next day." She giggled and shook with excitement. "I kept that secret real good, didn't I, Leah?"

Pride beamed from her eyes, her mouth, the entire posture of her body. She had done a good job secret-keeping. Problem was, she'd sent Jesse a letter promising things that I doubted were possible anymore. I didn't know what had happened with Michael Henry, how long he'd waited, if the missus found out, if he would be willing to try it again another day. In that moment, as pain gripped my stomach and questions of family swirled in my head, I didn't know where home was anymore or if I'd ever see it again.

And that was when the tears started. All those nights alone in the dark, I hadn't let the tears come, couldn't let them come because I didn't know if I could stop them once they started. In that moment, not even letters and reminiscences could undo or distract or return me to the time before the wave came crashing and carried me farther away than I'd ever wanted to go, too far to hope that home existed, too far to wish for more when I had been stripped down to even less.

Mary Ann crawled onto my bed with me. She rested her head on my shoulder, her body curled into mine and her arm hugging me across my chest, not pushing or restraining, but soothing. My sobs shook her little body, but she said nothing. She didn't shush me. She didn't tell me it would be alright. She lay beside me in bed until I fell asleep.

I don't know how long she was there or when she left, but when I woke in the morning, she was gone. That's the thing about kids. Adults always try to tell them to grow up, act their age, that there's no sense in crying. But kids know that sometimes the only thing to do is let the tears wash out of you. Sometimes tears are the only words worth sharing.

CHAPTER TWENTY-TWO

I lay alone in my room for the next few days, nursing the pain of healing from both secrets revealed and wounds afflicted. I curled beneath my quilt, blanketed in the darkness, too ripped by grief to want to go outside. I barely had the energy to eat the sandwiches and drink the water that someone left outside my door. I wanted answers, but what I wanted more was for my stomach to stop hurting, my heart to stop breaking.

My solitude ended with a knock on Saturday morning while I stared at the picture of my parents, wondering how much more I didn't know.

"Leah?" I didn't expect to hear Mr. Griffin's voice. The door creaked as he opened it. "Good. You're up." He stepped partly into the room, not fully committing to coming inside. "Feeling better?" I nodded. "Good. Mrs. Griffin asked everyone to give you a few days to heal." He said it as if she'd done me a favor. "I know this isn't great timing, but tonight's the dance—ball—and we could really use your help."

Mr. Griffin looked tired that morning, his hair a mess. But most of all he seemed uncomfortable. When I didn't respond, he said, "Take a minute if you need to, but there's a lot we have to do."

Before he could leave, I wanted some answers. "Why didn't

anyone tell me?" Mr. Griffin blinked a few times, his eyes flitting around the room as he stammered to respond. "Why didn't you tell me we're family?"

"Uh," he crossed his arms around his stomach, shifting his weight from one foot to the other. "I'm sure you have a lot of questions. For now, let's just make it through this day. You know how Mrs. Griffin's been preparing for it. Eva Jane's excited." His voice began to trail off as he muttered through what the day meant to so many. "Vivian's all in a tizzy," he rambled on. "It has to be perfect. I don't know if it's because she never had one of her own or, well, you know how she gets. Anyway, let's just get through today."

She never had one of her own.

What did that mean? A dance of her own? But she'd told me about her cotillion. Not a lot, but some. She and Mama had gone, I'd thought as friends, but apparently as sisters.

The back door slammed shut, startling both of us, stopping me from piecing together the puzzle right then.

"It's the day of the ball!" Mary Ann skipped across the porch and into my room. "Can you believe it?" She jumped up and down, her hair still wild from sleep. She skipped past her father, who nodded at me as if we'd agreed that later would do. I wanted answers then. I didn't want to let him get away, but I couldn't ask what I wanted to in front of Mary Ann. And he knew that. He used that moment to back out of the room and escape into the house.

Having no idea that she had interrupted anything, Mary Ann took my hand in hers and tried pulling me out of my room and into the house. "Come on, Leah!"

I used to do that to Daddy. When the ferry would stop on the island, I'd put my hand in his and pull, eager to get to the ocean's

edge, to see the sea spread out in front of us, feel the breeze blowing my curls any direction it pleased. How long had it been since
I had stood free at the edge of the ocean instead of tucked away
in that ramshackle room? Just like Daddy would let me pull him
across the sand dunes and to the tips of the water's ripples, I let
Mary Ann pull me back to life.

Before I stepped into the kitchen, I got myself together. Didn't
need Mrs. Griffin seeing any struggle. I stood up tall, smoothed
my hair and pulled back my shoulders. I'd probably need to bathe
later; my hair had gotten so greasy from lying on a pillow for so
long, but I knew chores waited for me on the other side of the
door. Not only the typical chores someone else had been carrying
on while I'd been trying to heal, but extra tasks as well.

For the rest of the day, we all did our part in acting like everything had always been normal, going through necessary motions
while avoiding conversation and eye contact.

That afternoon, I thought that, maybe, I could lie down for a
few minutes. My body cried for rest, my stomach aching all over
again, like it had the day of the procedure. Before I could make
it out the back door, I found Mrs. Griffin waiting for me in the
kitchen. Next to her, draped over the back of one of the kitchen
chairs, hung the blue dress from Eva Jane's closet.

Mrs. Griffin fidgeted with her hands before she touched her
pinned curls.

"I'll take those out for you in a moment," I said, expecting to
hear about how I'd forgotten.

"It's not time for that yet," she said, still not looking at me.
Her hands moved to the dress draped over the chair. "You'll wear
this tonight."

I looked from the dress to her, trying to understand.

"Tonight?" I asked.

"Yes, tonight. What we've spent all day preparing for?" She inhaled and exhaled loudly, finally looking at me.

"I didn't know I was going," I said.

"Well, 'course y'are." Her accent began combining words. "Who else's gonna serve the punch?"

I must've forgotten. Well, I hadn't forgotten, but I had assumed that, given my situation, Mrs. Griffin would prefer I stay at home, tucked away instead of present with her friends and neighbors.

A lot of questions bounced around my mind, but I didn't ask any, whispering a quiet, "Yes, ma'am," instead.

I went out to my room, sliding the lock into place so I could rest alone for a few moments until I needed to remove the pins and set the ladies' hair before we headed to the ball.

After I helped Eva Jane into her gown and I held each shoe for her as she pointed her toes and slid her feet inside, I put on my dress by myself. I reached behind me, contorting myself despite the stabbing pain in my stomach, until I could pull the zipper all the way up to the top of the neckline. I had to stop to catch my breath, wondering how I'd make it through that night, but I couldn't think about it for too long since I needed to be getting to the church. I combed through my hair without a mirror, not seeing from the outside how I looked, not giving myself time to admire the dress's fit.

I walked down the street as dusk began to settle and the streetlights started turning on. The Griffins would follow in the car at the appointed time. By then, I'd be stationed behind the punch bowl, ready to quench the thirst of the attendees, ready to serve them while wearing a smile and an apron to protect my secondhand dress.

The girls looked radiant that evening, all in long, white gowns, gloves up to their elbows, and pearls around their necks. Eva Jane looked so elegant in her satin dress. I'd seen her in it many times since she'd bought it in Charlotte, but because of the smile on her face, the way she held her chin high and her shoulders back, and perhaps the few inches her shoes gave her, she seemed so much older.

Sally's dress outmatched all the others. The skirt billowed wide, the bodice shaping her small torso. Her shoes lifted her higher, and though she was still shorter than the rest of the girls, she somehow seemed taller than them all.

As I stood behind the punch table and watched the couples dance their box steps, I paid no attention to the boys, the escorts all similarly dressed in suits, one looking as forgettable as the next. I watched the girls float around the dance floor, their gowns so long few shoes poked from underneath the hems.

Eva Jane and Aiken swayed and swirled their way around the center of the dance floor. When they ended the first song with a deep dip, she nearly fell to the floor, but he held tightly to her and pulled her upright. They recovered well enough that the adults around the edges of the dance floor applauded. Eva Jane took a bow and laughed, but as the music for the next dance began, I saw the look she gave Aiken. He didn't attempt to dip her again that evening.

Of course, I didn't get to see all the dancing. I had to make sure that punch filled each glass halfway to the top—no more, no less. I took the job seriously, hoping that Mrs. Griffin would stay on the other side of the room if she didn't have to tell me to correct a mistake I'd made.

I must've closed my eyes for a few minutes, taking in the sound, swaying with myself in the dark corner of the church hall. No one required my assistance for a few moments, so I got lost in my own imaginings until Sally brought me back.

"It looks like you're enjoying yourself," she said. Sally picked up a cup of punch and took a small sip.

"You look beautiful!" I said.

"Oh, thank you!" She looked down at her dress and then back to me. "So do you! I simply love that color!"

It was a beautiful blue that stood apart from the sea of white dresses the girls wore that night.

"Listen," she said as she leaned across the table. "I have to go powder my nose. Can you tell Michael Henry I'll be back in a minute if he comes looking for me?"

I told her I would. As she walked away, I closed my eyes again, trying to get lost in the music, trying to imagine Jesse there with me.

"Leah." His voice carried above the music, my imaginings, and the chatter of the hall and startled me back to reality. "Have you seen Sally?"

"She went to powder her nose." The words came out almost a whisper.

"What?" Michael Henry asked, leaning over the table and closer to me.

I put all my effort into my voice to carry it over the background noise. "She's in the bathroom!" I yelled as the song ended and the conversations quieted. The entire room looked at me as my cheeks burned. I wanted to recover from the embarrassment as well as Eva Jane had, to offer a bow and a giggle. More accurately, I wanted to walk up to the flowered wallpaper that hung in the church fellowship hall and blend right in, lean against it and let it absorb me. But Michael Henry wouldn't let me melt away into the wall just then.

He glanced around the room before whispering to me, "Are you okay?"

I looked up from my ladling. His eyes pleaded with me to be okay. I wanted to tell him I was, but the roundness of his eyes, the intensity of his look grabbed hold of me, and I struggled with words, so I nodded my head yes.

"I waited the other day," he said, as he twisted a cup of punch in his hands. "In the cemetery."

"I'm sorry. I didn't know what she—"

"I know," he interrupted my apology for something I had no control over. "It's okay. I just wish we could've gone." We looked at one another as the music continued, both of us daring to smile as we weighed each other's intentions. "We could try again."

I poured a ladle full of punch into a glass—except I didn't. My eyes had locked on his. My body finally waking up to the possibility that I could still leave.

And then I felt the cold punch trickling down the front of me, the wetness seeping through the apron and the dress and onto my stomach.

I startled and jumped back, spilling the rest of the ladle full of punch onto myself. It slid down the blue satin of the dress, and what the apron and dress didn't absorb pooled into a puddle on the floor.

"This is why I didn't want to let you wear that dress!" Mrs. Griffin growled as she grabbed the ladle from my hand. "Go get yourself cleaned up!" Then she turned to Michael Henry, "And you! Go find your date and dance!"

As I walked away, she knelt down to the ground with a stack of napkins and began sopping up the pool of punch.

I walked into the kitchen and to the sink. Thankfully, the accordion closure above the sink separated me from sight as I soaked up as much of the mess from myself as I could. The apron had caught much of the spill, though the red did bleed through to the dress in some parts.

As I dabbed myself with cold water, the sounds of the hall carried through that closure. Mrs. Griffin must've forgotten that the sink was located right behind the punch table.

"That girl is going to be the death of me, I swear!"

"At least you have a girl." I recognized Mrs. Wemberton's voice even if I couldn't see her. "I've been trying to talk Harold into a helpmate for years now."

"Well, they aren't all they are cracked up to be," Mrs. Griffin replied. "We had no idea what we were getting into. The social worker didn't give us much information. Said something about some spells, but if I'd have known the trouble she'd be, I'm not sure I would've gone through with it." Mrs. Wemberton sighed. "But, now? What're we to do? I mean we took in this child. We said we'd give her a home. It's not like we can put her out on the street. We're stuck with her."

"You try to do something good."

"Exactly."

"Well, aren't you just thankful for Dr. Foster?" Mrs.

Wemberton began. "Could you imagine the risk she'd be if he hadn't sterilized her?"

My breath caught in my throat. I stumbled backward, catching myself on the counter behind me. There was that word, that thing that Dr. Foster had talked about during the meeting and at the fair, with the posters behind him and the black-and-white rats on display. The talk of the betterment of things, the advancement of society by preventing some from procreating. And what was procreating other than making families of their own?

"I mean a girl of her kind," Mrs. Griffin said, "there's no telling."

"No telling at all," Mrs. Wemberton agreed.

I'd heard enough from behind that partition, and I didn't want to hear any more, so I threw my punch-stained apron onto the floor. It hadn't protected the dress. The stain showed large and red all across my midsection, feeling damp on my stomach where the wound throbbed. I walked out the kitchen door and into the night.

The bright moon lit my path, guiding me back to the Griffins' house, beckoning me to return home. Daddy said we could only see the stars in the dark. I didn't look to see the stars and constellations and the cosmos overhead. I knew they were there, as steady as ever. What needed my attention more was figuring out how I'd get back to where I'd wanted to be all along, a place lush with a forest path I'd carved out with the one who loved me most, a place where I could run free and wild. As I marched along the sidewalk that night, I decided that when they got home, I'd be ready to go, ready to leave behind this place where secrets mattered more than people, especially people like me.

CHAPTER TWENTY-THREE

I might not've had as much schooling as Eva Jane, Michael Henry, nor Sally, but one thing I wasn't was stupid. Of course, I hadn't figured out that this family was my relation. When I was pushing aside mourning for acclimating, I had other things on my mind besides noticing if their features looked a bit like my own. Yet, I had known one thing for sure: that procedure had nothing to do with appendicitis. Still, it took overhearing those whispers for me to understand what happened that day and why I'd carry a scar on my midsection for the rest of my life.

And why I'd never be a mother.

Seems I had been right when Miss Heniford asked us to write those essays. She'd thought motherhood was the feasible option for us girls. I guess she hadn't heard of Dr. Foster.

Those whispers at the ball made it clear that I'd never belong there, at least not in the way I longed to, not in the way I used to belong. I went straight to my room when I got to the Griffins'. I kicked my shoes into the corner, my toes dancing with freedom as I pulled off the punch-stained dress I'd borrowed from Eva Jane, the one I had so longed to wear. When I had first arrived, I'd delighted in the thought that the dress could transform me, make me one of them, make me a part of who they were. But now I wanted nothing more than to be the girl so free that fireflies shined as her night-lights, cicadas sang her symphonies, and the forest stood as her cathedral.

I pulled on my old dress, which looked more ragged and stained than the day I had arrived. It hung shorter, well above my knees, yet it felt more comfortable than the blue dress I'd so badly desired. Ashamed that I'd ever thought I could be one of them, I marched into the house with the dress trailing behind me. I walked to the fireplace that had yet to be used in the time I'd been there, and I lit a fire, coaxing it to start with whatever kindling I could find. Once the flames had taken root, I grabbed the dress and added it to the fire.

The fabric singed and scorched, turning orange and brown, falling away before melting into nothingness as it fed the flames that grew taller, smokier. I coughed. My eyes burned. My lungs rejected the smoke, but my spirit delighted in watching the dress burn.

"What on earth?!" Mrs. Griffin's voice rang through the billowing smoke as the fire continued to feed on the remains of the dress.

"What's going on?" Mr. Griffin ran into the room. "The flue. Open the flue!"

The missus and I stood staring at one another as Mr. Griffin reached to open the hatch so the smoke could escape up the chimney instead of into the room. I wanted to keep glaring at her, to watch her mind make sense of things, to see her realize that while she had been trying to prevent her children from being like me, she hadn't thought to consider maybe I wouldn't want to be like her. But then I heard their voices, especially Mary Ann's.

"Daddy, what's happening?" A cough followed her question as she stepped into the parlor. I hadn't seen her yet that evening, not up close, until that moment. As she stepped through the haze, her hand to her mouth to cover her cough, I finally saw the resemblance. I saw myself appearing, the younger version of me that Daddy might recognize more than how I'd changed in the time since he'd gone.

"Get out of here!" Mr. Griffin waved his arms in the air, trying to move the smoke out of the room, while motioning for Mary Ann to also leave. "Michael Henry, open the door. Get the windows!"

As the smoke began to move outside, I stood near the fireplace, absorbing the gaze of all five Griffins, commanding the center of attention. They stood in their suits and dresses, their hair still perfectly coiffed after their evening of dancing and socializing with others who had looked so similar to them. Michael Henry fidgeted side to side. Mary Ann had been the only one to remove her shoes so far. She stood barefoot, like me.

"Are you okay?" Mary Ann asked. She walked toward me and reached for my hand, but Mrs. Griffin pulled her away.

"Run along upstairs," her mother told her. "It's all under control now."

"But Mama."

"No buts!" Her voice rang high and loud. "All of you. Upstairs. Now."

No one spoke until the children had left.

"What happened?" Mr. Griffin asked. He removed his suit jacket and sat at the edge of his chair, too tired to stand but not comfortable enough to recline.

I looked at Mr. Griffin and told him, "I want to go home."

Before he could speak, Mrs. Griffin responded, her voice low and tired, disrupted by coughs, "You don't have a home. Why else would you be here?"

Mr. Griffin jolted. He looked to his wife, who didn't notice his astonishment as she kept her gaze on me. She was right, of course. I didn't have a home. At least not a house. I didn't have a front porch and a parlor, a staircase, and decorations. I didn't have siblings and parents to sit around a dining room table with me. But I did have something.

"There's someone who wants me," I said.

A laugh full of breath escaped as she asked who. "That Barna family?"

I nodded my head yes.

Mrs. Griffin rolled her eyes as her husband finally spoke, "Leah, I know you don't understand things like guardianship, but we're responsible for you. We can't just call them up and ask if they'll take you back."

I wanted to stand firm and calm, be nothing more than patient and persistent, but that notion of calling and asking made me so hungry to leave that desperation oozed from my voice as I asked, "Why not?"

Mr. Griffin stumbled to explain. "That's not how things are done."

Again I asked, "Why not?"

"Why would you think they'd even want you?" Mrs. Griffin cut off the back-and-forth between me and her husband. Maybe she didn't mean for me to answer the question, but I did anyway. And I did it in a way she hadn't thought I would.

"Because of Jesse's letters." Mrs. Griffin's eyes grew wide as Mr. Griffin wondered what I'd meant. "The letters you stole from me."

"What's she talking about?" Mr. Griffin asked his wife. She

merely shrugged her shoulders. "You took her letters?" His eyebrows pinched together as he wondered what had been happening within the walls of his own home. "Why?"

"Because," Mrs. Griffin spoke to her husband as if I wasn't standing there with them. "Her place is as our helpmate now. Why would she need to be reminded of where she came from?"

Mr. Griffin ran his hands through his hair. His voice was low as he said, "Vivian, not everyone wants to forget like you."

Mrs. Griffin's lips scrunched together and her eyes blazed as she looked at her husband. The room remained quiet for a moment, other than the crackle of the fading fire, which warmed my backside. I wanted to step away, to find a cooler place, but my feet stayed rooted to that place as Mrs. Griffin began to prowl around the room, removing bobby pins, her dark hair dropping out of its controlled style, but not fully uncoiling. Her hair scrunched up short, dark strands threaded through with silver ones.

"Why do you hate my mama?" I finally asked.

Mrs. Griffin stopped pacing and shouted, "Because she stole my brother!"

Brother?

"What?" the word exploded out of me as I tried to understand what she meant. "But you were sisters." My voice trailed off, not sure what the truth was anymore.

"Where'd you get that idea?" she sneered.

Then I looked at her again. As the flames cast a warm glow across her face, a spark of a resemblance came to mind. The dark hair. The gap in her front teeth. The eyes similarly shaped.

Daddy.

"You're *Daddy's* sister?" Of course. That explained the accent she always tried to hide. The cotillion she never attended. The embarrassment of anything having to do with being poor. The fight to prove she was always better.

"Don't remind me," she snarled.

"Why not?" How could reminders of Daddy be anything other than a gift?

If I looked hard enough, I could catch glimpses of familiarity. But their manners were so different, him with such a deep kindness, her with something dark and bitter.

"I don't know what he ever told yuh," she began. "But our childhood wasn't like this, like theirs." She pointed up the stairs. "They don't know how good they have it."

Daddy had told me some stories, but very few, mostly about him and Mama, not much about when he was little. He had always promised to tell me more when I got older. He'd thought he'd have more time to fill in the gaps.

"Us," Mrs. Griffin continued, "we had nothing. And I mean nothin'. Not so much as a pot to piss in."

"Vivian, please." Mr. Griffin started.

I warned myself to not believe all she said. I knew enough to know her version suited herself more than anyone, but then I thought of how Daddy had longed for more despite himself. And while his definition may have differed from Mrs. Griffin's, perhaps their desires were birthed in their shared childhood.

"It's true. And you know it." Her emotions blurred her words together like she had spent the evening drinking. "Daddy was worthless. Couldn't farm worth a darn, couldn't afford the doctor when Mama got sick, couldn't stop your Mama from talking

Harley into running away with her. Her. I never understood her." Despite the warmth of the fire, I felt a cold sweat starting to form on my body. "I don't know what she ever saw in him anyways. She had it all…family name, money, any marriage she wanted, I'm sure." Mrs. Griffin shook her head and looked to the ceiling before continuing, "They ran off. 'Course her parents weren't happy, and our daddy was too drunk to care." She paused for a moment and looked at the fading fire, the flames reflected in tears that had begun pooling in her eyes. "After he left, I had no one but myself."

The room stood still until Mr. Griffin got up from the chair, walked to his wife, and spoke quietly into her ear. "Vivian, they did the best they could. At some point you've got to forgive."

"Forgive?" She shook free of her husband. She paused for a minute, looking at my bare feet, her eyes staring without a single blink, her head shaking side to side. "How can I forgive when I'm still cleaning up after 'em?" Her eyes met mine as she hissed, "Fixin' their burdens?"

My hand went to my stomach. Those words were no mistake. I knew what she meant. I knew what she'd done—what she had convinced the doctor to do to me. I was one of those rats hanging on the poster board. I was one of the tainted ones, the burden needing fixing.

"You said we had to help," she cried to her husband.

"You wanted a helpmate. It's all we could afford."

My presence came down to practicality. Tears began to pool in my eyes, but I rubbed them away before they could fall down my cheeks.

"No one would work for Alma's wages," Mr. Griffin said. "And after you fired her—"

"So now it's my fault!" Her voice echoed through the parlor.
"I didn't say that."

"You said we had to take her, that we'd keep the secret, that
it would all be okay. But what was I supposed to do with her?
With those spells? The wildness? The boys? Even Michael Henry!
I didn't have a choice."

The room got quiet again—eerily quiet like an ocean with no
seagulls laughing and waves crashing—so all we could hear were
the pops of the fire that had simmered to a low, steady burn. I
watched the Griffins for a moment, the firelight illuminating
their faces while also casting shadows, a combination of light and
dark places beside one another. Mr. Griffin walked to his wife
again and put his arm around her. She kept hers tightly bound
around her own body, but she closed her eyes and rested her head
on his shoulder, the most contact I'd ever seen between them.

I let the quiet go for a moment. Like with Michael Henry that
night we stargazed, I thought maybe I could offer her something,
so I swallowed hard, breathed deep, and said, "Sometimes family's
not who you've been given. It's who you choose."

Mrs. Griffin opened her eyes but kept her head on her husband's shoulder, her voice quiet and without the energy to fight
anymore. "No. Family's what you make. It's what I've built here
despite all of them. You may be part of them, but you'll never be
part of me."

Mrs. Griffin began to shake and sob into her husband's
shoulder. He grabbed her in a hug and held her to him as she
hiccuped and gasped for air. I stood alone in the room, the one
who had been tucked away, the one who had been separated, the
one who had been cut open. But no one offered me comfort or

an apology. As if the isolation and the slap and the surgery hadn't told me enough already, her refusal to see me as anything other than a burden once again proved that she would never choose me as anything other than an opportunity, but certainly not as family.

I had no words nor anger to give just then. All I gave them was my silence as I watched them cling to one another.

"Go on to bed," Mr. Griffin finally said. "It's too late tonight, but I'll phone the Barnas in the morning"

My legs began to shake. My shoulders dropped as my body exhaled as if it had been holding on to that breath since the afternoon Mr. Barna had dropped me off. I didn't have voice enough to respond. I wanted to hug Mr. Griffin. Truth be told, I wanted to grab him by the hand, rush him to the phone, and make him place the call that moment. But after months of being there, what was one more night?

Before I walked out of the parlor, I heard the creak of Mary Ann's door open. I'm sure she heard the commotion. I wouldn't have doubted that Michael Henry and Eva Jane sat on the steps, watching and listening to it all unfold, but I didn't look up. I chose to walk out of the house, to walk away from this family that I didn't know I had. But of course I knew they were never meant to be mine.

Not wanting to spend another minute under their roof, I gathered my quilt into a tight ball in my arms and I walked down the street and into the cemetery, my softened feet feeling every acorn and twig along the path. I found the bench along the back side, near the railroad tracks. I pulled my blanket around me, thinking of how my life had been like a quilt—remnants of moments stitched together, some beautiful enough I'd want to be reminded of, others I'd rather discard into the scrap pile.

I fell asleep there in the quiet rustling of the tree branches that swayed in the breeze. I slept alongside the souls of those I'd never known, as the stars sparkled overhead like glitter and the crickets sang their song to the Carolina girl in their midst.

Mr. Griffin called for me from the back porch the next morning. He didn't ask where I'd been when I walked into the yard, wrapped in the dew-dampened quilt. I fell to my knees when he told me he was taking me home. I cried alone in the grass before I ran to my makeshift room and gathered the couple of items I had.

I met Mr. Griffin at the car, not stepping foot inside the house again. I didn't say good-bye to anyone. To this day, that's a memory I'd rewrite if I could. I would have gone to find Mary Ann. I would have let her run to me and hug me. But I didn't want to see her hurt just then. I didn't want to see her fat tears falling from her eyes, rolling down her cheek. I wanted to see her as the little girl on the Ferris wheel, her arms in the air, her fingers touching the sky as she yelled, "Let go, Leah! Let go!"

Mr. Griffin and I didn't speak much as we drove the long route I'd been on months before, but this time in reverse. It took us hours before we pulled up to the house. He stopped the car and didn't look at me at first. He looked beside me as he said, "I'm sorry."

This seemed to be the place where people told me their "I'm sorrys." But sorrys don't heal the wounds that gather within the soul and make us the people we never knew we'd be.

I looked across the yard to the home I'd been missing, but

what I'd come to know was that home wasn't so much the place but those who fill it. The sight I needed more than a fixed house was the family next door.

Standing atop the porch was Tulla. She held her hand above her eyes, shielding them from the sunlight. It had only been a few months, yet she looked older somehow. In a few minutes, she'd say the same of me.

In that moment, it all looked the same as the day I'd left. Tulla on the porch. Maeve sunning herself. The second-story shutter outside Jesse's window still hanging at a bit of an angle. It all looked the same. Though I didn't feel the same as the day I'd left. I guess that's the thing about coming home; it's not the home that's changed, it's the person coming back who has.

Before I opened the door and stepped out, I turned to Mr. Griffin—my uncle—and said, "Thank you." Those were the last two words I spoke to any of the Griffins. In the years and decades to come, I'd think about finding Mary Ann especially, but she had been so young when I'd been with them that I thought it best to let ghosts settle where they may and not resurrect them in the future.

As I stepped from the car, Maeve saw me. She was stretched on the front porch, her tail twitching in the afternoon sun. I couldn't believe Mrs. Barna let her on the porch like that. But maybe things had changed since the winter.

Tulla slowly walked to the edge of the porch. Maeve had already started running to me when Tulla caught sight of me and called, "Miss Leah!" She took the first step slowly until I stepped out from behind the car door and stumbled. After hours of sitting, my stomach ached, and I struggled to stand upright. Tulla began to run.

She reached for me, tucked her head beneath my arm, her arm around my waist, and began half carrying me to the house. How a woman so small could give such strength, I'll never know. That's when Mrs. Barna walked outside. With one look, she tossed her knitting to the ground and ran to my other side. I tried telling them I was okay, that I'd be okay, but they wouldn't let me go, not until we got inside the house and they sat me on a chair and asked me what had happened.

But before the story got started, Jesse ran into the room. "Leah!" He wrapped both his arms around me. We held each other for a minute, and before he let go, I began to cry.

Our last afternoon together in the Barna house we had been kids racing down the oak path. Though only a few months ago, so much more had come to pass since that afternoon, more than we could understand, yet enough for us to feel. As Tulla prepared biscuits and Mrs. Barna watched with uncertainty, I wept in Jesse's arms as he told me again and again, "You're home now, Leah. You're home."

Epilogue

HOLDEN BEACH, NC
2006

The best glimpse the future ever gave me came from an apple peel. And as slowly and methodically as I'd removed the skin from that piece of fruit, the future took its time revealing its fate.

I stayed with the Barnas and took over caring for their garden and orchard, growing them bigger each year until Mr. Barna suggested I start a produce stand. About the time Jesse finished high school, the harvests had gotten so plentiful that Mr. Barna had started selling the produce at the country store.

When Jesse went off to college, I moved into the house I'd shared with Daddy. The mug without a handle and the chipped plate were still on the shelf, the dresser with Daddy's extra clothes just as he'd left them. I wasn't concerned about the ghosts of the place. After all, by then I knew the ghosts of the real world were scarier than the imagined ones. I even wore

Daddy's old flannel shirts from time to time, and Tulla never said anything about it.

I walked that oak path anytime I wanted. Five always amazed me in how it overshadowed all the others, how it consumed the space that Four had left vacant. I often wondered if it would've been as big if Four had survived. We never planted another tree along that path, never rearranged the shells after the day I'd first left the Barnas'. It seemed best to let the memorials be what they were.

The saving of each other bound us up as tight as Jesse's lace was that morning on the railroad track. So, I waited for Jesse to finish up his studies—that's what we did in those days, we waited. Then I waited for him to come home from the War, checking each day for a new letter from him. This time I got to read each and every one he sent. We waited a few years after the War before Mr. Barna took us to Holden Beach, walked us to the empty lot, and told us it was ours. We waited to build the cottage until we had enough money saved.

My story, or parts of it, unfolded over time, though I never told Tulla and the Barnas all of it. They didn't need to know it all. What was done was done, and there was no reason to bring more grief to the ones who had let me go. But how were they to know? I was the orphan next door in need of a new home. All they knew was the way of things as far as they could see.

Over the years, Jesse heard the story. He'd ask me to tell him some days, saying he didn't want to forget. Sometimes I'd oblige him. Other times I'd tell him I was too tired for it. But he had to know the whole story. He had to hear it all before I agreed to marry him. He had to know why he'd never be a father, why he'd never have his own child to teach to fish the beach at sunset. He had to choose not just me but that future too. And he did.

Forgiving and forgetting are two different things, and I can't say with certainty that I've done either one particularly well. What they did was wrong. Another seven decades of life can't make up for the ones they prevented from ever existing.

I spent a lot of years not able to look at babies without a rage boiling up inside of me, like the swell of waves on an angry ocean. I learned how to smile through it and force a compliment, while keeping the tears from crashing, at least until I got someplace quiet. It was in the loneliness of the night when the sadness would force me awake, the false sense that a baby was crying somewhere and she needed me to comfort her. When I'd wake, it was my own cries that I could hear.

But now, I can tell my story. I tell it as if relaying the account of someone else, not someone I know too well 'cause then there's emotions that want to get involved. Maybe I gained the strength through the repetition of retellings that Jesse requested. Or maybe it was because I let him be the keeper of the feelings, while I told a narrative from a long distant recess of my mind.

The flashes eventually faded over time before full adulthood. The Barnas insisted we get to the bottom of them, and they arranged a lot of appointments shortly after I'd returned. I got looked at, poked at, hooked up to machines and wires, but no doctor ever could say why my body would stop for a moment, nor could they say why the absences eventually went away.

One day just before Tulla passed, she told me her thoughts. "It was like yuh had a way of being some place all your own, somewhere no one else could be."

I can't tell you how many sunsets we watched from the porch of our beach cottage, how many times we saw the sky light up in orange and pink and purple before the stars would turn on and the darkness would come. In all the years of all those sunsets, I never again saw one like I did that time with Daddy when the double rainbow stretched across the horizon and the waves washed the sand fleas about the shore.

As we'd walk the beach, I'd see sand fleas from time to time, scurrying and hurrying, falling over themselves as the waves unearthed them, pulled them from their homes, disrupted their protection. I'd watch them as they'd resettle and find their new place, bury themselves in the comfort they'd found and forget about the waves that had pulled them out. Even though the waves kept coming, nothing could stop them from finding their homes.

AUTHOR'S NOTE

While Leah's story is uniquely her own, the inspiration for her sterilization came from the real-life experience of one of my great-aunts. Born in 1919, Aunt Virginia was sent to an orphanage at the age of five where she was separated from her siblings. She was placed with a foster family a few months later. While we don't know her exact age, sometime around adolescence, she was sent to an institution where she was labeled "feebleminded," giving them cause to sterilize her. After the procedure, she returned to her foster family where she stayed until she married my great-uncle.

She passed away in 2011, and one of the lasting memories I have of her is when we were gathered together as a family one holiday. My oldest was an infant, and as usual, he was fighting sleep, so I asked Aunt Virginia if she wouldn't mind rocking him. Her face lit up, and she tenderly took him. A sweet smile radiated across Aunt Virginia's face as she lovingly watched my son fall asleep. At one point, she said, "I always wanted to have one of my own."

At that time, our family had no idea what had been done to her.

After she passed at the age of ninety-two, I heard Aunt Virginia's story. She was one of the kindest, gentlest, sweetest people I have ever known. She lived a simple, normal life as a homemaker, gardener, and avid Bible reader. She had so much love to give, and even into her nineties, she longed to be a mother. Her experience set me on a journey to explore the history of forced sterilizations and eugenics.

The American eugenics movement began in the early 1900s as an effort to remove genetic "defectives," including the insane, the "feebleminded," criminals, the promiscuous, and those in poverty. The thought was that those "traits" could be removed from the gene pool, thus creating a better society through selective breeding. But for the program to work, eugenicists needed to test the legality of the practice.

In 1924, at the age of seventeen, Carrie Buck was raped by her foster parents' nephew and was subsequently committed to the Virginia Colony for Epileptics and Feeble-Minded on the grounds of feeblemindedness, incorrigible behavior, and promiscuity. She was sterilized and then used to strengthen the legality of state-mandated sterilizations through the *Buck v. Bell* case.

The lawsuit was filed in Carrie's name but not for her benefit. The purpose was for the court to approve the legality of forced sterilizations. In 1927, the Supreme Court ruled to uphold a state's right to forcibly sterilize a person. This decision was considered a victory for America's eugenics movement that sought to "breed out" undesirable traits for the "betterment of society."

According to Adam Cohen's book *Imbeciles: The Supreme Court, American Eugenics, and the Sterilization of Carrie Buck*, "Carrie never got over what the state of Virginia did to her. When reporters tracked her down five decades after the fateful procedure, she told them she was sad about it—once she found out what it was. 'I didn't want a big family,' she said, but she had wanted 'a couple of children.' Sadness was not the only feeling she was left with. 'Oh, yeah, I was angry,' she said. 'They done me wrong. They done us all wrong.'"

As the American eugenics program took shape, the Nazis looked at the practice in America and used it as inspiration for its cleansing of "genetically inferior" races.

Supporters of eugenics created and disseminated propaganda through books, pamphlets, and events. One display at a fair read, "How long are we Americans to be so careful for the pedigree of our pigs and chickens and cattle—and then leave the ancestry of our children to chance, or to 'blind' sentiment?" They even held "better baby" and "fitter family" contests at fairs where contestants were judged on desirable traits in an effort to educate the public about raising a better and healthier breed of humans.

In *Better for All the World: The Secret History of Forced Sterilization and America's Quest for Racial Purity*, author Harry Bruinius explained, "In states without laws, doctors trained in the latest theories of mental health—or racial hygiene, as many called it—sterilized untold more of their patients. Often, in the face of public opposition, these operations were recorded simply as 'medical necessities' or unspecified 'pelvic diseases.' The number of appendectomies recorded at state institutions at this time is also suspiciously high."

I sat with Aunt Virginia's story for a few years before I began researching this history. I assumed the story would be set in Indiana—Aunt Virginia's home state and the place I knew well. But my first search engine results changed that assumption.

The first result showed me that North Carolina sterilized more than 7,000 people, and my own county, Mecklenburg, sterilized 485—three times the rate of any other NC county. This fact is why I chose Matthews, NC, as the location of Leah's sterilization. I decided that Leah's home would be Holden Beach in part because I officially started the manuscript on that island during a writer's retreat and because during the time period of the novel, "love of the sea" was a reason to question someone's sanity.

While the North Carolina Eugenics Board was formed in 1933, it wasn't disbanded until 1974. The state began making reparations in 2013 when it allocated $10 million to be split among living victims.

Between 1907 and 1983, an estimated 60,000 to 70,000 were sterilized in the United States. In the 1960s, sentiment toward forced sterilization shifted as attitudes toward marginalized groups changed. By the end of the twentieth century, legal sterilization ended.

But remnants and sentiments persist today. Here's only a short sampling from recent years:

- Between 2006 and 2010, California sterilized 148 female prisoners, according to a 2013 report from the Center for Investigative Reporting.
- In 2014, a Republican Arizona state senator was forced to resign after he publicly called for the sterilization of women on public assistance.
- In 2015, the AP reported that Nashville prosecutors were making sterilizations part of plea negotiations with female defendants.
- In 2020, a whistleblower claimed that an ICE facility for immigrants in Georgia had performed hysterectomies without informed consent.

Mark Twain said, "History doesn't repeat itself, but it rhymes." I hope Leah's fictional story can remind us of this sometimes forgotten piece of our history so that our present and our future will not rhyme with this past. May this be true for the sake of those tens of thousands who were sterilized against their wills, and for my aunt Virginia and the children she never had the chance to rock to sleep.

READING GROUP GUIDE

1. What role does nature play in Leah's life? How does it set her apart from the other characters in the story?

2. Describe Leah and Jesse's friendship. How are the characters similar? What sets them apart? How does their relationship flourish over the years?

3. Early on, we learn Leah's daddy wanted "more" for his daughter. What do you think that means? How does this idea affect Leah? Does this idea of "more" change over the course of the novel?

4. At the end of chapter four, Leah says of Maeve, "But part of her surviving was finding family. She had chosen me, but right then I had nothing for her. And in that regard, the two of us became kindred spirits, two strays without a place to call home." How are Leah and Maeve similar throughout the story?

5.   Imagine you are Leah and you arrive at the Griffin household. What questions would you have? What would be your first instinct: trying to fit in with the family or trying to get back to the Barnas?

6.   How would you describe Leah's relationship with the Griffin children? How do you believe they view her?

7.   What do you make of Mrs. Griffin? Where do you think her deep resentment for Leah comes from? How does it connect to the expectation of women in society at that time?

8.   Why do you think Mrs. Griffin uses Leah as a helpmate instead of letting Leah continue her education? How does Mrs. Griffin try to present herself and her family to others?

9.   Why do you think Mrs. Griffin ultimately decides to involve Dr. Foster in Leah's life? What was her excuse?

10. Near the end, Leah says, "I guess that's the thing about coming home; it's not the home that's changed, it's the person coming back who has." What do you think Leah's return home was like? Have you ever experienced a similar sentiment?

11. What parallels can you draw between Dr. Foster and the eugenics board, and body autonomy today?

12. Leah is a poor orphan who prefers the wild to societal norms. How does that set her up for being a candidate for forced sterilization? How does Mrs. Griffin's views of society justify her actions?

13. What does Leah ultimately learn about home and family over the course of the novel?

14. What do you think the conversation between Leah and Jesse looked like around the traumas she faced in the Griffin household? How would you approach that conversation?

A CONVERSATION
WITH THE AUTHOR

This novel is such an emotional read. What was your inspiration?

Unfortunately, my inspiration came from my great-aunt Virginia. She was such a sweet and loving person, and it was obvious that she had always wanted to be a mother, but she never had children. I remember one holiday when my oldest was an infant. He was fighting sleep, as usual, and I was not having success with getting him to sleep. I asked Aunt Virginia if she would like to rock him to sleep. She was so happy to help. She took him in her arms and said, "I always wanted one of my own."

I didn't know until after she passed away at the age of ninety-two that sometime during adolescence, she was sterilized by the state of Indiana. She was sent to an orphanage at the age of five, but instead of protecting her, society subjected her to an atrocity that had lifelong implications. I wanted to learn more, so I began researching forced sterilization and eugenics and soon learned that Aunt Virginia was far from the only person to experience this. And I was shocked by how long the practice continued in our nation. As my research and questioning continued, Leah began to develop and her story emerged. One evening at Ocean Isle Beach, North Carolina, a double rainbow appeared in the sky and sand fleas scurried about on the shore. Leah's voice took that moment, and the prologue wrote itself.

Do you have any other personal connections to this story?

Like Leah, my father was also a lumberjack. Actually, it was a family business that my grandfather started. Grandpa, Dad, my uncle, a few cousins, and my brother all worked as lumberjacks at different points in their lives. Dad was a great resource for me to understand how they logged before modern technology. It is a very dangerous job, and unfortunately, the incident Harley Payne experiences was inspired by a tragic event within my own family when I was quite young.

You really bring this time period to life. What research did you have to do?

Perhaps the most intimidating part of this story was the research, both in regard to the history of eugenics and the time period. Up until this novel, I had written in the present day. The thought of exploring another time period at first overwhelmed me. But then I began reading, especially about eugenics and the *Buck v. Bell* case that solidified the legality of forced sterilization. Having taken place ten years prior to Leah's story, reading about the case and Carrie Buck's history put me in the mindset of the time. Watching documentaries and movies like *It's a Wonderful Life* and *Our Town* helped me visualize the era. During much of my writing time, I listened to music from the 1920s and '30s. Perhaps one of my greatest resources was my next-door neighbor, who was born around the time the novel takes place. While she was not the same age as Leah, she helped me with terms and historical aspects as best as she could remember.

The nature aspect of the book is so beautiful and really paints

a clear picture of the landscape. Why did you choose North Carolina as the setting?

I moved to North Carolina shortly before I started writing the book. An observer by nature, I had been absorbing the setting, taking in what my new Southern home had to offer. From the coastal waters of the east to the Appalachian Mountains in the west, this state is so full of a range of beauty. I have always loved nature, and North Carolina provides the perfect landscape—green canopies, blue skies, white-capped water—for a tree hugger like me.

I settled on Matthews as one location when I learned that its county had one of the highest rates of sterilization. I chose Holden Beach as Leah's home after spending a writer's retreat there. Plus, I had learned that "love of the sea" was reason enough to question someone's sanity during that time period, which could possibly lead to sterilization. Being a sea lover myself, as I considered what sort of home would be the hardest to leave, a coastal one seemed right.

How did the story evolve over the course of your writing?

Perhaps it's best to ask my early readers that one! After so many drafts and revisions and years of fine-tuning this story, I forget what the initial iteration looked like. But I do remember that in the beginning, Leah was quite alone. She had no allies other than Tulla, Mary Ann, and Maeve. Jesse was more foe than friend. The Barnas did not care about her, and Michael Henry was a straight-up villain like his mother. I suppose I was working out how a community of people could allow such a thing to happen to her, but nuance was missing in those initial drafts. And so was

Leah's agency. Over multiple drafts, I explored how a girl at the bottom of the societal ladder could still be independent and fight for herself instead of simply being passive to the forces of the world around her.

We have such an incredible cast of characters. Which was your favorite to write?

Certainly Leah. I felt like I was seeing the world through her eyes and that I was along for the journey with her. But runners-up would be her father and Mary Ann. My own father was a lumberjack like Harley Payne and has a similar quiet spirit. And I enjoyed the levity and sweetness that Mary Ann brought to the story. I couldn't help but root for her, hoping that her light continued to shine brighter than the darkness within the Griffin house.

And of course I have to mention Maeve. Being a cat lover myself, I had a lot of fun writing and picturing Maeve. She not only is the companion Leah needs but one that softens and wins over everyone she encounters: Harley, Tulla, Mrs. Barna, etc. She loves unconditionally and softens the hearts of those around her.

What's your biggest bit of advice for aspiring writers?

Keep going. My writing professor, Frances Sherwood, said that the key to success as a writer is perseverance. And I know that to be true. I wrote two novels before this one. They will never see the light of day. But that's okay. They were practice, and practice is necessary. Creating and developing a cast of characters and a story line for eighty thousand words is no easy task. If you are a writer, you must keep going—despite distractions, disappointments, and rejections. Persevere one word at a time.

Who are your author inspirations? Any books we should be adding to our reading lists?

I've been spending a lot of time with Madeleine L'Engle and Sue Monk Kidd over the last couple of years—both their fiction and nonfiction. My all-time favorite is Wallace Stegner's *Crossing to Safety*. He tells a brilliantly subtle story of friendship over time that immerses me as a reader and inspires and challenges me as a writer. Elizabeth Wetmore's debut novel, *Valentine*, continues to impact me and is one I cannot get off my mind. I got lost in the poetic prose—impressively executed, rich detail without being cumbersome—of Kelly Mustian's *The Girls in the Stilt House*.

What're you working on next?

Leah's story started me on a journey to unearth overlooked stories and to chronicle the plight and fight of unheard voices of the past. My current work in progress explores the Baby Scoop Era of the 1960s, asking the question: What happens when the darling girl next door learns that love is conditional and ambition has its limits? The novel takes place during a time when parents could send their "wayward girls" to maternity homes to hide their pregnant daughter's secret shame, forcing a girl to give her baby up for adoption and then return to society as if nothing ever happened. This novel juxtaposes the breakthrough technologies of the Race to Space with the societal realities that kept girls grounded.

ACKNOWLEDGMENTS

Writing a book can be seen as a solitary undertaking. And while I spent plenty of hours tucked away in my writing loft in the company of only my golden retrievers, the truth is that this book would not exist without the village of people who have come along beside me. These acknowledgments will be anything but exhaustive, but here goes…

Leah's story would not exist if it weren't for my aunt Virginia and those who lived through this societal atrocity of forced sterilization. Aunt Virginia, I will never forget the way you rocked Jonas to sleep, lamenting never having had a child of your own. I will always remember your sweet spirit, your kind smile, and the laughs we shared over rounds of Uno.

I cannot say thank you enough to Rachel Cone-Gorham, literary agent extraordinaire. Thank you for falling in love with Leah's story and for believing in me. Your constant enthusiasm and encouragement have been a balm for a weary writer's soul and a catalyst to keep telling stories.

MJ Johnston, thank you for seeing the potential in this manuscript. Your keen editor's eye improved and deepened Leah's story. I am grateful for all you and the entire team at Sourcebooks has done, including Cristina Arreola, BrocheAroe Fabian, Ashley Holstrom, Caitlin Lawler, Valerie Pierce, Stephanie Rocha,

Meaghan Summers, Jessica Thelander, Heather VenHuizen, and Molly Waxman.

Thank you to each and every one of my early readers: Dawn Beery, Laurel Brown, Jocelyn Chrisley, Heather Donahue, Emily Gopikrishna, Kristi Lawrence, and Jennifer Lowke. You saw this book in various forms of completeness. Your feedback and honesty helped shape this story into something better.

Special thanks to Ann McCain, an early reader and historian next door. Thanks for helping me find the Southern term for Hoosier cabinet, among other things.

Thank you to Barbara Peden and Laura Jones for reaching out to our family and making us aware of what happened to Aunt Virginia. Thanks for digging through files and piecing together as much of her story as we still have available to us.

Much appreciation goes to my constant cheerleaders: George and Joanna Azar, Adam Beery, Josh and Tara Casper, Bev Church, Ted and Amy Church, Jeanne Laney, Jodi Kayser, Stephanie Rizk, and Maria Swett.

I am grateful for my author friends who have offered encouragement, wisdom, and advice along the way: Joy Callaway, Lisa DeSelm, Erika Montgomery, Marybeth Whalen, and Kim Wright.

So many thanks to Gary Pethe for being a writing mentor to me in the various stages of my career, including as a copywriter for RV toilets. Your constructive criticism back in our ad agency days not only helped me craft press releases and marketing materials but also improved my ability to write fiction. Thank you for taking the time to give detailed feedback and for always pushing me to improve.

To all those who celebrated the journey of this debut novel, from family to friends and friends of family/friends, and people my mother randomly met and shared the news with. I can't begin to list each and every one by name. Please know that your enthusiastic support and impatience to see this book in print has meant so much to me.

To my parents, whose support I have never doubted, thank you for a quiet childhood that gave me room to explore, imagine, and even be bored. But most of all, thank you for your constant and unconditional love. And, Mom, thanks for being my biggest fan. I'm sure I owe many book sales to you.

Many thanks to Jonas, Kenna, and Adelyn for your encouragement and the privilege of being your mother. Kenna, thank you for your notes and suggestions. I apologize that this was not set on Mars, but I'll save that feedback for another story.

Perhaps the most incomplete thanks go to Matt, my husband. My high school sweetheart. My fellow traveler through this journey called life. Words cannot aptly describe all you mean to me. Your patience, pride, and constant belief in me have been a scaffolding of support that has surrounded me through all the ups and downs of this career. Thank you for being solid, steady, and unwavering.

And thank you, dear reader, for taking the time to read this story and even to the end of this page. May you know the beauty of home and the comfort of family as surely as Leah does in the arms of her daddy.

ABOUT THE AUTHOR

© Bethany Callaway

Meagan Church is an author, wordsmith, and storyteller by trade. She received a BA in English from Indiana University, and her work has appeared in various print and online publications. A Midwesterner by birth, she now lives in North Carolina with her high school sweetheart, three children, and a plethora of pets. To follow her storytelling, visit meaganchurch.com.